MW01489082

WHEN THEY DISAPPEARED

A MAK AND WILTON THRILLER
BOOK 1

ADDISON MICHAEL

PAGES & PIE PUBLISHING
Author Services

2024 Pages & Pie Publishing

Copyright © 2024 by Addison Michael

All rights reserved.

No part of this book may be reproduced in any form or by any electronic or mechanical means, including information storage and retrieval systems, without written permission from the author, except for the use of brief quotations in a book review.

ISBN: 979-8-9862920-7-6

Library of Congress Catalogue-in-Publication Data

Michael, Addison

When they disappeared: a mak and wilton thriller/Addison Michael

Cover Design by Art by Karri

Editing by Tiffany Avery and Jayne Hankins

While set in real places, this novel is a work of fiction. All characters, events, and police agencies portrayed are products of the author's imagination. Any resemblance to established practices or similarity that may depict actual people, either alive or deceased, are entirely fictional and purely coincidental.

www.addisonmichael.com

Thank you to my readers who love mystery thrillers as much as I do

PROLOGUE

MADDOX

Despite the chilly weather outside, the real cold was the stony atmosphere coming from inside the Aston Martin that the Casa Cipriani hotel had provided to the popular star-crossed lovers. When the shiny, black sports car rolled to a stop in front of the Battery Maritime Building located on the edge of the East River, Selah Lablanc flung open the door without hesitation.

She stuck one long shapely leg out of the car, then the other. Her Christian Louboutin black pumps with signature red soles touched the ground. She stood regally for a moment, like a queen assessing her subjects. Her vintage black blazer and pantsuit had been a steal from Saks Fifth Avenue. But her perfectly coordinated handbag was easily worth over twelve thousand dollars. She smiled at the group of fans huddled outside their hotel. She winked and gave them her famous double-hand wave.

Maddox Miller, an NFL football player, who had also been dressed by the best, wore an Armani double-breasted suit custom tailored for his six-foot-four-inch body and fit to accommodate his 220 pounds of lean muscle. A gold hoop earring winked from his ear. Maddox was a little more reluctant to leave the limo, trying not to let his irritation over the public adoration show. As per his agreement with Selah, Maddox made the choice to do what was expected of him. He got out, came around the car, and grabbed Selah's hand, making sure to stand close enough that their shoulders touched.

The crowd went wild.

"Kiss her!" someone shouted.

He laughed in mock surprise and leaned over to gently kiss Selah's signature red lips. He even swept her long blonde hair to the side and put an arm around her shoulders, which he kept there as he broke the kiss. He put his free hand up in mock humility.

"Okay, okay, we've gotta get in there," Maddox said.

Though Selah looked at him with adoration in her eyes and smiled that brilliant, red-lipped smile that used to make his heart somersault, he felt her body tense. He knew he would never hear the end of this one.

He dropped his arm and grabbed her hand again, gently leading her forward, but it felt like they were clinging to each other in more of a death grip. They walked through the crowd, all smiles and waves to the fans.

Once they were in the hotel, they barely noticed the luxurious lobby with its Art Deco features, jazzy music playing in the background, and chic Italian vibe. The ceilings were vaulted and there was a tiled fireplace along the wall. This was the kind of place where Maddox would love to relax and hang out if only they could ditch their trail of paparazzi.

The concierge greeted them crisply, smoothing the front of his Italian suit, and immediately ushered them into a private elevator which took them directly to the Riverview Penthouse Suite.

The room had cashmere wall coverings. Like the lobby, Art Deco fixtures and pictures on the wall adorned the suite with matching Italian tiles. But the view from the private terrace is what sealed the deal for Selah. She adored a good view.

Once they were alone in their hotel room and the door had swung shut, they dropped hands as though the touch had been burning them.

It was supposed to be a private getaway after a special appearance on *The Entertainment Today Show*. One last fling before Selah went on tour and Maddox went to play in the big rivalry game.

"This is over," Maddox declared in a low and strong voice.

"I know. What a relief!" Selah responded, her eyes on the Statue of Liberty, which they could see from their room. She kicked off her Louboutins. "The fans are getting worse, I think. Speaking of which, what in the world were you thinking by talking to them? You know you can't give them too much attention!"

"I don't think you understand what I just said to you. I'm saying this is over. Us. We are over. I'm done." He looked deeply into her eyes, making sure she understood his words.

She froze, standing stock still with wide, surprised eyes and stared at him like she could not comprehend his words. Maddox braced himself for what he knew would come next. Selah liked to get her way and she would do anything to get it. This was not going to go well. But they'd been on the brink of a break-up for a while. She shouldn't be surprised.

"But what will everyone think?" she asked in a whisper, her eyes full of fear.

"That's what you have to say right now?" He shook his head and picked up his phone. He dialed and put the phone up to his ear. "I need an exit out of here. Can you put together a quick plan?" He paused, listening, before he continued. "I'll be leaving separately. We definitely don't want this to leak, so if you could be extra discreet here, that would be great. Thanks!" Maddox hung up the phone.

He turned back to Selah. Her eyes seemed to be swimming with tears. He hesitated for a moment. He'd never seen her cry before. Was he making a mistake?

"Hey," he said softly as he closed the gap between them and put his hand on her shoulder. "You're gonna be just fine."

She wiped her tears with irritation. The moment was gone. She put her shoulders back and stood up taller, her composure firmly back in place. "I have no idea how we're going to spin this one," she snapped bitterly.

He felt his wall go back up and irritation settled back in its normal place. He should've known that all she would care about was her public image. He had fallen for her manipulations so many times to get him to so many events. The truth was, he was tired. He was a football player, so that was saying a lot.

"Can we end this amiably, please?" Maddox asked. Then he ducked to avoid the pillows she began throwing at him. She seemed to throw anything within reach. He was lucky pillows were all she had at her fingertips at the moment.

"Get out!" Selah screamed loudly. "I don't need you. I never did."

"Gladly," he said, feeling resigned. She didn't seem to notice he had not even brought a bag. This had been his plan from the beginning.

He checked his phone as he opened the hotel door. He glanced back and could see Selah's back to him, her shoulders shaking. So, she *was* crying. Maddox felt a wave of sadness wash over him.

On cue, as the door swung shut behind him, his phone started ringing. It was his publicist—a person he'd never needed before he met Selah. She had an escape plan for him. Relief flooded through him as he stepped onto the elevator and out of Selah's life. He realized he was done with the limelight, even if just for the moment. The NFL was different from Hollywood. He had figured that out the hard way.

As the elevator doors closed behind him, he sighed and pushed down his emotions. He wondered if she could have just been her, without all the fame, and if he could have just been him, a successful tight end for Kansas City, would they have actually had a chance to make the relationship work?

He supposed he'd never know the answer to that. He pushed open the door to the back entrance of the hotel. Limo in sight, Maddox stepped into the daylight. He looked around, satisfied that there were no paparazzi peeking over the privacy wall behind the hotel and that the limo was wedged comfortably on a one-way street that would lead to his freedom.

He never saw it coming. He squinted at the bright sun overhead, thinking he must have left his sunglasses somewhere. He nodded to the limo driver, who was standing by the door the driver had opened for Maddox. As Maddox stepped forward to duck into the limo, he felt a slight sting on his neck which he assumed was a sweat bee. He swiped at his neck as he settled himself in the comfortable seat of the luxury car, unaware that sweat bee was really a needle with fluid in it.

The door closed beside him.

Peace settled over him as he sat in that quiet, nondescript limo. The next minute, he was unconscious.

1

WILTON

Stephen Wilton rolled over and put a hand on his girlfriend's bare shoulder, scooted over to it, and then kissed it. He smiled when Kristie mumbled something incoherent. She wasn't a morning person. He was, but he thought he could watch her sleep all day.

Her eyes flickered open. "Are you watching me sleep again?"

"Guilty," he smiled.

Kristie threw the comforter off and sat up in one graceful movement. He could see the swan-like arc of her back and the curve of her firm bottom. Her shapely legs were long and slim. She reached for the clothes she had been wearing last night and began pulling them on.

For a moment, her long, brown hair that waved down her back reminded him of *her*. Yes, perhaps he had a type. Brown hair, green eyes, stubborn, and independent. Kristie slid her pants on and turned around as she snapped her bra into place. She hesitated.

"Honestly, Stephen." She took three steps back to the bed and laid back down. She rubbed the comforter suggestively. "I could do this with you all day. I mean, look at you. You're easily the hottest guy I've ever met. With your curly blond hair, baby blues, and that body…" She trailed a finger over his six pack.

"But?" he asked, knowing what was coming next. *Love 'Em and Leave 'Em* was his nickname at the office. That's because he always seemed to be dating a different girl. What the people at the office didn't know was that it wasn't Stephen who was doing the leaving.

"*But* I'm not what you're looking for." Kristie picked up a picture off his nightstand. It was a picture of Paige, who was laughing with a younger version of his daughter, Anna.

"That's a picture of my daughter. It was a good memory—"

"Right, a picture of your daughter *and* your baby mama, Paige. Come on, Stephen. Don't you think that's weird? It's like you're advertising that you're still in love with your ex. And by the way, all you want in life is a family. *This* family."

"That's not fair," Stephen protested weakly. Her words stung because they were true.

Kristie shrugged, leaned over, and kissed Stephen. "Like I said, I could do this all day long. You call me if you want a good time. But I'm not the girl you're going to put a ring on."

"Oh no!" Stephen sat up, suddenly horrified. "You found the ring?"

Kristie's long, perfectly manicured fingernails tapped the nightstand drawer. "You don't keep it very well hidden. Good gosh, Stephen, we've been seeing each other for three months!"

"It's not—it's not what you think," Stephen defended himself.

"Well, either it's for me or it's not—and I'm not sure which is more disturbing—but the fact remains, you have a wedding ring in your nightstand drawer." She got up again and pulled on her shirt.

"It wasn't for you," Stephen said quietly.

"Was it hers?" Kristie pointed to the picture of Paige. She adjusted her shirt, smoothing it against her body.

"No, actually." Stephen got up out of bed and pulled on a pair of boxer briefs. He sat down on the edge of the bed and wondered if he looked as rejected as he felt.

Now Kristie hesitated. "There was a second potential missus? Do tell."

Stephen sighed. It wasn't a story he wanted to relive. It wasn't something he talked about. He'd met Carley Smith a few years ago, long after Paige had ended things with him. They'd lived together and raised Anna for a year before she'd broken up with Stephen. But Carley quickly decided she couldn't live without Anna and kidnapped her while Stephen was away and Anna was with his parents. In an attempt to keep Anna and make the police stop looking for her, Carley faked her and Anna's deaths. Stephen was left in agony that two people he loved in his life were suddenly dead. When he realized they were actually still alive, he'd found and tracked Carley down. Except he had arrived minutes too late. She had been shot in the abdomen and then died in his arms. He found Anna minutes later, unharmed—physically. They found out later that four-year-old Anna had witnessed the murder.

"No?" Kristie replied to Stephen's silence. "That's the thing about you, Stephen. You fall hard for a woman, start planning a wedding, but you don't know how to be vulnerable or open enough to get her down the aisle."

Stephen's phone started ringing. He glanced at the screen. It was the office.

"Then there's that." Kristie pointed to his phone. She slipped on her shoes, walked a few steps to him, and kissed him a long good-bye. "Call me if you need a little fun."

Stephen watched her go, thinking sadly about why he couldn't ever make them stay. Was he really that unlovable?

His phone rang again, and he answered this time.

"Stephen? How fast can you get here? We have a new case." Deputy Director Rob Sikes was all business.

"I can be there in twenty minutes," Stephen said, knowing it would take him five to shower. He hung up. As he quickly showered, turned off the hot water, and toweled off, he thought about Kristie's words.

While his daughter, Anna, was his family, she didn't live with him. He did want to have a full-time family of his own someday. He would love to get married and maybe even have another child or two. But right now, he was married to his job. That would have to be enough.

2

SELAH

Her signature red lipstick was smeared up the side of her face and her head was tilted as if she'd been thrown forward, her chin resting on her chest. Her long blonde hair, which gave the angelic look she strived for, was flipped over her head. She didn't know there was blood matted in her hair.

She woke slowly, groggily at first. Her neck was hurting. She lifted her head, seeing only the hair in her face. She shook her head to clear the obstruction to her sight when she found she could not use her hands. They were tied behind her back. She yanked a few times to discover they were bound securely.

Then she gasped as her eyes noted her surroundings. She was limited in what she could see. From her vantage point, a layer of dust covered a cement floor and one stack of boxes piled on top of each other all the way up to the ceiling. It was a small room, and she was in the center of it sitting on a folding chair. It looked like she was in a basement. An empty basement, save the boxes and the chair she sat on. Her eyes roamed, looking for a door, but she could not find one. There weren't any windows either. There was a staircase against the wall that led up higher than Selah could see. She assumed there was a door at the top.

A groan erupted from behind her.

"What the—" she gasped, surprised to hear the groan so close to her. She tried to look behind her, but she couldn't crane her neck far enough. It sounded like... "Maddox," Selah said.

"Hello?" came the abrupt response.

Her heart sank. He was the last person she wanted to see right now.

"You? You tied me up? Selah, are you crazy? This is way over the line—"

"Umm, I'm tied up too. In case you haven't noticed. Do you really think I could kidnap you?" her voice dripped with sarcasm.

"Are we kidnapped?" Maddox's voice sounded panicked. He started pulling on the ties. Selah only knew this because when he yanked at the rope, her rope moved as well.

"We're tied together," she sighed in response. With this knowledge came the sense that they were tied back-to-back. His body heat radiated against her back, keeping her warm.

"Great! That's just great. I have a big, important game to play. It's the first time we've played this team since they beat us in the championship last year. This is personal to me! What day is it? How long have I been gone?" His words were coming out in angry, emotional bursts. He was now yanking with all his strength at the ropes. "Where are we? Is this some kind of a joke?"

"First of all—ow. I don't want to be here either, you know," Selah said, feeling more annoyed than hurt. She chose to believe his reaction wasn't aimed at her. He was just scared, like she was, and reacting. But the more he pulled, the more the ropes rubbed her wrist. She'd woken up before him, so she'd had more time to process the situation. "No, I don't think this is a joke."

"Does it really hurt when I yank the ties?" he asked, his voice a little softer. "Because I'd like to get out of here alive. What's a little wrist burn compared to death? I knew letting your bodyguard go to have some alone time was going to bite us in the—"

"You're right. I can handle it. Keep trying the ties," Selah's voice dropped to a whimper. "Do you really think we're going to die? Don't you think we'd already be dead if so? We need to think this through. Did someone kidnap us? We weren't even together at the time... Who would kidnap us and put us in a small room together—"

"Half of America!" Maddox retorted angrily. "I swear to God. Everyone told me not to date you. *She's too big city for you,* they said. *She's too big of a star.* America will never let you have privacy. Why didn't I listen?"

"Too big city?" Selah asked drawing her words out, feeling the sharp sting of indignance. "I'm from a smaller town than you. You would know that if you ever listened to anything other than yourself at dinner time! Besides, *you* sought *me* out. You knew what you were getting yourself into."

Maddox was now yanking the ropes fervently.

Selah took a deep breath in, working to ignore the rope burn. Maddox was right. The pain in her wrists would pale compared to what someone might have in store for them.

"They forgot to warn me what a diva you were. A real piece of work."

"Oh, poor Maddox," Selah mocked, reacting to the pain his words were causing her heart. He had clearly held a lot back prior to the breakup. "The multi-million dollar diva was more popular than you and made more money than you and was actually self-made and independent. It's not my fault it hurt your feelings when I opened my own car door or reached for the check at restaurants, I—"

The room went silent. The silence stretched on for an uncomfortable minute.

"What?" Maddox asked. He'd stopped yanking the rope and was trying to crane around and see what had caused Selah to stop talking mid-sentence.

Selah was looking at a woman in her early thirties. The woman was sitting at the top of a staircase that had been hidden behind all the boxes. The woman had brown hair from what Selah could see in the dark, and black, beady eyes. She was thin. She was staring at her and Maddox with a strange fascination in her eyes. She looked familiar.

"I know you," Selah said slowly, recognition dawning. But she couldn't place where she knew her from. Was she a fan? A stalker?

"What's going on?" Maddox asked, still trying to see behind him.

"Shh," Selah shushed him. "I'm talking to the woman at the top of the stairs."

"The w—"

Clapping erupted and the woman stood up. She clapped slowly as she took the stairs one at a time, excruciatingly slow.

Selah's heart beat faster. The woman was dressed from head to toe in black. She carried an ominous vibe. She moved like she was floating. Almost like walking in slow motion. Her eyes, which never left Selah's, were piercing and soulless. The effect was terrifying. Selah watched, stiffening her body to prepare for whatever came next. Finally, the woman stood in front of Selah. She reached out a hand and Selah flinched, expecting a blow. Instead, the woman inspected Selah's head.

"Ouch," Selah exclaimed as the woman touched a tender spot.

"Sorry," the woman said disingenuously without the hint of real emotion. "I didn't want to hit you. I just couldn't see any other way…"

"I feel like we've met before," Selah said warmly. If she'd learned anything in her career, it was how to fake it with her fans. This one probably needed to feel known. If Selah didn't acknowledge her, she knew things would go very bad very quickly.

"You remember me?" The woman stood back and gazed at Selah in admiration. "I'm Elle. I helped you with makeup before *The Entertainment Today Show*."

"Oh! Elle. Right, I do remember you!" Selah didn't really remember the woman doing her makeup at all, but she knew how to play it up.

"Well, I'm actually way more than a makeup artist. This proves it." Elle smiled triumphantly. "I'm part of a way bigger plan. But *this* was all me. I got you here all by myself."

"Oh, come on!" Maddox interrupted insolently. "There's no way you got me here all by yourself."

Elle stomped over to face Maddox. "Fine," she snapped angrily. "I have a cousin. He's a big guy. He has a limo. He helped get you out of the car."

"Did he also hit me over the head? I have a massive headache," Maddox whined.

Elle laughed. "No, that's from the drug we gave you. You're the best part of my plan."

"Why?" Maddox asked. "What did I do?"

"It's not what you did. It's what you're going to do." Elle waved her hand like the details didn't matter.

"She's the one you want," Maddox said, his voice loaded with bitterness. "She's way more popular than I am—"

Selah sucked in a terrified breath. *Cowardly move, Maddox*, she thought.

The woman smacked Maddox across the face hard enough that his whole body moved sideways. That stopped him from talking for the moment.

"You!" the woman spat contemptuously. "You are some

piece of work. *You* are the reason she's so heartbroken. You couldn't even keep her happy for more than four months. That says a lot about you." The woman poked a black, pointy acrylic fingernail in his face.

Selah could feel the back of Maddox's head tap the back of hers as he reacted to the finger in his face.

"How did you know about that? We just broke up in the hotel," Maddox asked. His voice sounded humble and fearful.

"I have my ways," Elle sang out cheerfully.

"Come on. Relationships are a two-way street. Everyone knows that. There was no way this was gonna last. She's on tour half the year. I'm playing ball or practicing most the year..." Maddox tried to argue.

"Shut up!" Elle snapped angrily.

Selah could feel her upper lip start to sweat.

"You could not do any better than Selah, and you'd do well to remember that. You two are not leaving until you learn to get along. America wants you together. Not to mention, together you can do great things."

"That's it?" Maddox asked. "You'll let me go if I just continue to date Selah?"

The woman hit him again. "See, that's where you're wrong. In a relationship, it's not about *me*, it's about *us*. You're a selfish bastard. I knew it. I could just tell."

Maddox was quiet now.

Selah was too horrified to laugh. But this woman had him pegged.

Elle turned and walked halfway up the stairs.

"Wait," Selah called out. "If we promise to keep dating, can we go free? He has the game to get to and I'm supposed to be on the *Pretty in Pink* tour..."

Elle paused, looked back, and snorted. "The game is in a week. I don't think he'll make it that long. I'm betting on the other team, anyway." She turned and went up the stairs.

Selah heard a door shut and lock at the top of the stairs.

"I'm the selfish one?" Maddox cried with outrage in his voice.

"Yeah, she's got your number alright," Selah said with a smirk.

"Looks like we're never getting out of here," Maddox growled.

"We could pretend, you know," Selah pointed out the obvious. "We did like each other once."

"No way in hell," Maddox stated emphatically. "I'm not pretending anymore."

Selah rolled her eyes. "I could call her back down and have her kill you if you would prefer?"

"You'd like that, wouldn't you?" Maddox snapped.

"Good God, Maddox. I think you're a jerk, but I don't want you dead."

"Well, I don't want to die either. There's one thing we can agree on."

"Do you think they're looking for us? The police?" Selah rolled her ankles which were surprisingly unbound.

"We're America's biggest stars right now. Of course they are looking for us. I bet they knew we went missing the minute we fell off the map—"

"Shh!" Selah sat up straighter.

"You, shh!" Maddox snapped.

"No, did you realize she used the exact same words you did? She said, *You are a real piece of work.*" Selah's eyes started roaming around the room.

"So what?" Maddox asked.

"What if she has a camera down here? Do you think she's live streaming us?" Selah whispered.

"No way," Maddox whispered back. "That'd be a good way to get caught."

"Maybe, but I bet she's got a camera on us. I think we're

going to have to work together to get out of here," Selah whispered.

Maddox grunted and grew quiet.

3

WILTON

Deputy Director Rob Sikes put a navy-blue folder with the official US Marshal emblem on the table and pulled out two five-by-seven professional photos, which he slid across the table in front of Stephen and his partner, Ethan Booker. Stephen glanced at the photos with instant recognition. Selah Lablanc was the number one American pop artist of the year. Maddox Miller was a tight end who played in the NFL for Kansas City.

He snickered. "What's this?" Stephen asked.

"This, gentlemen, is the case the Attorney General has assigned us," Sikes answered.

"I don't get it," Booker said.

Stephen watched Booker lean over and study the glossy headshots earnestly. Booker was serious most of the time. He was shorter and stockier than Stephen. Not that it mattered. Stephen still believed he was stronger than Booker. Booker's intellectual brain and the way he handled his gun made him an excellent partner to work with.

"Selah Lablanc and Maddox Miller, America's hottest new couple," Stephen cracked with his best announcer voice. Then he got serious. "What about them?"

"Wait, Selah is dating Maddox Miller?" Booker looked devastated.

Stephen smirked and shook his head. "Sometimes, buddy, I swear you live under a rock."

"Well," said Booker, still flabbergasted by this news, "she can do way better than Maddox Miller!"

"Haven't you seen his football stats this year? Without Maddox Miller, Kansas City wouldn't have the winning record they have. Just wait your turn, Booker. It'll be over any day now. You may get your shot yet."

Booker's face reddened a little. "I guess I haven't been watching the games lately."

Stephen laughed at his partner's baffled expression.

"You two done?" Sikes asked.

Stephen got serious.

"Good." Sikes rapped his knuckle on the wood table where they sat in the conference room. "Both Selah Lablanc and Maddox Miller have disappeared. They were last seen three days ago at Casa Cipriani hotel in New York. We have testimonies that Selah screamed at Maddox so loudly in the hotel, the people in the suite next door heard her—"

"What does that have to do with us?" Stephen interrupted, feeling confused. "Marshals don't get involved with adult kidnappings."

"Very good, Rookie," Sikes smirked. "Six months out of the academy, so you still remember exam answers. But there's something you're forgetting."

"Oh?" Stephen sat up straighter and thought a minute.

"We step in when police, FBI, and marshals are at capacity working other cases. Maddox Miller is from Kansas City—he's one of our own. Further, they have a suspect for the kidnapping and don't have the time and resources to apprehend her. A woman known as *The Fan*. She posted bail after a failed kidnapping stunt but never showed up for court. She's had a warrant for her arrest for over three months. This kidnapping case has her name written all over it. We need to find *The Fan*. Where we find her, we likely find Maddox and Selah. Though Maddox lives in Kansas City, he and Selah were last seen in New York—which was where *The Fan* was last seen as well."

"So, we go to New York, find *The Fan,* and bring Maddox and Selah home," Booker summed up.

"Gold star to Booker," Sikes agreed. "If you'll direct your attention to the screen…" He had grabbed the mouse on the table and pointed it to the large screen on the wall casting from the MacBook Pro in front of him. He clicked on the Zoom app.

Stephen saw two names on the screen waiting to be admitted. Sikes clicked on the first name—*Devon Peterson, FBI Director.* Then he clicked on the second name—*Jack Tigress, MCPD Chief.*

Sikes sat down. Stephen and Booker followed his lead.

"Good morning, gentleman," Sikes greeted.

"Sikes," Peterson returned.

"I don't know how good the morning is, but I'll take your word for it," Tigress bit directly. He looked wound tight, like he was ready to spring into action.

Stephen gulped. He didn't know how he was expecting this day to go but he certainly hadn't expected an impromptu meeting with the heads of the FBI and the MCPD which he knew stood for Manhattan County Police Department, a precinct in New York. He felt like he'd been blindsided and wished someone would have given him a heads up. He sat up taller, his whole focus on the men on the screen. Was this a task force?

"Peterson and Tigress, these are two of our finest marshals, Wilton and Booker," Sikes indicated who was who as he spoke their names. "Wilton, Booker, meet Devon Peterson, FBI Field Officer Director for Manhattan, and Jack Tigress, Chief of Police for the MCPD."

Finest marshals? Stephen thought. *More like most available marshals...* Still Stephen appreciated Sikes throwing his support behind them in front of these officers.

They all said a round of *hellos*. Introductions over, they got right to business.

Tigress took the lead. The kidnapping had, after all, happened in his city. "Approximately three days ago, Selah Lablanc and Maddox Miller were reported missing. Maddox had been spending time with Selah during his bye week. Now these are grown-ass adults, and half of us in the office have a working theory that Selah and Maddox finally figured out a way to allude the paparazzi and media. Most likely they ran away together—"

"But we have reasons to think the opposite is true," Peterson broke in. "The publicist says she created a get-away plan to sneak Maddox out the back door of the hotel. Apparently, this wasn't uncommon. Turns out America's sweethearts aren't so sweet on each other anymore."

Tigress grudgingly shrugged his shoulder. "The other half of the office is operating under the theory that a crazed woman, whom we like to call *The Fan*, found a way to kidnap these two. She's attempted kidnapping stars before and managed to get away before she could be convicted. Though I have no idea how she could manhandle a guy Maddox's size anywhere unless she had help. Regardless, no one has seen or heard from Selah after her scream. The publicist can't confirm that Maddox got in the car she sent for him. We know he didn't show up for the first practice after bye week, but we've got a call in to the airport to check if he actually got on a plane that day."

"That's right," Stephen said. "If he doesn't play—"

"They won't win," Sikes repeated Stephen's earlier words. "There's a lot riding on this game. They lost the championship to the team they're scheduled to play, didn't they?"

"Well, that's motive right there!" Booker exclaimed, throwing his hands up. "Anyone who gambles big money and puts it on the other team could gain by taking Maddox out of commission until the game is over!"

"Don't forget about Selah's scream," Stephen mused. "Any background of assault on Maddox? Was there any evidence of foul play in the hotel room?"

"MCPD made a routine check and found no blood, no DNA, and few fingerprints," Tigress answered. "Other than a few pillows strewn all over the room, nothing was amiss."

"Pillows!" Booker smirked. "What, did they have a pillow fight?"

"Actually," Stephen said while staring at Booker, "that scream could have been playful. We should keep our minds open to possibilities. What if Selah ended up slipping out of the back of the hotel with him? To your point, Chief, they could have left together and found a way to hide from the media, and everyone is panicking while they finally managed to find a little privacy."

"Regardless," Sikes pinned Stephen with his gaze. "We definitely need to find *The Fan*. And I don't need to tell you discretion is of the utmost importance here."

"What can you tell us about *The Fan*?" Booker asked.

Peterson fielded this one. "She starts by sending fan letters to her favorite star. It seems innocent enough. Her first two kidnapping attempts went terribly wrong—probably due to inexperience—but on her third attempt, she succeeded. Until her victim got away. She had three big-name witnesses take the stand and testify against her. It would have been an open-and-shut case, but the judge allowed bail and *The Fan* disappeared."

"Does *The Fan* have a name?" Stephen asked dryly. He knew from recent training that tracking and apprehending criminals fell under the jurisdiction of the marshal services but they sure seemed to be putting a lot of energy into the theory that this person had the means to kidnap two well-known stars.

"Elle Jones," Peterson stated.

"Who called in the disappearance and why did they wait three days?" Stephen challenged, still holding on to his gut feeling.

Peterson cleared his voice. "Her sister, Stacia, reported Selah missing. She had also assumed Selah and Maddox were off somewhere together until Selah missed the jet to her first concert stop on the new *Pretty in Pink* tour. Shortly after, Maddox's family called to report him missing. When the coach called asking where Maddox was because he didn't show up for practice, his family was concerned. With the big game coming soon, Maddox was due back on the field. He's not the kind of player who will just miss practice randomly. He hates paying fines and loves the game, so he's hasn't missed one this year. Turns out, no one in either family had seen or heard from either of them for over three days."

"Did Selah receive any letters from *The Fan*?" Stephen asked, still puzzling over this supposed connection.

"None that we know of but we haven't had a chance to interview her mom, yet," Peterson answered.

"Booker, Wilton, any other questions or do you have enough to get you started?" Sikes asked.

"What are the protocols for investigating in New York?" Stephen asked.

Tigress responded. "You've got full support and cooperation from MCPD. You need anything, like backup, we're a phone call away."

"Is there any other information we need to be aware of while we investigate?" Booker asked. "I'm still unclear on why we're heading to your city when you probably have a staff full of detectives and marshals who are perfectly capable of investigating—"

"A-hem," Sikes cleared his throat, but it sounded like he was annoyed.

Stephen felt his pulse speed up at Booker's bold, direct

question. It had come across like a challenge. To his surprise, Tigress laughed and looked a little proud.

"You may have seen something in the media, but we've had a string of corporate CEO's showing up dead recently. What originally looked like random deaths appears to be connected. We've all been working overtime. In fact, Peterson's team has been helping us connect the dots. We're crossing our fingers that the connections stop in New York. We don't want to think about the resources we would need if this became an international investigation."

"What else?" Sikes asked while looking at Stephen and Booker.

"I think I have enough to get started," Stephen answered. "We can touch base when we land."

"Great," Deputy Peterson answered. He signed off the screen with a wave.

"Sounds good," Tigress said. His screen went black.

"What else?" Sikes asked again now that it was just the three of them.

Stephen scratched his head, feeling a little starstruck and confused. "Why me? I know Booker has been with the marshals for over eight years, but I'm not exactly a senior marshal in the office."

"You're becoming a bit of an expert on kidnappings, Wilton," Sikes responded.

"I am?" Stephen asked, feeling surprised by the news.

"Sure are. You saved your daughter who had been kidnapped—"

"Glad that nightmare is over!" Stephen exclaimed.

"You followed a lead to find your friend, James, who had been kidnapped in Canada, and you brought him back home safely."

"But what about Demitri Abbott?" Stephen asked, wondering about his priorities. They still had a murderer on the loose who had ties to the mob and that was Stephen's personal priority.

"Don't worry, you'll be the first to know if we get a lead on Abbott," Sikes confirmed.

If Demitri Abbott ever shows up again, Stephen thought.

Sikes scooped up the glossies and put them in a file along with the names and testimonies of the people the MCPD had already talked to. Sikes slid the file across the table to Stephen and Booker. "You'll find your plane tickets in there along with the address for your hotel, a vehicle rental confirmation number, contact information for the folks in New York, and other logistical information. You leave this evening."

Stephen grabbed the file, his mind going down the rabbit hole that happened every time he thought of Demitri Abbott. He was glad no one was saying what they were all thinking. There was a good chance the criminal Demitri Abbott would elude them just like he had a number of times before.

Demitri Abbott had killed Stephen's ex-girlfriend, Carley Smith. The story was Carley and Demitri were seeing one another when he killed her. The motive for the murder was unknown. Stephen believed Demitri had met Stephen's daughter, Anna, during that time. When the murder went down, Anna had been hiding there in the room.

Stephen worried constantly that Demitri would eventually come for Anna. But he hadn't so far. In the meantime, Stephen had Anna in karate and had given Paige, her mom, strict instructions to teach Anna how to use a gun when she was old enough.

Stephen worked out of the Kansas City office, which put him hours away—too far away to help if anything happened to his daughter. His only comfort was that his *baby mama*, as Kristie had called Paige, knew how to shoot a gun and had spent time working in a police office. Paige was also teaching her husband, James, how to shoot. They believed Anna was safer hidden away in a small, country town than with Stephen in Kansas City.

Booker slapped Stephen on the back. "We'll find Demitri Abbott. Don't you worry, my friend."

Booker was lying, but Stephen appreciated the gesture. Stephen felt deep in his gut, which he was learning more and more to rely on, that Demitri Abbott was long gone.

"How will you be able to keep this from Kristie?" Booker grinned as he stood up from the table. "Isn't she a huge Selah fan?"

"Trust me, I won't be talking to Kristie anymore," Stephen said lowly, bracing himself for the inevitable ribbing.

"Another one—"

"Bites the dust, yeah," Stephen attempted to beat him to the punchline.

"Oh man!" Booker shook his head with a wide grin. "That's rough."

"Yeah." Stephen gritted his teeth. Booker had no idea how hard it was on Stephen to invest time into someone only to be dumped. But harder still was the fact that it happened repeatedly.

"When?" Booker asked.

"A few days ago," Stephen admitted.

He thought he saw admiration in Booker's eyes as he repeated the nickname Stephen was growing to hate, *Love 'Em and Leave 'Em Wilton.*

But Stephen was beginning to wonder if his problem went much deeper than that. He wondered if he was worthy of love. He walked back to his cubicle. All his intrusive thoughts paused when he saw that he had a visitor.

The visitor stood looking out the window with her back to Stephen. Her five-foot-four-inch frame barely took up the corner of his cubicle. Long, thick brown hair waved halfway down her back. She was slim and appeared toned under her white blouse.

The pencil skirt she wore accentuated her curvy hips and back-side. His eyes scanned down her muscular calves to her practical black high-heeled pumps.

"Are you taking the case?" the woman asked as she turned.

Stephen's face reddened as he realized she had known he was there, and she must have seen him checking her out through the reflection of the window.

"The case?" he asked blankly. He now found himself staring into a pair of large, green eyes that assessed him coolly. She was beautiful, but what left him breathless was her resemblance to someone he had once loved.

Her pretty, heart-shaped lips pursed in disapproval. It occurred to Stephen that this woman, whom he had never met before, did not like him.

4

WILTON

"I said, are you going to take the case—the Selah Lablanc and Maddox Miller kidnapping?" the pretty female repeated the question impatiently.

"Have we met?" Stephen responded, feeling confused because the case wasn't supposed to be common knowledge. "I wasn't aware I had a choice in what cases I accept."

Her eyes were like emeralds. Big, deep-green sparks of anger flashed at him. Was she angry with him or just angry in general? He searched his memory for what he could have possibly done to this woman.

"You do," she answered bluntly. She studied him for a minute. A silence stretched to the point of discomfort. Her eyes roamed intrusively the length of his body down to his shoes and back up again to meet his eyes. He was on the verge of asking again if he could help her with something when she stuck out her hand.

"Alyah Smith," she said crisply.

"Stephen Wilton," he replied, taking her hand.

Her hand was warm, and Stephen held it half a second too

long. Irritation flashed in her eyes again as Alyah reclaimed her hand abruptly.

Recognition triggered Stephen's brain. "Wait, I know you," he said.

"No. You don't. We've never met. I'm the District Attorney—"

"Ah," Stephen said, thinking that must be how he'd recognized her.

"I came to talk to you about the Selah and Maddox case," Alyah's voice was curt, her tone was direct. "You don't have to take it."

"I see." Stephen didn't know what to make of this feisty little woman in his office glaring at him. "I'm trying to figure out why a District Attorney would care whether I take this case or not."

"I have my reasons. So, with this case, I'm giving you an out. This is a high-profile case and I need to make sure we do everything by the book. There will be a lot of attention on us." She crossed her arms over her curvy chest and glared at Stephen. "It requires the *right* US Marshal."

"I'm sorry, I'm confused. I think I need more information. Are you up for re-election or something?" Stephen asked. He was starting to feel irritated. A district attorney would only be here for one reason. Had someone complained about him? "What makes you think I'm not the *right* US Marshal for the job?"

Alyah Smith stepped out of his cubicle and beckoned him to the conference room with the crook of her finger.

Stephen followed her, feeling curious and a little worried.

Once she shut the door and they were alone in the room, Alyah turned back to him. "You're the newest marshal on our team and you don't have the best prior track record. You got lucky when you were hired on as a US Marshal. I did my research. You were fired from your last job as a detective, Wilton. I know all about you."

"I was promoted to my next opportunity!" Stephen protested weakly, quoting the words his lieutenant had used at the time. He felt his eyes widen in disbelief. His pulse was racing. The truth was, he *had* been fired. But the lieutenant he worked for had given him a glowing letter of recommendation.

"Sounds like a fancy way to say you were fired." She tapped the toe of her pointy shoe for emphasis.

"Unbelievable," Stephen said, shaking his head. Going sideways with the District Attorney in the first six months on the job was not a smart way to jump start his career. "Why were you looking into me in the first place?"

Alyah shrugged. "It's my job to make sure we have reputable US Marshals who are doing what they're supposed to be doing and not cutting corners. I'm not sure how you got caught up in the Demitri Abbott case. Something tells me there's a lot more to that story than you let on."

Stephen crossed his arms and shrugged.

"Your first job here with the marshals was to get to know Scott Milternett, the Kansas City crime boss, and make him feel comfortable with you. There's a hole in your statement about what went down the night you found your kidnapped daughter. How you ended up in pursuit of Demitri Abbott is a complete mystery. He wasn't a part of your assignment. The fact that you *miraculously* found your missing daughter while in pursuit of Abbott is not lost on me. You had your own agenda that night and I think it got someone killed."

Stephen's mouth dropped open. "I didn't... I wasn't—" Stephen had no idea how to respond.

Scott Milternett was Carley's uncle. Carley was Stephen's ex-girlfriend and the woman who had taken his daughter. Stephen had suspected Scott had something to do with Anna's disappearance and Stephen had been correct. But he had chosen not to disclose his personal interest in the case in the statement. No one knew he was personally involved in the case until he trailed Carley to the hotel where Demitri Abbott had just put a bullet in her abdomen. Carley had died in Stephen's arms that night.

"Articulate." Alyah smirked meanly.

"Wait a minute. Carley Smith. Alyah Smith," Stephen said slowly. His eyes slid closed, and he groaned as the recognition of her name dawned. "Carley was your sister?"

"And your ex-girlfriend," Alyah snapped as she pointed at Stephen's chest.

Stephen stared at her. All of his earlier irritation melted away. Compassion and sorrow filled him as he gazed at her stiff, angry countenance. He wanted to hug her. He wanted—no needed—the connection to grieve this loss with her. No one else knew how bereft he had felt. Not only would a hug be highly unprofessional, it would also be a little like hugging a porcupine.

"Alyah, I'm so sorry for your loss," Stephen whispered. He watched as surprise filled her eyes, followed by a flicker of sorrow, then snapped back to anger.

"We were told her car went off the side of a mountain. We didn't know she was still alive. We had a funeral. So, to be told, *Surprise, Carley's been alive all this time but now, for sure, she's dead,* well, surely you can understand the whiplash of emotions. Not to mention the questions that no one can seem to answer."

"Alyah, I'll answer your questions any time."

"No!" she snapped. "I don't want to talk to *you* about it. Truth be told, I don't trust you. Which brings me back to the Maddox and Selah case. You don't have to take it. I work closely with the Attorney General and you should know that if you do take the case, I'll be watching you very closely. Because someone in this office needs to."

Stephen nodded slowly, processing her words. *Maybe she's up for re-election and feeling stressed*, he thought, *or maybe, she's taking her grief out on me*. He knew all too well that anger was a form of grief. He understood her pain. Pain in the form of anger was easier to control than sadness. Everything he'd said had come out wrong, so he chose silence as Alyah abruptly turned around and exited the conference room.

Despite her obvious dislike for him, Stephen knew Alyah Smith, with those flashing, angry eyes, would haunt his dreams. He couldn't wait.

5

WILTON

The sun was setting and casting a beautiful array of colors across the sky as Stephen exited his car that afternoon and walked to his two-bedroom home. He'd left work early to come home, pack, and maybe sleep an hour before he headed to the airport.

The home was big enough for Stephen, the eternal bachelor. It was a little plain with white siding that wrapped the house and black trim around the windows. The door was black too.

He paused after walking up three stairs to his front door and before walking in. There would be no dog to greet him. No children would run to the door and scream, *Daddy's home*! No beautiful wife or girlfriend would yell, *Hi, honey, how was your day?* There would be nothing on the other side of that door. A quiet, lifeless silence would welcome him home.

As he had expected, the silence met him at the door. With a quiet sigh, he walked in and locked the door behind him. He immediately turned on the TV. Noise filled the quiet space and drowned out his thoughts. At least, for now.

Stephen pulled off his clothes. The office was business casual, which had consisted of a plain blue button-down shirt, a pair of dark jeans, and black Brooks. Stephen had argued for the tennis shoes on account of the number of times he found himself running after criminals in this line of work.

He unholstered his gun and laid it on top of the toilet tank. He got in the shower and immediately turned on the hot spray of water. Most days a shower was enough to wash away the grime of work sweat, along with the stress of his thoughts. Today, it didn't work. He couldn't stop thinking about Alyah.

He didn't fault Alyah for her anger. He even understood now why it was directed at him. He was surprised to find she had gone through the trouble of looking into his past. He should be irritated over the assumptions she'd made about him losing his job. He wasn't. He was impressed. She was right.

Still, he hated to be at odds with anyone. He wondered how he could win her over.

Not gonna happen, buddy, he told himself. *You can't win 'em all.*

What really got under his skin was how much she looked like Carley. She was her sister, after all. Carley had spoken very little about her family. What she had said had been very negative. Still, he remembered that Alyah was Carley's half-sister. Which meant Alyah should only half resemble Carley. Alyah was petite and curvier than her sister. But those eyes took him back to a time when Carley had been the center of his world.

He thought about his irksome office nickname, *Love 'Em and Leave 'Em Wilton.* He felt embarrassed as he pondered if Alyah had heard that nickname as well. Well, they were half right. Stephen fell in love too easily. But it was always the women who did the leaving. Impressing a woman into his bed wasn't hard for Stephen. It was keeping the woman in a relationship that Stephen couldn't seem to figure out.

But Alyah certainly wasn't impressed by him. She saw straight through him. She knew who he really was. He'd been fired as a detective and immediately took the job of US Marshal, which he still felt he'd gotten by sheer luck.

Unlucky in love. Lucky in work. Which is precisely why he preferred to spend the majority of his time there.

Stephen turned off the shower and toweled off. He immediately went to the living room and turned up the TV. He'd do anything to drown out his thoughts. He headed to his bedroom and got dressed in a new pair of jeans and a t-shirt. He preferred to be more casual while traveling. He threw a coat on the bed next to a suitcase he'd pulled out. New York in November would be cold.

His cell phone rang as he went to the freezer and pulled out a frozen dinner with the word *Healthy* on it. He snickered to himself. Was there really such a thing in a frozen dinner?

"Hello?" he answered.

"Daddy!" Anna, his four-and-a-half-year-old daughter squealed.

"Hey, honey!" Stephen greeted. He smiled despite his earlier thoughts.

"Are you coming to my karate tournament?" Anna asked, sounding breathless.

Alarmed, Stephen looked at the events on his calendar. This was the first he was hearing about a tournament. "When is it?"

"Two weeks, silly daddy!" she giggled.

Stephen smiled. "Right, of course."

"Momma says she'll get me a new puppy if I get another belt!"

"A puppy!" Stephen exclaimed, thinking this was overkill.

"Yes!" Anna squealed again.

"Put your mom on the phone," Stephen requested.

"Okay," Anna agreed. He imagined she went skipping off to find her mom.

The phone went quiet for a moment.

"Hello?" answered Paige, his ex-girlfriend and baby mama. Her voice sounded like warm honey.

"Hey," Stephen greeted, willing his heart to slow down.

Regret often washed over him when he talked to her. "Did you tell Anna you were getting her a puppy?"

Paige laughed. "Kind of, but it's not what you think. I told her I'd take her to a puppy show if she gets her next belt at the tournament. Not to get a puppy, just to go look at them. Right, Anna?"

Stephen could hear Anna giggle again and knew his clever daughter had been working him and her mom simultaneously.

"When is the tournament, Paige?" Stephen asked.

"It's in two weeks..." Paige wasn't talking to him anymore. "Oh, James, can you grab Aurora? She's crying... Sorry, Stephen."

"It's okay," Stephen said but felt that familiar pang in his heart. He was glad to see Paige so happy. She and her new husband had twins recently and she seemed to always be juggling the three kids these days. It was hard for him not to think *I saw her first* when he was around her husband.

"Can I get back to you with the date?" Paige asked, sounding distracted.

"Sure. Before you go, you should know I'm going out of town on a case."

"How long?" she asked.

Stephen didn't pretend it was because she was worried about him. It purely had to do with tempering Anna's expectations.

"Not sure. I'll be back in time for the tournament," Stephen gave a promise he knew he had no right to give.

Paige sighed over the phone and lowered her voice. "She misses you all the time, Stephen. Today's a good day, but her nightmares are still steady."

Stephen nodded, forgetting for a minute Paige couldn't see him. "I'll be back in time. Can you please put Anna back on the phone?" Stephen asked. He put his frozen dinner in the microwave as his smart, spunky daughter came back on the line.

"How's school going, Anna?" Stephen asked. He watched the meal spinning in the microwave.

"Jaime Sisco is a bully!" she announced.

"What did she do?" Stephen asked.

"*He* pulled my hair," Anna said.

"Did you punch him?" Stephen asked, knowing the last time she dealt with a bully she'd taken matters into her own hands and punched him in the nose.

"No!" Anna said solemnly. "Sensei says I'm not supposed to hit or kick anyone at school."

"Right. I'm glad Sensei taught you that," Stephen said with a smile, knowing he had taught her that long before her sensei had. He pulled out his dinner and sat down to eat and talk.

"I told my teacher," Anna announced proudly.

"Great! That's exactly what you should have done," Stephen praised.

"I know," Anna responded.

After a few more minutes, and a long story about Anna's new best friend, Anna stopped storytelling.

"Mama says I need to go wash my hands for dinner."

Stephen said *goodbye* and hung up the phone, feeling a big pit in his stomach. He found himself wishing for his phone to alert that he needed to come back in to work.

Work would save him from this empty house, but he wasn't sure what would save him from the emptiness in his heart. He finished his bland dinner and sat on the couch, willing himself to relax as he stared at the TV screen. Chances of a nap before the flight were small.

Instead, he was trying to calculate exactly where he would be and when so he could be back for Anna's tournament. He could hear the excitement in Anna's voice as she invited him.

Anna needed to be the one female relationship in his life that didn't end in disappointment.

Booker sent a text to ask if Stephen was ready for the big trip to New York. Despite Alyah's admonishment to not take the case, and his current fear of missing Anna's tournament, Stephen had decided to take the assignment. He'd be ready. He just needed to throw the rest of his clothes in a small suitcase.

After all, work was Stephen's comfort zone. He'd be back for Anna's tournament if he had to get on a plane in the middle of a case and make a special trip home then fly back to resume his involvement.

Nothing would keep him away from his daughter's tournament. Nor would he miss the opportunity to prove to his very attractive District Attorney that he was just as qualified as the next guy to find Selah and Maddox and put their kidnapper behind bars.

He could do it all. He always had. His eyes were getting heavy as he watched the TV screen flicker. Within minutes, he was snoring. But his sleep was restless.

He would make it home in time for Anna's tournament. With the exception of his relationship with women, things worked out for Stephen. This would be no different.

He had no other choice.

6

SELAH

Time was dragging on. When they had been down in the basement for a day, Selah's arms and legs tingled, and her bottom had started going numb. As luck would have it, she'd had time to change out of her pantsuit before she was nabbed. She wore a pair of black leggings with a sweater that fell off one shoulder. But she had a problem that was worse than tingling and numbness. The need to relieve herself made the situation more urgent.

She would have thought the worst thing in the world would be to find herself tied to her ex-boyfriend who seemed to hate her. It was also horribly awkward that Maddox hadn't said more than two words to her since the deranged kidnapper had introduced herself.

But Selah's concerns had been for herself. Her most basic needs were not being taken care of and she had no idea how to fix that.

"Maddox?" she whispered, breaking the silence.

"Yeah?" he grunted.

"I need to pee," Selah announced with a sigh of embarrassment.

"Thanks for telling me," he answered.

He had stopped yanking on the ropes that bound them hours ago. Selah assumed his quiet state came from the fact that the big game was fast approaching, and Maddox wasn't there to practice. She had learned from him that missed practices equaled big fines. Instead, he was tied to her, the last person in the world he wanted to be with. It had been hard enough to convince him to come to New York during his bye week.

"Don't you have to go?" she asked.

"Yeah, I do," his voice was gruff and impatient. "Maybe we just agree that whatever happens in captivity stays in captivity?"

"You mean?" Selah was horrified. There was no way she could just relieve herself right here with him so close to her. She began to cry.

"Shit, Selah. Don't cry. We have to think of a way out of here," Maddox said, though his voice had softened considerably.

"What if we don't ever find a way out? What if we die down here?" Selah sniffled.

"You're such a pessimist. For someone who has so much good luck in life, you were always such a downer!" Maddox stated.

Selah's mouth dropped open. "Not true!" she protested.

"True."

"Give me one example!" she challenged.

"When you told me we would never have privacy and we might as well accept that even in our most private moments, someone would be watching."

"Well, that's just common sense—" she scoffed.

"It was constant. It was as if you didn't want to even hope we could have a normal life together."

"We wouldn't have," Selah said flatly. "I thought you might as well accept the life you were stepping into."

"Then there was the baby situation," Maddox spat out with disdain.

Selah froze. Pain radiated from the core of her heart and stiffened her joints. *The baby situation*. That was the real problem. That was the actual place where they'd gone wrong.

"I don't want to talk about that," Selah whispered.

"I bet," Maddox's voice was hot and angry. "I wouldn't either if I'd made such a horrible play at manipulating someone to stay with me."

Selah sucked in air as if she'd been slapped. "Is that what you think?"

"Yes."

Selah was spared from an answer when she heard, and then saw, footsteps on the stairs. She could feel her lip and forehead sweating. She had been dizzy, tired, and her stomach hurt from a long time of holding it when she needed to pee so badly. At that moment, watching her kidnapper come into view, Selah just felt terrified.

Selah tried to control her shaking, convinced she'd never felt so afraid in her life. Elle, their kidnapper, was standing in front of Selah and staring at her with her pupils dilated. There was a manic energy about her. Elle's dark brown hair was messy, falling out of her ponytail.

In one hand, Elle held a bucket. In the other hand, she held a gun. Selah jumped as the deranged woman dropped the bucket on the floor and it hit the ground with a loud clatter.

Elle began circling the two like a vulture circling a dead carcass. Selah tried to control the tears that sprang up over the imagery. Her stomach hurt so badly. Selah didn't want to die.

Elle paused in front of Selah, pointing the gun at her face. Selah squeezed her eyes shut in fear. This could be it.

"Open your eyes, I'm not gonna kill you today. But if you do something stupid, I'll have no choice. It would be such a waste." Elle smiled with meanness in her hard eyes. Then she continued. "Here's the deal. I'm going to untie your hands. Here's a bucket to relieve yourselves. This isn't Hollywood, this is the real world, and you'll need to suck it up. I'll bring you food a couple times a day. Don't try to rush the door. I'll know and I'll shoot you on the spot. Don't test me on this. It would be a bummer to have to kill America's sweethearts."

"What's the point?" Maddox asked harshly.

Elle stalked angrily to confront Maddox.

"Is there a ransom?" Maddox followed up his question. "If so, my mom will pay it."

"Yeah, mine will too," Selah chimed in eagerly.

"Don't you worry, there's a plan bigger than *you* in play." With that announcement, Elle took out a knife.

Selah flinched but couldn't make herself close her eyes now. She was frozen. If this was the end for her, she was going to have to watch every excruciating minute.

Instead, Elle cut Selah and Maddox free.

"Thank you so much!" Selah said as the ropes fell away. She rubbed her wrist where the ropes had made them raw. She could see the angry red marks on them.

Maddox kept silent.

Gun trained on the two, Elle went back to the staircase and walked slowly up the stairs.

When the door shut behind Elle, they could hear a deadbolt click into place.

Selah turned to Maddox, her eyes wide with shock. To her surprise, Maddox was now standing and grinning broadly at her.

"Your lipstick is smeared." He reached out to touch her cheek.

Selah jerked away angrily.

Maddox got serious then, his eyes filled with concern. "You have blood in your hair."

"I do?" Selah asked.

"Yeah, come here," he ordered, his voice soft. He stood in front of her as he investigated the small lump on her head. He touched it gently.

Selah winced.

"It's not bleeding anymore. I think it's okay. Do you remember getting kidnapped? Did she hit you on the head?" he asked.

Selah shrugged. "I don't remember anything, Maddox. One minute I was screaming at you to come back and the next minute, everything went black. Until I woke up here."

"It was similar for me too." Maddox nodded as his eyes searched the room, presumably for a way out. Then they settled back on Selah who could feel the tears welling in her eyes as she reached out to feel the sore spot on her head.

"Come here, Sey," he said. "Don't cry. I'm gonna get us out of here."

Selah walked into his outstretched arms. "How?"

"I don't know. I'll find a way. What do you think about that?"

"I think I need to use the bucket," Selah's replied.

7

WILTON

As he usually did on an airplane, Stephen reclined his seat back with his eyes closed, pretending to be asleep. Which is why he was so surprised when he felt a hard poke in his ribs.

"Hey," Booker said. "You awake?"

"I am now!" Stephen answered irritably.

Booker didn't seem to notice or care about his irritation. "Hey, do you think Kristie would be interested in me? I might actually have a chance since she's on the rebound."

"Booker, did it ever occur to you that I wasn't the one who did the dumping?" Stephen felt like Booker was rubbing salt in a wound.

"No shit? No, it wouldn't have occurred to me. What happened? I mean look at you. You're incredibly detailed—you don't miss a thing. You lift more than anyone else on our team. Best looking guy in the office. You're like the US Marshal golden boy—"

"Looks aren't everything, you know," Stephen grumbled.

"No, but you can overlook a whole lot of crazy when someone looks like she does and like you do."

Clearly, Booker was not going to let this go.

"She thinks I'm still in love with my ex-girlfriend," Stephen stated matter-of-factly, hoping that he would drop the subject.

"Carley?" Booker asked.

"No, Paige," Steven corrected, shifting in his seat.

"Ah, the baby mama," Booker nodded. "I could see that. I don't know as much about Paige. But I knew you were pretty broken up about losing Carley."

"Kristie found a ring in my bedside table. I had bought it for Carley before she decided she didn't want me. She only wanted my daughter."

"Brutal," Booker said. "This is gonna kill your reputation, you know."

Stephen shrugged. He was quiet a minute as if debating how much to say. "You know, I watched my parents be extremely happy all the years of my life. Even through some really awful times..." Stephen paused, remembering when his older brother, who was something of a bully growing up, had popped off to the wrong person, at the wrong place, at the wrong time. A bigger bully had pulled out a gun and shot his brother, Greg, in the face. That single instance had changed the course of Stephen's life. From that point on, Stephen wanted to be in law enforcement to try to control those situations and reduce the chances of that happening again. "I just want what they have."

"A family?" Booker said in astonishment. "Yeah, women can smell that a mile away!"

"Thanks. I'll take that into consideration," Stephen said with sarcasm. But then he got real again. "I guess I'm pretty unlovable."

"Nah, just needy and clingy. You just have to guard yourself, man. Don't fall in love so easily. Girls like a challenge."

"Thanks, I'll keep that in mind too," Stephen quipped.

"Seriously though... do you know how hard it is in this job to have a family?" Booker asked.

Stephen thought of Anna, the daughter he saw way less than he wanted. "Yeah, I have a pretty good idea."

Booker just shook his head in disbelief.

Stephen pulled out his phone and flashed Kristie's number at Booker so he could save it in his phone for when they landed. "Here, I think she's just looking for a good time."

"Thanks," Booker grinned boyishly at Stephen. "That's one thing I'm better at than you."

"Indeed," Stephen agreed as he closed his eyes again, hoping Booker would leave him alone for the rest of the trip.

8

WILTON

The penthouse in the Casa Cipriani hotel was immaculate, save the pillows strewn everywhere. Against the protest of the hotel general manager, Deputy Director Rob Sikes had requested the room be left exactly as it was so they could dust for prints and investigate the room.

The haughty manager had protested that the room was always in demand. He argued he needed to clean the room and book it immediately.

Besides, he'd continued, *MCPD has already been here and cleared it.*

The deputy director had shut the man down with threats of obstruction of justice. Which is why Stephen and Booker had been sent straight to the penthouse suite upon landing in New York.

"I say they staged a fight and ran away together," Stephen stated as he half-heartedly looked around. He used a gloved hand to pick up each pillow and inspect it carefully. Then he put the ones he inspected into a tidy little pile.

"Just think," Booker said, his voice sounding dreamy. "Selah Lablanc stood in this very suite just three days ago."

"Yeah, that's as close as you're ever gonna get to her, too—"

"Blood," Booker interrupted.

Stephen dropped his pillow and swiveled around.

Booker was now crouched down the hallway and peering at the floor. Stephen followed his gaze. He approached slowly and carefully. Sure enough, there was a smear of blood on the dark hardwood floor.

"Where there's blood, there's usually a—"

"Blunt object nearby," Stephen finished as he took a few steps back and began to look around.

"Unless she was hit with the butt of a gun," Booker stated. "How tall is Selah?"

"She seems tall in pictures," Stephen answered. "You know that could be Maddox's blood. Don't rule out any possibilities." Stephen walked away from his partner.

"Right," Booker said. He pulled a cotton swab from a kit he'd brought with him and generously swabbed the blood.

"Eureka!" Stephen yelled. He had pulled out the trash can that was hidden in the cabinets. The only thing inside the trash can was a marble drink coaster, which he now held with his gloved hand. "What are the chances that we get a fingerprint?"

"No way," Booker breathed. "That would make our kidnapper an idiot."

"Maybe." Stephen grinned at their good fortune as he placed the coaster in a plastic bag. "I'm more concerned about MCPD and why they missed this."

Booker nodded. He stood and joined Stephen. "Let's look through the place one more time."

Another thorough search proved fruitless. Stephen was now convinced there was foul play which meant Selah Lablanc and Maddox Miller might have been kidnapped after all. And if they'd been kidnapped, time was not on their side. They'd already been gone for three days.

Unbidden, Alyah's beautiful, angry eyes flashing at him

came back to mind. Dead celebrities would not bode well for the US Marshal's office. Especially on an election year. Nor would it help Stephen's new career.

Stephen shuddered imperceptibly. Would Selah and Maddox be alive when they found them?

9

WILTON

In the morning, after a quick conversation, Stephen and Booker both decided the next best step would be to go see Selah's mother, who lived forty-five minutes outside of the city. They gave her a quick call to make sure she would be home when they got there.

The further they drove outside of New York and the closer they got to Mrs. Lablanc's neighborhood, the more the houses started to resemble family homes. The moderate-sized homes were well-kept. They sat on quarter-acre lots and were well-maintained. The noise level dropped and there was a quiet peace about the area. Within the hour, Stephen and Booker found themselves in front of Selah's mom in her nice, cozy living room.

"Thank you for inviting us in, Mrs. Lablanc," Stephen said as he and Booker took the seats the woman had indicated they sit in.

"Would you like something to drink?" Mrs. Lablanc asked. Her blonde, shoulder-length hair was tied back in a low ponytail. It was easy to see where her daughter got her looks. Mrs. Lablanc was a shorter, older version of Selah. Her blue eyes were astute but kind. She was curvier than Selah, too, but carried it well in her blue jeans, flowered blouse, and matching blue cardigan sweater. In fact, her style suited her doting personality.

"No, thank you," Booker immediately responded.

"Do you have any coffee?" Stephen asked.

Booker gave him a strange look which Stephen ignored.

"Oh! Sure. I have a Keurig. How do you like your coffee?" she called as she left the room.

"Black, please. And thank you." Stephen responded as he immediately got up. The large room was airy. It smelled new. Either it had been flipped recently or they'd done some remodeling. The wood floors appeared shiny as if they were new or had just been polished. The walls were painted light gray, and the pictures were impeccably placed with pops of vivid orange, yellow, and red flowers. All the colors tied together with a beautiful faux flower arrangement on the twelve-foot dining room table they could see from their place in the living room.

Stephen began looking at photos. The large stone mantle held at least fifty framed pictures of Selah's family and Selah in multiple stages of childhood. The mantle took up a good portion of one wall. It was the warmest piece and the focal point of the living room.

Stephen could surmise which people in the pictures were family. They all bore a strong resemblance. Especially a girl who looked a lot like Selah but was older and taller than Selah in all the pictures. Then there was one that showed Selah with a girl her age with long black hair and brown eyes. Their feet were bare, and they both looked dirty, like they had been playing outside. The young Selah held a big fish and looked proud. The other girl held her nose and looked a little green. He picked up the picture frame, smiling at it, just as Mrs. Lablanc came back in the room.

"Oh!" Mrs. Lablanc smiled sadly at the memory the picture

had evoked. "That's Selah with her former best friend, Sarah. Sarah thought the fish was stinky, but Selah was so proud. Her first catch."

"Former best friend?" Booker asked.

Stephen put the frame back on the mantel and accepted the steaming cup of coffee before sitting back down.

"Thank you," he said.

Mrs. Lablanc nodded. "Cost of fame, I suppose. She and Sarah were friends up until senior year in high school. Selah never went into detail about what went wrong, but I'll tell you what I think. It all happened about when Selah started gaining popularity. Sarah thought Selah was getting too big for her britches."

"That's too bad," Stephen commiserated.

Mrs. Lablanc nodded.

"Where's Sarah now?" Booker asked.

"I don't rightly know," Mrs. Lablanc replied thoughtfully. "After Sarah swore off Selah, I never saw her again. She really cut her out of her life. I think Selah tried a couple of times to reconcile, but Sarah wouldn't have any part in it."

"Sad," Stephen said.

Mrs. Lablanc nodded.

"Your home is lovely, Mrs. Lablanc," Booker changed the subject. Now Stephen gave Booker an odd look.

"Oh, thank you. It's my forever home. I couldn't bring myself to leave after my husband died five years ago. Selah kept trying to move me closer to her place—she lives in the city on the Upper East Side. Even tried to get me to move in once. But this is my home. I let her send a crew out to do a little remodeling. We just freshened it up. But I couldn't bring myself to make too many changes."

Stephen nodded.

"Does Selah still have a room here?" Booker asked.

Mrs. Lablanc looked surprised.

"It might seem strange, but sometimes when people are kidnapped, the truth lurks in unresolved pasts," Booker explained.

Stephen had never heard that and wondered what Booker was up to.

"Okay." Mrs. Lablanc looked skeptical but got up to lead the way.

The two men followed her.

"Did Selah have any enemies?" Stephen asked, trying to get this interview back on track.

Mrs. Lablanc shook her head and smiled sweetly, clearly her daughter's biggest supporter. "Selah is lovely. She's kind and the success really hasn't changed her much. She's a little more confident. But she did have an awful lot of those darn paparazzi..." Mrs. Lablanc clicked her tongue and shook her head. Her eyes showed displeasure.

"Anyone in particular?" Stephen asked.

"No, I can't remember anyone Selah ever named. *Use it to your advantage, mama,* Selah would say to me. As if a mob of rude photographers were ever an advantage." Mrs. Lablanc opened a bedroom door to reveal a spotlessly clean room with the same gray walls as the rest of the house.

A light blue comforter was smoothed perfectly in place with a mound of pillows with words like *Happiness, Joy, Live, Love* all sitting on top. There was a computer table in the corner of the room with a few journals stacked neatly on top.

Stephen would love to get a look at those journals.

"Can we look through the journals?" Booker asked as if reading Stephen's mind.

"No," Mrs. Lablanc's tone turned icy. "Those are Selah's private thoughts. Her songs in brainstorm mode. I'm sorry gentlemen, that's where I draw the line."

Seeing nothing out of order and nothing else of interest,

Stephen nodded. "Thank you, Mrs. Lablanc, you've been a big help."

"What's next? How will you find her?" she asked, worry etched on her brow as she ushered the boys down the hall and back to the main room.

"Perhaps you could give us a list of people you think might have seen or talked to Selah in the last week?' Stephen asked. "That will give us a place to start."

"Certainly," Mrs. Lablanc grabbed a pen and paper out of an end table. "Only…" She looked worried.

"What's the matter?" Booker asked.

"I didn't talk to Selah this past week. Her sister did. I'll give you Stacia's information," Mrs. Lablanc started scribbling on the pad. "Maybe you could check in with Emily, her publicist, too. She knew exactly where Selah was going to be—it was her job to know and schedule her." She scribbled on the pad of paper again.

"Thank you, Mrs. Lablanc," Stephen reached out and accepted the paper from her hand and put it in his pocket. They opened the front door and the three of them walked out on the front porch.

Stephen heard it before the impact hit. Everything began to move in slow motion. There was a quiet pop. He imagined the whiz sound of a tiny piece of brass with copper and zinc combined. The smell of gun powder. There was no time to scan for its source. In the time it had taken to blink, a shot had been fired.

Instinctively, Stephen reacted. He immediately dove toward Mrs. Lablanc. He could feel her body fall. The force of his body against hers pushed them back into the house. He landed protectively with his body covering hers.

Stephen jumped to a crouch beside the older woman, whose eyes held a shocked expression. He pushed the front door shut, using it as a shield.

"Stay down," he ordered gently. "Are you hurt?"

"No." Mrs. Lablanc rolled to her side, then to her knees. She crawled away from the door to a nearby hallway without windows.

Stephen nodded. He did a quick scan and pat down of his body. He felt no pain. But something was wrong. Someone was missing. Stephen looked around for Booker.

Still squatted down, Stephen drew his gun. He pulled the door, edging it open a crack and glanced out.

"Booker?" Stephen called out quietly. Stephen was still crouched in a squat and using the door as a shield, careful not to make himself a target.

Booker's silence lent to Stephen's growing concern.

"Booker?" he called. "You okay, buddy?"

Stephen scanned the horizon. Not seeing a threat, he opened the door wider. That's when he noticed that Booker was lying face down on the porch, just out of Stephen's viewpoint behind the door. His breath caught in his chest.

Time froze and slammed still.

Booker wasn't moving.

10

SELAH

Selah watched Maddox pace the room and occasionally stop to investigate a crack in the wall or a place in the concrete that he thought might just be a secret trap door.

The door opened and Selah could see his muscles tighten as he wound up to pounce. Except the crazy kidnapper only came halfway down the stairs to place two bowls of hot soup on the staircase.

The woman said nothing before she turned around and ran back up the stairs. Maybe she knew better than to take her chances with a six-foot-four-inch NFL player who outweighed her by seventy-five pounds.

Selah went to the stairs, climbed a few, and grabbed her bowl. Her stomach rumbled. She knew it wouldn't matter what the soup tasted like. She hadn't eaten for some time and she was hungry. She put her nose down and smelled it. It was tomato basil, her favorite.

"Selah." Maddox's voice broke through her actions.

She had just taken a spoonful of soup, brought it up to her mouth, and was about to drink it.

"What?" her voice came out so sharp she almost flinched

herself. No way was he going to judge that she was eating right now. It wouldn't be the first time. Sometimes Selah hated that she was a star. She had her figure to worry about after all. She almost snorted to herself. That was about to drastically change.

"How do you know that's not laced?" Maddox whispered with urgency.

"No way," Selah stared at the red soup with suspicion. "Wouldn't we already be dead if they wanted us to be?"

Maddox hesitated and looked from Selah to the stairs. He seemed to be considering her words. "Wait, they? Do you know something?"

"Of course not!" Selah's voice was sharp again. "Do you still think I had something to do with this?"

"Look me in the eyes and tell me this isn't because of you. You were famous way longer than I was. I might have just been along for the ride."

"We weren't together when we were kidnapped, you idiot. If they only wanted me, why are you here? They were after both of us," Selah snapped. She took a spoonful of soup and slurped it greedily.

She refused to acknowledge why she was really so angry with Maddox. She had the best news a girl could ever hope for and she couldn't tell him. She couldn't even trust his reaction. Besides, she had made her choice. He didn't get to weigh in on this. His first reaction to her telling him the truth had been a bad one. It told her everything she needed to know.

"Why do you keep saying *they*?" Maddox challenged.

"Because more than one person had to have taken us. We were in two different places. Everything went black after the fight. After you left me, I changed my clothes and walked out of the room. I was standing in the hallway, debating going after you. That was my last thought before I woke up here. Someone must have hit me over the head—"

"You debated going after me?" Maddox's eyes softened.

"Focus, Maddox!" Selah snapped her fingers. "None of that matters anymore. All that matters is us getting out of here. Where were you when you were taken?"

Maddox scratched his head and stared at Selah as if he was trying to recall. "I remember going down the elevator. I walked out the back door. I saw the limo. Then nothing." Maddox looked confused.

"So, someone got you just outside the hotel. Someone hit me in the hotel room. What's the common denominator? Who knew where you were going to be and where I was?" Selah asked.

"Your publicist!" Maddox shouted.

"No way!" Selah protested. "Emily and I are practically sisters. She's seriously closer to me than Stacia. She would never do anything to hurt me—"

"Yet she had access to our schedules at that moment," Maddox argued.

Selah rolled her eyes and spooned the warm soup into her mouth defiantly. "Are you sure you didn't text someone that you were leaving? Your team knew your flight was scheduled to bring you back to practice."

Maddox groaned at the mention of practice. "Who on my team wouldn't want me to play?"

"Anyone who wanted to bet on the game and win!" Selah was eating the soup with more urgency. She had never been so hungry in her life. She was light-headed from not eating enough today. She began to think about every bite of rich, gourmet food she'd ever left uneaten on a table at a restaurant. All the times she stopped eating because she was afraid she might gain weight though she exerted over a thousand calories a show with all her dancing and singing.

How ridiculous and shallow, the thought flitted through her mind.

"So you're blaming it on me? Typical," Maddox spat. "It's always my fault, isn't it?"

"Finally," Selah answered with sarcasm. "It must feel so good to finally be real with yourself. Admitting you're the problem is the first step."

Maddox huffed but said nothing. Instead, he stared hard at Selah until she finished her soup. He waited at least fifteen minutes. Seeming satisfied that Selah hadn't keeled over, he reluctantly stalked up the stairs and grabbed his bowl of soup.

He had just finished when Selah felt her stomach turn. Selah didn't even make it to the bucket before her stomach started heaving.

Maddox looked horrified. He froze to the spot.

When Selah finished throwing up in the corner, she wiped her mouth and glared at Maddox.

"I'm okay, thanks for asking," Selah snarked as she sat in the chair with her back to Maddox. She didn't have any desire to explain that her upheaval had nothing to do with the food.

Maddox and Selah had worse things to worry about than a case of the stomach flu.

In fact, Selah would consider herself lucky if she lived to experience the next time she got sick.

11

WILTON

Booker was lying face down on the porch.

Stephen scanned the road slowly. He scanned the rooftops. He looked for open windows within range or curtains that swayed as if someone had just been up to no good and rushed away. He tried to remember if he'd seen any passing cars at the time of the gun shot.

Stephen knew better than to expose himself to a possible threat, but he had to risk it. Hyper aware, his eyes re-scanned his surroundings as he moved. Stephen crawled to Booker's side and felt for a pulse. Feeling no pulse, he cursed. Fear and panic clawed at his chest. Stephen knew he shouldn't roll Booker over, but he thought there might be a chance he could save him. He knew firsthand that just because a person didn't feel a pulse, it didn't mean there wasn't one. Booker's pulse could be faint. Stephen had to try something. His brain refused to accept what his gut was telling him.

Stephen's plan stalled when he rolled Booker over and saw a bullet wound to the middle of Booker's forehead. Blood poured out of the hole in Booker's head, creating a large red pool underneath him. It had only taken one shot. Stephen could no longer deny it. Booker was indisputably dead.

Stephen gulped back the lump in his throat. There was no time for that right now. The realization that he and Mrs. Lablanc continued to be exposed every moment he stayed out there caused him to act. Stephen dove behind the front door as another bullet slammed into the door exactly where Stephen had been crouched minutes before. He could hear the bullet splinter the wood. He stayed low as he shut and locked the door.

He peeked out the window in time to catch a black sedan burn out on the road. Funny, he hadn't noticed the car until now. Before it disappeared from sight, he saw the last three numbers on the license plates—542.

"Are you okay?" Stephen asked Mrs. Lablanc, who sat huddled in the hallway.

She nodded with big, scared eyes.

"Your partner—is he..." her voice trailed off and her eyes got watery.

"Yes," Stephen said. He pulled out his phone and called Chief Tigress. Staying down and avoiding windows, Stephen made his way around the house, looking in closets and under beds. "This is Wilton. We need back up and a way out of here. My partner has been shot and killed. I'm at the home of Mrs. Sally Lablanc." He rattled off her address.

He listened as Tigress gave the okay. Convinced the house was clear, Stephen came to guard Mrs. Lablanc in the hallway.

Next, Stephen called Deputy Sikes.

Sikes reacted quickly. "What's happening?"

"Not sure. We were leaving Mrs. Lablanc's home when we heard a shot—"

"Please tell me Mrs. Lablanc is okay," Sikes interrupted.

"She is and so am I. But Booker's not. He was shot. He didn't make it, sir."

There was a deafening silence on the other end. Stephen waited, his dread filling the silence.

Finally, Sikes spoke, his voice barely above a whisper. "Ethan Booker was a good man."

"Yes. The best," Stephen paused. "I don't think the danger has passed though. I ducked another shot. I called for backup, which is on the way… But we need an extraction plan."

"Okay, I'll get another marshal on a plane. We'll get Mrs. Lablanc to a safe house and put a guard there with her. We don't know who the shooter was after, but we have to assume she's not safe."

"Right. When we have cover and backup, I'll escort Mrs. Lablanc to the safe house. I'll wait with her until you get someone here."

"Good thinking. We'll be in touch," Sikes agreed as he hung up the phone.

"Now what?" Mrs. Lablanc asked. Her eyes were wide with fear, and she kept looking around into the living room where there were plenty of windows as if she suspected someone would break in at any moment.

"Now, we wait," Stephen announced. "We can't leave until we have cover. The MCPD will come and do a thorough search outside. We'll get Booker moved. Someone will come and clean up the porch. You won't be able to stay here tonight."

"Oh!" Mrs. Lablanc cried out in distress. "Where will I go?"

"We'll hide you in a safe house. You'll have a guard or two with you to keep you safe."

"How long?" Mrs. Lablanc asked.

"Until we find your daughter. We were naïve to think she was the only target," Stephen answered. "It seems like someone is targeting more than just Selah. Where is Selah's sister?"

"Stacia should be at work right now," Mrs. Lablanc whispered with fear in her eyes.

"Can you please call her and put her on speaker phone?" Stephen requested. "We need to give her a heads up."

Mrs. Lablanc's eyes filled with tears. "What should I tell her?"

"She needs to assume she's in danger."

12

MAK

"This little piggy went to market. This little piggy stayed home. This little piggy had roast beef. This little piggy had none. This little piggy went *wee-wee-wee* all the way home." Mak finished the nursery rhyme by tickling her three-year-old daughter, Harper, and was rewarded with giggles.

"Your turn, mommy!" Harper announced as the laughter died down. Her big brown eyes were hopeful, and Harper's straight, reddish-brown hair hung limply in her face.

"My turn for what?" Mak asked, knowing her own eyes were a mirror of her daughter's. If only she could get her own reddish-brown hair as straight as Harper's...

"Where are your piggies?" Harper pointed to her mother's feet.

"Oh no you don't. It is way past bedtime, little missy." Mak pulled the covers up and tucked her precocious toddler in tight.

"I can't move!" Harper protested.

"Good!" Mak responded with a knowing smile. "You won't be able to get out of bed until morning, will you?"

The nightlight was on, and the light overhead was off when

Mak finally made it out of her daughter's room. Mak paused outside in the hallway and leaned her back against the wall.

She took a deep breath in and exhaled it slowly. Mak loved moments like these with her daughter. She would never regret the memories they were making. But life these days was a little *too* normal. She missed the thrill of the chase. She missed the feeling of putting missing pieces into place and solving crimes. She missed her life as a US Marshal. Immediate shame and guilt filled her the minute the thought hit her brain.

As if she had willed her phone to ring, her cell started buzzing in her back pocket. She pulled out her phone and checked the screen. It was Deputy Director Sikes.

Mak held her breath as she answered. It was a little late, but time had never dictated calls made by the US Marshals. Nothing could ever wait until morning. She answered on the second ring.

"Cunningham?" Rob Sikes was all business.

Mak snapped to attention at the sound of his tone. "Yes, sir?"

"There's been an incident. Are you ready to come back in?" he asked.

You tell me, she thought, *you're the one who put me on this bullshit leave in the first place.* "Of course. Do you need me now?" she asked.

"No, no, you can come in the morning. Make it bright and early though, would you? I need to get you briefed so you can be in the field as soon as possible. Be prepared. You'll be traveling tomorrow."

"Yes, sir," Mak hung up the phone and stared at it in wonder. She'd been going to the psychologist regularly. She knew Deputy Sikes got copies of the reports. She had been wondering what was taking him so long to call her back in.

"Makayla?" John's sudden voice and nearness broke into

Mak's musing. She jumped a little and pulled a defensive stance.

John laughed. Her husband's deep, sexy voice still sent shivers up Mak's spine after six years of marriage. His height and broad build made Mak feel petite at five-foot seven-inches tall. Mak had no shortage of dates back in college but once she joined the US Marshals, the dating pool had shrunk considerably. It took a real man to be in a relationship with a female US Marshal.

It took a man who was loaded with self-assurance to step up and volunteer to stay at home with their daughter three years ago while Mak continued her dangerous career after Harper had been born. Mak adored John for stepping up to keep stability in Harper's life while mommy went off to *fight the bad guys*.

But then, the inevitable happened. Mak had made one bad judgment call in the field during a kidnapping case involving a child. As a result, Mak was placed on leave. For the past seven months, Mak had settled into a very normal routine of family life and psychology visits. She had made her peace with what had happened. But she didn't know if Deputy Sikes would ever make his peace with it. Until now.

"You okay, babe?" John asked in a whisper, aware Mak had just put their daughter to bed for the night.

Mak took his hand and led him downstairs to the living room. She sat beside him on the couch. She could see the organized piles of paper on John's desk in the office from where she sat. Since Mak had been on leave, John had started some consulting work. The timing worked out perfectly.

"Sikes just called me back in," Mak told John as he cuddled beside her.

"That's great news. When do you go back?" John asked.

"Tomorrow morning. Early." Mak put her hand in his. She knew her eyes betrayed the excitement she felt. "He told me to be prepared to travel."

John laughed. "Well, hallelujah!"

"What do you mean by that?" Mak looked offended.

"You know what I mean. I could see the way you paced around the house looking for things to do for the past seven months. You can only work out for so many hours a day. I was about to suggest you get a hobby."

Mak smirked at her husband. "Very funny. You know I've loved every minute of the time I've had with Harper. It's just—"

"Harper doesn't need to be saved," John leaned over and kissed Mak lightly. "I'm happy for you, babe. You ready to go back?"

"Funny, Sikes asked the same thing. Yes, I'm more than ready," she responded.

"PTSD is a real problem in the field, you know," John got serious.

Mak shuddered. "You don't have to tell me. It's all I've talked about for the past seven months. I think I'm good. I'm in a good place mentally. Time will tell if I freeze up on the job."

"Think Sikes will let you have a say in the type of cases he assigns you?" John asked.

Mak shrugged. "He always has the final say, but I'll bet he steers me away from cases involving kids for now."

"Probably smart," John nodded.

Mak nodded back but hated the thought that she now had a handicap. A glaringly obvious defect that she didn't know if she could control. She was quiet as she thought back to the case that had put her on leave for seven months. A child had been kidnapped. Rather than wait for the *go-ahead* from her superior, Mak had rushed in. She'd always trusted her instincts, but she had admitted over the course of her counseling that her viewpoint might have been impaired on account of thoughts of her own daughter.

Mak had gotten stand-back orders, but she'd disobeyed them. She didn't think they had time to wait, so she'd kicked in the door where they suspected the child was being held. They'd found the child dead. Mak's stomach knotted just thinking about it. There was no way to know how long the child had been deceased because the parents refused to allow an autopsy. Based off the condition of the little body, the child had been killed within an hour of their sting operation. After an interrogation into the situation, the Attorney General had made the determination that the problem had been Mak's inability in that moment to follow the stand-back orders. But Mak knew Deputy Sikes was more concerned with the fact that she'd seen her first child fatality and PTSD was a very possible result. He'd wanted her healthy before she returned.

"Why tomorrow morning?" John asked, bringing Mak back to the present.

"There's been an incident," Mak responded.

"There always is," John rubbed her knee affectionately.

Mak put her head on his shoulder, loving the way it fit perfectly between his muscular pec and shoulder. "Have I told you today how much I love you?"

"Multiple times," John said. He gently guided her chin up with his hand, so she had no choice but to look up into his face. He was irresistibly handsome with his blue eyes, square jaw line, and Romanesque nose. His black hair had premature gray strands that only added to his dignified look. He tilted his head down and kissed Mak.

Mak deepened the kiss in an unspoken acceptance of what was to come next. She broke the kiss just long enough to take her shirt off and throw it on the floor. John followed her lead. *This* was never a problem in their marriage. They loved each other as if they only had today. With Mak's dangerous job, they knew that might not be too far-fetched. Mak kept her focus on her husband for now.

Tomorrow she could think about what new, dangerous situation she would be placed in.

13

WILTON

Stephen stared out the window and blinked his eyes rapidly, working hard to keep them open. He could hear Mrs. Lablanc snoring in the next room. He went to the kitchen and poured himself another cup of black coffee. Him falling asleep on the job had cost a life before. He couldn't ever fall asleep on duty again.

His mind drifted to the last all-nighter he'd attempted to pull. That was a memory he'd rather forget. Though he couldn't relive that night. It would live in his brain forever. His sleeping had cost Carley her life.

He'd been brand new to the marshals. By day, he was working as a US Marshal. By night, he was stalking a house where he suspected Carley and Anna were living. The only solace he took in his theory was that if Carley had loved Anna enough take her, Carley would treat Anna like gold.

It was Carley's uncle, Scott Milternett, who had woken Stephen up. Carley was on the run from Demitri Abbott, a man Scott would have called his right-hand man. Until Demitri went feral. Unbeknownst to many, Demitri suffered from multiple personality disorder, and he had allowed one of his more terrifying personalities to take control.

By the time Stephen had arrived at the hotel where Carley had run to, it was too late. Demitri Abbott had shot Carley in the abdomen while Anna had watched from her secret hiding space in an armoire. While Stephen grieved the instant and unexpected loss of Carley, he was overjoyed to find Anna.

Thinking about the past was enough to wake Stephen right up. Snippets of that time played on repeat in Stephen's nightmares. He could never get Carley back. Of all his past fails in his roles in law enforcement, this fail was one no supervisor would ever need to hold him accountable for. They didn't need to. Stephen did a good enough job of beating himself up over this one.

He scanned the text message again and noted the names of the two marshals. Jonas Petry, the marshal coming to relieve Stephen of protective custody duty, would be on a plane at an obscenely early time in the morning. Mak Cunningham was coming later. Stephen flipped to the text from Sikes. He was always so curt and to the point in text. Stephen knew he hated talking this way. Sikes felt information could be compromised via text.

Sikes: *Mak Cunningham will be your new partner. Text you when Mak's plane leaves.*

Who is Mak? Stephen wondered. He'd tried to call Sikes to inquire, but the one time Sikes actually answered, he'd explained to Stephen he was too busy to talk because he was putting out fires and arranging a funeral.

Thinking about the funeral made Stephen's eyes well up. Booker had been a great partner and had been on his way to becoming a good friend. He wondered about his new partner. He understood why they wouldn't send Stephen out on his own. Stephen hadn't even made it out of rookie status yet. But the marshals in his office worked in pairs. He wondered how well he would work with his new partner.

Stephen had never met Mak at the office. He'd now been with the marshals long enough to have met them all. Even the ones who'd been on vacation when he'd first arrived. A transfer, maybe?

Stephen watched the sun rise. Just about when his eyes were blinking and he was zoning out again, Jonas Petry showed up at the door of the safe house. Jonas took one look at Stephen and told him to go to bed. He didn't have to tell Stephen twice.

For once, Stephen was asleep the minute his head hit the pillow.

14

MAK

Mak Cunningham walked through the doors with the regal emblem of the US Marshals etched on the outside. Pride welled up in her chest each time she saw the emblem. It reminded her of the hard work it had taken to get here. The rigorous training, the exams, the relationships she'd had to let go of. The payoff had been worth it. She'd never regretted her choice to serve. She was made for this.

Sikes didn't have to ask her to come in early to ensure that she would. Mak was an early riser. Today was no exception. Mak was up, dressed, and out the door by six in the morning. She threw her carry-on bag in the back seat of the car before she raced to work. Sikes had asked her to be ready to travel. She was.

When she had backed out the driveway that morning, she had realized her rearview mirror was in the wrong place. It was pointed at her. For a moment, she'd critically eyed her auburn hair that she'd thrown back into a neat ponytail. She couldn't help the short, stray pieces of hair that refused to stay back and framed her face instead. She didn't care about that. Her ponytail was good enough. She also guessed she was pretty enough. She really didn't need to wear makeup. Long, black eyelashes framed her large expressive eyes. Her nose was a little small for her face, but it would be stupid to complain about that.

Her brown eyes were what kept her glued to the mirror. She could see the excitement in them. It was the excitement of promised fulfillment—something that had been missing in her life for the past seven months. Her eyes held a depth of wisdom and hope beyond her years. She lived to save people.

Now, as she pushed through the door to the office that had been her home for over eight years, Mak paused and breathed in the smell of cedar, office furniture, and hard work. She knew this office wasn't where the blood, sweat, and tears happened. Still, it was home base.

"Mak."

Mak whirled around to see Sikes approaching with two cups of coffee.

"Thanks." Mak smiled and accepted the steaming mug and with her free hand, shook his. She followed him into the conference room and sat down in her favorite chair. It was still dark outside. There was something important about having a meeting before the sun came up.

Sikes sat across the table. He didn't smile back. In fact, Mak could see the strain on his face and the red that rimmed his eyes. He rubbed his bald head, a sure sign of distress. He wasn't a tall man, but his title of *deputy* fit him well. His serious stature was enough to command respect.

Mak waited quietly. She wasn't naïve. She knew if she was being called back in, there was a reason. Something had gone wrong.

"Mak, there's no easy way to tell you this so I'm just going to come right out with it," Sikes began.

Mak nodded and squared her shoulders. She'd put on her

big girl pants this morning. Sikes knew blunt was the best way to approach Mak.

"Ethan Booker was killed yesterday."

For seconds, the air left Mak. She resisted the urge to double over. Denial clouded her brain. Did Sikes say *killed* or *gone*? Booker couldn't be dead. He was just gone, right? She replayed his words. *Ethan Booker was killed last night.*

"Damn it!" Mak finally reacted. Unbidden, the memory of her first day flooded back to her.

Hey, sweetheart. Are you lost? a man named Cranz, who would become her co-worker, had greeted when she'd walked through the front door. His eyes roamed appreciatively over her body.

Sweetheart? Geez, Cranz, I thought you were more progressive than that. Booker intercepted Mak while scowling at Cranz. He turned to Mak. *Makayla Cunningham, I presume?*

Mak, she'd corrected immediately. She shook Booker's hand.

Booker, he responded. *Good to meet you. Deputy Sikes is stuck in a meeting but asked me to show you around. Hey, I saw your test scores. Impressive. You'll be a welcome addition around here. We could use someone with smarts...*

Mak snickered and glanced back at Cranz, whose face held a perplexed look.

Booker had been the first marshal to treat her not like a woman but like a comrade. They'd become partners on the force. He'd trained her and taught her everything she needed to know. They'd become friends when he'd demanded respect be given to Mak every time their co-workers tried to get her to take a seat when situations got dangerous. Cranz hadn't lasted there past the end of the year. She'd suspected Booker had something to do with that. Mak hadn't been sorry to see him go.

In fact, Booker had been her partner up until things went south with the kidnapping seven months ago. They had been after a sexual predator. The obvious objective had been to free the child. Mak had gotten emotionally compromised. Booker hadn't. She hoped she had learned from that situation. Time would tell.

She shook her head. She couldn't believe she would never see Booker again. She wondered if she'd ever thanked him for the difference he'd made in her life.

Mak took a deep breath. "How?"

"I sent him and Wilton to New York for a kidnapping case. They were talking to the mother of the victim. When they stepped out onto the porch, a sharpshooter hit Booker." Sikes pointed to his forehead. "We can only assume they were targeting Mrs. Lablanc."

"Lablanc?" Mak managed to croak. She took a big sip of coffee to swallow back the unshed tears. The coffee was hot and scalded her throat. She didn't care. Maybe it would burn away the lump that had formed.

Sikes nodded. "Selah Lablanc and Maddox Miller have been kidnapped."

"And?" Mak didn't miss a beat. "Adult kidnapping isn't us."

"It is when the Attorney General appoints it. The MCPD and the FBI are too busy to take the case. They think they know the perp. A woman they call *The Fan*. Find *The Fan*, you'll find Selah and Maddox."

"They're too busy to save American icons?" Mak's voice sounded sarcastic.

Sikes shrugged. "They have a rash of New York CEOs who have started popping up dead and appear connected. They need to figure it out before the next one dies."

"I see," Mak said, as her brain processed all that information. "So, you're assigning me to take Booker's place?"

"Yes."

"Who did you say Booker was partnered up with?" Mak asked.

"Wilton. He's a rookie. I need a senior marshal to partner with him because he's new," Sikes stated.

Mak nodded. "How new?"

"Six months," Sikes answered.

"Is he good? Reliable?" Mak wondered.

Sikes nodded. "He has a lot to learn, but he was a detective for six or seven years. He's not new to law enforcement. He's got a good head on his shoulders. Detailed—"

"Think first and rush in too late?" Mak snorted.

"Yeah, he'll be the perfect partner for you. Maybe you'll learn to rush in a little less."

Mak felt her face flame, and she bit her tongue to stop from rushing to her own defense. She knew he wasn't just referring to the child kidnapping case. Rushing into situations was common for Mak. Though Mak still wasn't convinced she'd made the wrong call in that situation, and she wouldn't grovel to him.

"I need to ask you a question, Mak." Sikes tapped a finger on the desk.

Here it goes, Mak thought. Wordlessly, she nodded.

"Is being back out in the field going to be a problem for you?"

"No, sir," Mak didn't hesitate.

"Good," Sikes said. "If it becomes a problem, can I trust you to do the right thing and remove yourself from the situation?"

"Yes, sir," Mak agreed.

"Good. I've got you on the plane leaving in…" Sikes checked his watch, "an hour and a half. Can you make that?"

"Yes," Mak agreed. "Let me look through the files and I'll need you to brief me on everything you know. Including Wilton's history."

Sikes nodded in agreement. He led her to his office, pulled out files, and handed them to her.

Mak took them and began to thumb through.

"I'm counting on you to bring Wilton back in one piece."

Mak nodded, but she felt her spine straighten. Mak was incapable of telling a lie. Thinking about Booker, a seasoned US Marshal, she realized that wasn't a promise she could make right now. As long as Wilton knew how to take care of himself, they'd get along just fine.

15

SELAH

Selah groaned as she woke up. She was feeling stiff and sore from spending the past several nights sleeping on a cold basement floor. She'd never been one for camping when she was growing up. Though she was exhausted, her sleep had been shallow and interrupted. She had been cold. Shivering at one point. She woke to find a long-sleeved t-shirt draped over her body. She snuggled into the shirt, using it as a blanket. She peeked at Maddox, who could sleep anywhere. He was only wearing an undershirt.

Her heart thawed a little. Then she remembered his body temperature always ran hot. He'd probably gotten overheated and when he'd shed his shirt, he just draped it over her. As she tried to get back to sleep, she remembered to feel grateful for the extra layer.

Still, the shirt made her remember that Maddox hadn't always been so selfish. In the beginning, he was wonderful. He was protective. He was creative with the ways they hung out to avoid the media. He told her his hopes and dreams. They were inspiring, and Selah had wanted to be a part of them.

That bubble burst when Selah had peed on a stick that told

her she was pregnant. It was miraculous. Both Selah and Maddox were double safe. There was no possible way she should have gotten pregnant. But she did.

The night she told Maddox, he had revealed his true self. All of his selfishness and intention not to make this a permanent relationship came to light. Maddox was mad about the news. She'd replayed it a hundred times in her head.

What do you mean, you're pregnant? he'd thundered at her.

Selah had actually felt a little scared. She'd waved the stick at Maddox.

Maddox jumped up and started pacing. He began mumbling about his career and Selah's career. *How can two people have a family in the middle of these lifestyles?*

I'm going to keep it, she'd announced with more courage than she felt.

What? he'd practically yelled back.

Maddox, you're scaring me a little, she'd squeaked.

Well, don't you think we should discuss that? he asked.

No, I don't. My body, my choice, she'd answered quietly.

The hell— Maddox had left the room then, mumbling irritably.

It was right there that Selah concocted a plan. She would tell Maddox she had lost the baby. She didn't want to be with him anymore after that. She just couldn't figure out how to spin the break-up so her fans and his fans didn't draw some weird dividing line. They had gained so many fans while they were together, breaking up might feel like asking the continent to pick a side in a divorce. She'd had to fight her way to where she was, and she hated the idea of losing fans and making people mad at her. But she just wanted out. Suddenly, nothing mattered more to her than this little life growing inside of her. She hadn't known she wanted a child. Until she had one on the way.

When she told Maddox a week later that she'd lost the baby,

he'd jumped to an ugly conclusion. He'd assumed she had been playing games to get him to commit. Everything spiraled downward from there.

Selah had actually felt relieved when Maddox broke up with her. She just wished he would have been able to sit down, be civilized, and come up with a PR plan with her. Instead, he'd stormed off. And now they were in this mess.

Hot tears sprang to Selah's eyes. Would they make it out of here alive? She had more to live for than her crazy fans.

She had to make it out alive for her baby.

16

MAK

Her flight was so early in the morning, Mak could have slept on the plane but she didn't. She was too wired. Too excited for this new adventure. It did feel weird flying by herself. She and Booker used to have the best conversations on planes. They used to take bets on how quickly they could find the bad guy. Mak was very good at that game. She often wondered if Booker got chatty on a plane because he was secretly afraid of flying. People acted weird when they got nervous.

Not Mak though. She loved everything about being up in the air. She loved the view from above the clouds. She'd take a window seat any chance she got. She loved takeoff and landing. Of course, she'd never been on a bad flight. She believed she was a good-luck charm to everyone on the plane.

Mak Cunningham is on board? You're welcome, ladies and gentlemen. Mak's flights are practically perfect. Mak smiled to herself. That was another thing about flying. Mak never got bored. She could easily entertain herself the entire flight.

Still, Mak got serious again as she eyed the empty seat beside her and felt instant sadness. Booker should be there with her. Mak jammed on a pair of sunglasses as she felt the tears well up. She sure hoped she could get her emotions under control before they landed. They were all over the place.

As usual, the flight was uneventful. Mak grabbed her carryon and backpack and made her way down the aisle of the plane, out the runway, and hit her Lyft app. A driver would be there in seven minutes.

Once in the Lyft, Mak pulled out her cell phone. She waited until she heard the sexy voice of the man she loved on the other end.

"Heya," she purred in a silky voice. "Whatcha wearing?" Mak noticed the Lyft driver look in his rearview mirror with wide eyes, alarm evident. Mak just smiled.

John laughed in response, his tone deep and masculine. "PJ bottoms and a t-shirt. You were gone very early this morning."

"Yep, before the sun came up," Mak chirped proudly. The excitement of a new case surged through her veins. "Well, anyway, my plane touched down in New York."

"Great. How was the flight?" John asked.

"Perfect as always," Mak said, looking out the window to take note of her surroundings. "Is Harper up yet?"

"That sleepy head?" John asked. "No way. I'll go get her up here in a few minutes."

"Sounds good. Give her my love when you do," Mak made a kiss sound.

"Will do. Be safe, babe," John said.

"Always." Mak hung up the phone.

Once she hung up, Mak took the rest of the ride to review the very little she had learned and heard about Stephen Wilton. It wasn't a lot. Alyah Smith had popped in before Mak left.

Odd, she'd thought. *Alyah usually kept to her side of the building and let the marshals go about their business.*

Mak had noted that Alyah tried to appear casual but seemed very on edge.

I heard about Booker, she'd started. Her eyes were sad.

Mak wasn't aware Alyah knew much about Booker, so Mak had just nodded, not trusting herself to speak.

I—ah—wonder if you could do me a favor? Alyah looked like those words rarely ever came out of her mouth and they tasted bitter. Mak respected Alyah. She was a powerful DA. Like Mak, Alyah was fighting a little harder than a woman should in today's world to make a name for herself. Alyah was fair and by the book. Mak had never crossed her. Not that they'd hung out either. As Mak eyed Alyah's expensive pantsuit and high-heels, Mak realized it was likely because they didn't have that much in common.

Sure, Alyah. What's up? Mak had asked, feeling impatient. She'd needed to get out the door.

Keep an eye on Wilton for me? A blush crept up Alyah's cheeks.

Mak wondered if this was a personal or professional interest, but Alyah's next words clarified that.

I don't know much about him and the jury's still out on that one, Alyah cracked.

Mak smiled but didn't drag the details out of her. Instead, Mak asked, *Is there something specific I should be watching for?*

Alyah quickly shook her head. *Just that you're the senior agent. Don't let him slip into the driver's seat. He's too rookie for that.*

Ah, Mak understood her meaning. *Thanks for the heads up. Us women need to stick together. If you don't mind, I need to go, or I'll miss my flight.*

Of course, Alyah agreed. *Be safe, Mak.*

It was weird alright. In fact, it was the most she'd ever spoken to Alyah in the time Alyah had become the DA, which was a few years ago. Mak assumed Alyah was younger than her, which made her respect the DA all the more.

Mak shrugged off the conversation. In truth, Mak often felt frustrated by women who were vague and cast hints at what they really wanted to say. Mak just said it. She was direct and blunt. In this line of business, those two attributes had served her well. She got out of the Lyft, hit tip on her app, and trudged around to the back of the apartment building where they had set up the safe house. Eyes up and noting her surroundings, Mak put her body protectively in front of a keypad and keyed in a code. She let herself in, feeling sure that no one was watching her.

The ominous thought occurred to her that if someone was watching, she'd already be dead. Like Booker was.

17

WILTON

Stephen woke to the sound of laughter. Loud laughter. For a minute, he was disoriented. He didn't recognize a thing. The ceiling was not his ceiling. The walls were white with no decorations. The bed he was lying on was a little springy for his liking. Bright sun streamed in despite the thick blinds on the windows. It felt like it was midday.

Then it all came back to him. He was on a case. His partner had been killed. The realization hit him like a punch in the gut that it could have been Stephen who'd been shot first instead of Booker. Life was fleeting. Especially in this line of work.

With mixed feelings, Stephen got out of bed. Gut wrenching sadness over his partner's death warred with the sudden gratefulness to be alive. He heard the laughter again and tried to remember who was in the house. The laugh sounded female. And it wasn't just Mrs. Lablanc. There seemed to be several females laughing.

Stephen curiously walked out of the room. He remembered Mrs. Lablanc's daughter Stacia. The plan had been for Mrs. Lablanc to ask Stacia to come stay with her until they found Selah and Maddox. Maybe Stacia had arrived.

When he rounded the corner into the living room, he saw Mrs. Lablanc and Jonas Petry sitting with a tall, slim female with auburn-colored hair that was pulled into a messy ponytail. The woman was wearing black cargo pants and a plain gray, long-sleeved t-shirt tucked neatly into her pants. Her shoes sat on the floor at the door. Her feet were pulled under her. She was grinning broadly.

"Mind if I join the party?" Stephen asked. He scratched his head, sure that he was ruffling his blond waves, but he didn't care.

The woman jumped to her feet and pulled back her shoulders as if standing at attention. She held out her hand.

"I'm—"

"Stacia, I presume?"

They both spoke at the same time. A look of confusion fell over Mak's face. Stephen heard Petry snicker as he watched from his place on the couch.

"I'm Mak," Mak smiled, her hand still extended. "Mak Cunningham."

"You're Mak?" Stephen finally shook her hand. Now his face held confusion. "I thought—"

"I was a guy?" Mak cut in. "You're not the first. Can we move past it?"

"Yeah." Stephen was taken back by her abrupt manner. Was she rude or just direct? He couldn't decide. He felt his heart sink a little as he processed that this was going to be his new partner.

"Stacia's not coming, by the way," Mrs. Lablanc said from her cozy seat on the couch.

Stephen turned and looked at the kind older woman. Her eyes looked sad, but she was resolute.

"Stacia doesn't think she's in danger," Mak jumped in. "She's not convinced Selah and Maddox aren't on some tropical island somewhere."

"Even after the gunshot?" Stephen's mouth dropped open a little.

"Yeah." Mak bobbed her head.

"She's stubborn, dear," Mrs. Lablanc said.

"Would you like one of us to talk to her?" Stephen asked. "We are short on resources and really can't assign a private detail to watch her. But we could try to convince her."

"It would be a waste of time, I'm afraid," Mrs. Lablanc said sadly.

"Petry, if Stacia changes her mind, can you text us and we'll escort her here?" Stephen requested.

"Sure," Petry nodded.

"You take good care of Mrs. Lablanc," Mak told Petry. She turned back to Mrs. Lablanc. "Try to keep yourself out of trouble here. We'll be back from time to time to check on you. And we'll crash here at the end of day."

"I would like that very much," Mrs. Lablanc smiled.

Stephen didn't know how Mak had done it in such a short period of time, but she'd managed to become best friends with the kidnapping victim's mother. Stephen couldn't wait to hear what Mak had learned.

He supposed if she'd had instant rapport with Mrs. Lablanc, Mak must be a very likeable person. It might be easy to work with her. But as they left the safe house and he watched Mak put her shoulders back, lift her chin, and jog down the stairs, his doubts arose. She was now on a mission. Stephen had no choice for the moment but to tag along.

He discovered that Mak must have gotten a Lyft because there was a car waiting outside for them as they stepped into the chilly fall air. Mak had grabbed a fleece jacket before she left. She wore it proudly. On the upper left corner, it said her name—*Mak Cunningham*—and underneath were the words *US Marshal*.

"That's a nice jacket," Stephen managed before Mak flung open the car door and Stephen went to the other side.

She grinned as he got in. "They'll give you one when you've been around for longer than a few months."

Stephen felt his face flame. "Six months," he corrected, resisting the urge to justify his place with the marshals.

Mak tossed out an address to the Lyft driver and turned back to Stephen, her voice all business. "I know your history. I'm sure it's been tough starting over with us when you had seniority as a detective. I'm also sure it's going to be tough to remember you're a rookie here. But I have as much time here as you had as a detective. You gonna be able to follow my lead?"

Stephen nodded but was thinking, *So much for being partners. Looks like Mak needs to be in charge.* For the moment, Stephen had no choice but to agree. Was she always this direct?

"Good, you can brief me on everything you know, and I'll brief you on what I know. We'll have a quick get-to-know-you talk, and we'll figure out our plan to move forward."

Stephen was quiet as he processed her words. "When you say you 'know my history,' what do you know?"

Mak speared Stephen with an annoyed look as she jerked her head toward the driver whose eyes kept straying to them. Stephen picked up her cue that there were big ears in the front, and they could finish the conversation later.

She grinned suddenly. Her voice took on a teasing tone. "I know they call you *Love 'Em and Leave 'Em Wilton.*"

Stephen cursed under his breath as the Lyft driver even snickered. Stephen really hoped they dropped that nickname sooner rather than later. In the meantime, he swallowed his irritation and stared out the window. He had to remind himself they were here for a bigger purpose.

Whether he liked his new partner or not, one thing was for sure. Time was running out for Selah Lablanc and Maddox Miller.

18

WILTON

Mak had rented them a black Ford Escape which Stephen had challenged immediately.

"Can't we get a Tahoe or something?" he asked.

"May I remind you we have a per diem, and we have to take what they give us," Mak responded. She smiled gratefully to the woman working behind the desk.

The woman behind the counter smiled shyly at Stephen with apology in her voice. "I'm so sorry, sir. It really is the best vehicle we have available for that price."

Stephen felt instantly bad. "Stephen," he corrected her. "And I understand."

"Oh, good," the woman smiled and batted her eyelashes a little. She picked up a business card and wrote her phone number on it. She slid it across the desk to Stephen. "That's my direct cell number in case you need anything else, Stephen."

Stephen picked up the card and looked at the name. "Thank you, Ivy."

Mak rolled her eyes as she scooped the keys off the counter and turned to go find the Escape.

Stephen jogged after her. "You're driving?"

Mak whirled around and stopped so quickly, Stephen almost bumped into her. "Let's just get this out of the way, shall we?" she asked sharply. "Is having a woman partner going to be a problem for you?"

Stephen felt instantly offended. He wasn't like that. The woman part wasn't the problem. "No, but your attitude toward me might be."

"Attitude?" Mak asked. She blinked blankly at him.

"From the moment we met, you seem to be working hard to put me in my place. You seem nice and outgoing to others but with me—" Stephen rubbed his neck knowing his irritation sometimes showed up in red at the back of his neck.

"Ah. Yes, that makes sense," Mak seemed relieved. "I have two modes. I love people, which helps when we're interviewing people in the middle of investigations. But there's a time and a place for that. Right now, we need to get shit done. I'm on a mission."

Mak started moving again. She clicked the key fob and turned in the direction of the beeping. She found the car and opened the back hatch. She threw in her bag and waited while Stephen did the same. She got in the driver's seat and waited for Stephen to slide in the passenger seat.

"We're at the disadvantage of being strangers thrown together as partners on an investigation that has already started. Having said that, it should be easy to get up to speed. You have information for me, and I have information for you. But make no mistake, you're still the rookie in the room—well, the car. Despite your years as a detective, you just reset your career. This is the big leagues, Wilton. Any questions?" Mak started the car and pulled out of the lot.

"Yeah, what could you possibly have learned about the case in the hour you've been here?" Stephen asked with genuine curiosity.

Mak flashed him a sudden smile. "This is where my people

skills come in. I got the hot gossip. Are you ready for this?" Mak didn't wait for him to reply. "Stacia, Selah's sister, who you know will not be joining her mother at the safe house, is Selah's business manager. Mrs. Lablanc thinks Stacia has chosen to be Selah's business manager as a way of inserting herself into her sister's life so she can continue to spend time with her busy pop-star sister. It's also Stacia's way of keeping tabs on Selah— Mrs. Lablanc thinks to protect her. She says Stacia has always been a protective older sister and thinks Selah is a bit naïve. Further, Mrs. L thinks Stacia feels responsible for Selah's disappearance and is feeling too guilty to remove herself from her role. Mrs. L thinks Stacia will continue to *man the ship* to keep Selah's disappearance under wraps from the public until Selah is back safely."

"Holy cow, you got all that in the short time you were there?" Stephen asked.

"I got more. Mrs. L also said Stacia doesn't believe Selah has been kidnapped. Stacia and Selah had a fight right before the disappearance. Selah pushed Stacia away and told her to stop trying to control her life. Selah said she's perfectly capable of making her own decisions without her sister. Stacia thinks Selah and Maddox ran away together to prove a point."

"I had the same thought," Stephen admitted.

"It was always a possibility," Mak nodded.

"Stacia told Mrs. Lablanc about the fight?" Stephen asked, wondering how close Mrs. Lablanc and Stacia were.

"No, Selah did. Selah is like this with her mother," Mak held up two crossed fingers. "Stacia keeps to herself. She doesn't talk unless she needs to. She's not shy exactly, just introspective. She stopped talking to her mom about her life the day she moved out."

"I see," Stephen said.

"Do you still think Selah and Maddox ran away together?" Mak asked.

"No. Booker found blood in the hallway of the hotel suite," Stephen answered.

"Blood?" Mak asked, her voice sounding incredulous. "Do tell."

"We took a sample and turned it in to the MCPD. The Chief's name is Tigress—"

"Cool name," Mak interrupted. She flinched. "Sorry, continue. I have a bad habit of interrupting. When will you have the results?"

"Any time. Just waiting on a phone call. Anyway, the theory about them running away together doesn't make much sense for Maddox," Stephen mused. "Why would he risk not playing in the big rivalry game?"

"Ugh! Right?" Mak agreed as she attempted to navigate locked down New York traffic. "Did you see the first game? It was a disaster without him. Worst blow-out in history. The announcers kept talking about Maddox being out with a torn rotator cuff."

"Media," Stephen shook his head. "Why do they always have to make the story bigger than it is? He was back the next game. It couldn't have been a torn rotator cuff."

"Control?" Mak asked with a shrug.

"Maybe. Where are we going?" Stephen asked. He eyed the way traffic didn't move. He didn't tell Mak what he thought— the rental car was a terrible idea in New York. Though they did have a confidential place to talk about the case.

"Speaking of media, that's the best part about today!" Mak paused for dramatic effect. "Mrs. L said Selah and Maddox had an appearance on *The Entertainment Today Show* and they met with the CEO of the EBC network. I want to get a first-hand account of their interaction and where Selah and Maddox were going after that."

"Selah and Maddox met with the CEO? Doesn't the network have production managers and assistants who would have prepared them for the on-air interview? Not to mention the on-air talent and the makeup artists... I wonder why they would meet with the CEO? They must interview hundreds of stars a year," Stephen scratched his head under his curly blond hair.

Mak shrugged. "Maybe the CEO is hands on?"

"Or maybe she's a superfan," Stephen added the possibility. He was starting to feel better about his new partner. Mak could be direct but if he put aside her abrupt nature, they might get along well. She moved fast and got things done quickly. He just needed to keep up. He pulled out his cell phone and did a quick search of the EBC network.

"What else did you and Booker have planned?" Mak asked.

Stephen didn't miss the way her eyes flinched a little when she said Booker's name. He wondered if they had been partners before Stephen showed up. "We were planning a visit to Selah's publicist. She was the person who would have known where they were going next. Right before they were taken. She reports directly to Stacia."

"Good thinking." Mak jerked the wheel and jammed the car into a small opening in the next lane. She was rewarded with an angry honk. She smirked at Stephen and shook her head. "New York."

"Yeah, we could probably get there faster walking." Stephen pointed to the packed sidewalk of busy people. They were jammed up but at least they were moving.

Mak shuddered. "I'm claustrophobic. Besides, we need a place to discuss the case in private."

"Okay." Stephen saw the logic. "Did you learn anything else?"

"Yeah!" Mak seemed to be enjoying herself.

"Come on, the suspense is killing me," Stephen coaxed.

"Selah is pregnant."

"What?" he was shocked though he wasn't sure why.

"Maddox is most definitely the father. But he reacted very badly when Selah told him."

"Well, that could change everything!" Stephen exclaimed.

"Right. Are you thinking what I'm thinking?" Mak asked as she finally made a turn on a busy street and into a parking garage.

"If you're thinking that Maddox just became suspect number one!"

"Yes," Mak agreed. They didn't have to quote the stat about boyfriends and husbands being the number one suspects in cases like these.

"So, maybe Maddox isn't kidnapped *with her*. Maybe he *kidnapped her*." Stephen stated the obvious theory.

"Right, and if that's the case, we might not be looking at kidnapping." Mak's mouth hardened in a line.

Stephen's eyes got big. They might be looking at murder.

19

MAK

Mak was about to throw open the car door when Stephen's cell phone rang. Stephen, hand on the door, looked at the cell screen and paused.

"I have to take this," he said. "It's my daughter."

"Okay," Mak said. She respectfully got out of the car to give him privacy. *What do you know, Stephen Wilton has a daughter,* she thought. *At least that's something we have in common.*

Mak leaned against the car and tried not to fidget. To her, patience wasn't a virtue, it was a curse. It slowed life down and she wanted no part of it. Though she did feel a small pang over not talking to Harper this morning.

She heard the car door open and slam shut. Then Stephen was at her side.

"I'm sure I don't need to remind you to keep your eyes up and be alert. Remember that we now have a fallen brother. If someone killed law enforcement once, they won't hesitate to do it again."

"About that," Stephen said as he fell in step with Mak's quick pace. "I'm sorry about Booker. I'm sure he meant a lot to you."

Mak paused and Stephen saw her eyes get moist. She took a deep breath and slowed her pace. She turned to Stephen. "Booker trained me. He was the first one to look past the fact that I was a female. He stood up for me on more than one occasion over it. He was a good man. And yes, he meant a lot to me. He was my partner until seven months ago." Mak was walking fast again as if she could stay ahead of the emotions. She knew she had long legs but felt a touch annoyed that Wilton had to practically jog to keep up. Still, she refused to slow her pace.

"I feel like there's a story there," Stephen said. "Why haven't I ever met you? Where have you been since I started?"

"That's a story for another day," Mak stated dismissively. She walked into the lobby and paused. She turned a slow circle.

Mak was standing in the building that housed one of the most powerful television networks in America. But it wasn't how Mak pictured it would be. Judging from the size of the outside of the building, which appeared to take up several city blocks, she knew the inside of the broadcasting building would be big. What she did not expect was how open it would be. She was also surprised that it was in need of an update. The large tiles on the floor were a dingy, off-yellow color from age. Despite the windows around the building, the décor and lighting was dark, oppressive even. There were a few tables that hugged the walls with a handful of people sitting at them with coffees and cell phones in front of them. Mak spotted a Starbucks serving coffee just beyond a reception desk.

Mak gave the receptionist her most winning smile and walked forward confidently. "Hi, we're here to see L. Taylor, the CEO of the EBC."

The receptionist smiled. "She goes by Lizzie Taylor. Is she expecting you?"

"No," Mak smiled again and casually flashed a badge. "We're US Marshals."

"Oh!" The receptionist's eyes widened as she quickly picked

up her phone and had a conversation with someone who they guessed was an office manager. She replaced the phone and turned back to them.

"Floor forty-one." She pointed to the elevator. "Lizzie Taylor is now expecting you."

"Great! Thank you so much!" Mak said as she headed for the elevator. Once on the elevators, Mak shook her head. "The CEO's name is Lizzie Taylor. Really?"

"What?" Stephen asked.

"Don't you know your Hollywood starlets from the forties?" Mak asked in surprise. "Everyone knows Elizabeth Taylor."

Stephen shook his head back and forth.

Mak sighed.

"Elizabeth Taylor was a big, glamorous movie star from the forties, fifties, and sixties…. *Cleopatra, Giant, National Velvet*… Bet you money Lizzie's not her real name and this CEO is playing off of Elizabeth Taylor's name." Mak felt smirky.

Steven shrugged. "Lots of parents name their kids things without thinking about the implications. Maybe they knew Lizzie was destined for greatness in the film industry. Instead, she *settled* for CEO of a major TV corporation."

"Maybe," Mak said, not convinced. "I am picking up on your sarcasm, by the way. Maybe this CEO thinks she's God's gift to the TV world."

"That sounds like an unfair assumption," Stephen said bluntly.

Mak felt her spine straighten and her respect grow a bit for Stephen. Direct was good. The fact that he wasn't afraid to contradict her was even better. He was probably right. Mak wasn't sure why she had drawn a conclusion when she hadn't even met the woman. In fact, she should feel some kind alliance with a woman CEO for the simple fact that Lizzie Taylor most likely had to fight her way to the top in her role as a woman.

"You're right," Mak said. "Not sure why I went there." She

decided to put her bias aside. Still, she might need to explore where that thought had come from later on. She recalled her conversation with Alyah. *We women need to stick together.* Mak would do well to remember that going into their interview.

Remembering the conversation with Alyah, Mak thought about questioning Stephen, but the elevator doors opened and she missed her moment.

As it turned out, Lizzie Taylor also looked a lot like the starlet Elizabeth Taylor. She had short hair that fell to her shoulders, and she wore it in big, fluffy waves. Her thin heart-shaped lips wore bright red lipstick. She was tall and thin. Every piece of clothing on her body was branded and top-quality material, down to her shoes. Not that Mak could have named the brands. Mak didn't care much about such frivolous things herself. She could just recognize the high-end quality of the clothes.

Lizzie smiled graciously and extended her hand. "Lizzie Taylor."

Mak flashed her badge. "I'm Mak Cunningham."

Stephen followed her example. "Stephen Wilton."

Lizzie Taylor was nothing if she wasn't hospitable. She delivered a water bottle to Stephen and a Coke Zero to Mak and graciously invited them to take seats.

"Thank you," Mak said as she opened her soda. "We're here to ask you some questions about Selah Lablanc and Maddox Miller."

"Whatever for? I mean, they were just here late last week—lovely people. Some stars are stuffy, you know. But not them. They're very down to earth," Lizzie said.

Mak noticed how often Lizzie's eyes seemed to stray to Stephen.

Oh no, she thought, *another instant admirer for Stephen?* Seriously, what was it with this guy? He was okay to look at in a charming, boyish way but personally, Mak didn't see the appeal.

"We're here because we want to ask you some questions

about your experience with Selah and Maddox when they were here. We understand they came for an interview?" Mak began.

"They did," Lizzie bobbed her head up and down.

"Ms. Taylor, did you personally greet and escort them around the day they were in the building?" Stephen asked.

"Please, call me Lizzie," she paused. "Yes, I did walk them from place to place that day."

"Is that normal? I'm sure you're very busy. Don't you have staff—like a production manager—who does things like that?" Mak asked.

"Things like what? I don't know how other CEOs run their broadcast businesses, but I prefer to play hostess and make sure our guests feel warmly welcomed while in my building. I'm sure you understand that we're nothing without the star power of Hollywood who agree to come interview and entertain our audiences. Not to mention the power of influencers in marketing. Without them we would be nothing. We'd have no content and no viewers. We aren't called Entertainment Broadcast Company for no reason. I personally like to ensure each of the entertainers have a top-notch experience." Lizzie's mouth curved up into a prideful smile.

Stephen smiled back at her and for a moment, she held his gaze.

"I'm a huge fan of Selah and Maddox. How did things seem between them?" Mak asked. She leaned forward and feigned interest like she was looking for the latest Hollywood gossip.

Lizzie sat down on the corner of her desk across from where Stephen was sitting. No matter that her skirt was a little on the short side. Come to think of it, Lizzie's blouse was unbuttoned just low enough to show a little cleavage too. Mak sighed. She didn't understand most other women.

Lizzie's eyes connected with Mak's. "Truth be told, they seemed a little distant. There was a slight chill to them. I swear, no one would notice, but I see things like that."

"You can spot that kind of thing?" Mak asked.

"Oh yeah. I work around actors and actresses all the time, and I see through it all. Not to mention, you don't get to where I am today without being able to feel the temperature in the room," Lizzie said. She looked at Stephen again.

"That's right," Stephen said. "Didn't I read somewhere that you're the first female CEO the company has ever had?"

Lizzie's eyes widened with pleasure. "Yes, you did. I am. Worked damn hard to get here, too."

"I bet." Stephen leaned forward with an appreciative gleam in his eyes.

Is he flirting with her? Where did he pull out that piece of information? Mak wondered.

"TV is still a good ole boy's club, though. But I worked hard to break down the walls and get in. Now that I'm here, I'm not going anywhere," Lizzie said.

"Impressive," Stephen said. "So, you noticed something off with Selah and Maddox, huh? What tipped you off?"

"Well, they walked in holding hands, all lovey-dovey, looking into each other's eyes. But when they left, it was like they forgot the act and dropped hands when they thought no one was watching. Someone is always watching. Really, though, what's this about? Are they in trouble?"

"We aren't sure—" Mak started.

"They seem to have disappeared—" Stephen said at the same moment.

Mak shot Stephen a disapproving glance. She hadn't wanted to tip that.

"Disappeared?" Lizzie's eyes got round with concern. "Disappeared where?"

Mak smiled sheepishly. "If we knew, we wouldn't be here. Do you have an agenda from their visit?"

"Yes." Lizzie got up and went to her computer. She clicked a few buttons and printed it out. She handed it to Stephen and gave him a smoldering look.

Geez, Mak thought, *should I give them some time alone?*

"Do you happen to know where they were going after the interview?" Mak asked.

"No. I was only responsible for what happened while they were here. They are grown, consenting adults. What they do with their time is up to them."

"Right," Stephen smiled, seeming to lay on the charm. "Can you think of anything they said while they were here that could give us any clue or indication of what was happening next?"

Lizzie smiled but shook her head back and forth. Her curls swayed with the movement. "No, I'm sorry. I really don't remember anything. But I would be happy to reach out if I remember something. If you'll just put your phone number in?" Lizzie handed her cell phone to Stephen.

Stephen took her phone without hesitation, put in his number, and handed it back to Lizzie. The department always gave the option of carrying a phone specifically for marshal business, but judging by the brand, Mak decided Stephen was using his personal cell. Some officers opted to use one phone for both personal and business.

Mak tried not to roll her eyes when Stephen handed the phone back to Lizzie and she looked into his eyes a second longer than was necessary. It was not lost on her that Lizzie wasn't asking for *her* number.

Mak stood. "Before we go, we would like to meet with each person who worked with or came in contact with Selah and Maddox the day they were here."

Lizzie took back her phone and hesitated. She frowned. "Everyone?"

"Yes, production manager, assistants, hair and makeup, on-air talent, and anyone else who pitched in for the interview. Will that be a problem?" Mak asked.

"Of course not," Lizzie said quickly. "I just need to remember who did what." She went back behind her computer and printed another schedule and cross-checked it with what Mak assumed was a calendar system of employees. She wrote names of employees by each task on the agenda. Then she motioned for them to follow her.

One by one, Lizzie helped them gather every person listed on the schedule. One by one, the employees came to the conference room. Mak and Wilton asked each employee about their experience with Selah and Maddox. They asked if anything had seemed off or if they knew where they were going next.

Only one woman responded with knowledge of future plans. The woman was young, mid-twenties, and identified herself as an intern. Her name was Maggie.

"I heard Selah say she couldn't wait to get back to the hotel. It was Casa Cipriani. She said it had a beautiful view of the Statue of Liberty. She asked Maddox if he'd ever been to the hotel. He wasn't very talkative. He just shook his head. He seemed preoccupied. Like his mind was on something else."

"Did Selah seem to notice?" Mak asked.

"I don't know," Maggie replied.

"Did she say anything about it?" Mak pressed.

"No, the conversation just dropped. I thought it was because I was there and Maddox is a private person or something. I just assumed it was none of my business. So I offered to take them to the studio," Maggie answered.

"You took them to the studio?" Mak asked, feeling surprised. "Where was Ms. Taylor at this point?"

"She had stepped out to take a phone call which is why I took them to the next stop," Maggie stated.

"Did anything seem off about them? Like did they seem to be fighting?" Mak led and then cursed herself silently. She never wanted to push a potential witness to fit into her theories.

"They did seem quiet and very serious when I walked up.

Other than that, they were fine. They put on big smiles and seemed excited when I showed them to the studio. But that's Hollywood, ya know? They turned it on for the cameras."

"Thank you, Maggie. You've been very helpful. Can you think of anything else?" Mak asked.

Maggie shook her head.

As she had with every other person she'd talked to, Mak asked for Maggie's contact information should she have any other questions. Maggie gave it with no questions asked.

When they were done, Mak and Stephen thanked Lizzie for her time. Mak reached a hand out to Lizzie. Lizzie, who only had eyes for Stephen, finally peeled them from him and accepted Mak's hand.

"Thank you for coming by today. I'll be happy to let you know if I remember anything else." Lizzie grabbed Stephen's hand and held on to it a little longer than seemed normal.

Mak waited until they were in the elevator before she spoke to Stephen. "Well, I guess I see your work in action now."

"What?" Stephen asked genuinely confused.

"You and your effect on women," Mak smirked.

"That wasn't—I didn't—she was—" Stephen sputtered.

Mak's phone rang and she looked at her screen. "I'm sorry, Stephen, I need to get this." She put the phone to her ear. "Hey, Harper!"

"Mommy!" Harper's sweet little chipmunk voice greeted her.

"How's my favorite daughter?" Mak asked.

"I'm your only daughter!" Harper squealed with a giggle.

"Oh yeah. Everything good?" Mak smiled.

"Yes, I just miss you," Harper said with a pout in her voice.

"I just left! You haven't had time to miss me," Mak protested.

"But I do," Harper insisted.

"Are you having fun with daddy though?" Mak asked.

"Yeah. But he makes me go outside and run around when I have too much energy."

"Oh, I see what this is. Daddy's harder on you so you want me to come back?" Mak teased.

"No. I just love you. When are you coming home?" Harper wondered.

"I'll be back this weekend," Mak stated. Her lips tightened as she remembered this Saturday was Booker's funeral. She and Stephen would get on a plane and come back for that regardless of where they were on the case.

"Good. I'll see you soon."

Mak hung up the phone and noticed Stephen giving her a funny look.

"What?" Mak asked. They had gotten out of the elevator and were walking in the parking garage.

"You have a daughter, too," Stephen acknowledged. "How old?"

"Harper is three."

"My Anna is four and a half—" Stephen said.

That's when they heard it.

The sound of a gunshot echoed through the garage.

20

WILTON

The sound of the gunshot magnified and warped, seeming to come from all directions. Stephen immediately ducked beside the nearest vehicle, which was an SUV.

Heart racing, he pulled his gun. He sensed, rather than saw, Mak react. She flattened herself against the other side of the SUV. The bullet had been intended for her. He was sure of it.

"Are you hit?" he called.

"No," Mak answered quickly.

That's when Stephen saw the shooter.

"Nine o'clock!" he shouted. A shadowy figure stood angled in their direction with his gun still pointed. He was wearing all black with black sunglasses. Stephen pointed his gun in the direction of the shooter. The shooter didn't have a clean shot.

Mak rolled her upper body out to the side of the vehicle. Both hands held her gun tightly in her grip. She, too, had the shooter in her gun sight.

The man froze and stared at them like a deer in headlights. Seconds crawled by.

"US Marshals, drop your weapon!" Mak called loudly, her voice echoing.

Stephen saw, then heard, the shooter's gun clatter to the ground. Then the man took off running.

"What the..." Before Stephen had time to process, Mak was sprinting after the shooter.

Stephen cursed and ran after Mak. Gun in one hand, Stephen grabbed his phone out of his back pocket. He tried to keep up. Mak was fast. Way faster than Stephen. She was easily outrunning him and gaining on the shooter.

The parking garage curved upward to the next floor. Both the shooter and Mak had disappeared from Stephen's view. He was still running uphill but falling behind.

"Call Tigress," Stephen told his phone after looking at it to unlock it. He hit the speaker button.

"Tigress," the curt voice answered.

"Wilton. In pursuit of an active shooter. EBC parking garage on—" Stephen panted, working hard to get the words out. He had no idea where they were. "I'll ping you."

Stephen could hear the sound of running feet above him as Mak and the shooter were steadily moving farther away. Stephen paused to ping his location to Tigress. He debated going back for the gun the man had dropped. He decided he needed to cover Mak. Following the sound of their footsteps, Stephen ran faster up the ramp.

"Mak?" Stephen yelled. He was out of breath and his lungs were burning.

"Up here," Mak yelled back. "I got him."

"Good deal!" Stephen panted as he continued his run upward. He came up on Mak who had a knee pressed into the middle of the shooter's back. The shooter was lying face down. Mak held the shooter's hands behind his back with one hand. She had a gun pressed into his back with the other hand. She was citing the man his rights.

Stephen's pulse beat faster as he approached the shooter. He scanned the rest of the parking lot quickly. He'd made the mistake of not seeing the shooter before. He wouldn't do that again. He needed to make sure there wasn't a second shooter before he studied this man.

When his gaze fell on the man, Stephen was shocked. He frowned. The man wasn't large. From where he was lying on the parking lot floor, he looked short and thin. His hair was dark but had a shock of gray running through it, indicating the man might be older.

"Not so brave or strong without your gun, are you?" Stephen asked. He resisted the urge to kick the shooter's leg, though he wanted to.

The man grunted and then moaned.

"You get it?" Mak asked. "His gun?"

"No, but I called Tigress and backup is on the way."

Mak nodded but got up off the guy. She jerked him to his feet. Indeed, the man wasn't much taller than Mak. He looked unassuming. He was casual in a pair of black jeans, a long-sleeved black t-shirt, and a pair of black Vans on his feet. His sunglasses were cheap, unbranded plastic frames. Mak held his hands tighter behind his back. The man grunted but Mak didn't loosen her grip.

Stephen wasn't sure if the man complied with Mak's perp walk because he didn't think he could fight back or because he knew she still had a gun at his back. Regardless of the reason, the man willingly walked back down to their Escape.

"Grab the gun, please," Mak called to Stephen as they got back to the level where they'd been shot.

Stephen grabbed the gun the shooter had dropped as they walked by the spot where this had all started. He ran ahead and opened the car door. He dug in his bag until he found the handcuffs.

"Why did you shoot at me?" Mak asked the man as she pushed him against their vehicle.

The man said nothing. He stared ahead vacantly. His eyes

were dark brown, but his pupils were enlarged, which made them look black.

Mak held a gun pointed at him while Stephen handcuffed him. Stephen's eyes scanned the parking garage again.

"You're a terrible shot," Mak tried again. "You do this for a living?"

The man flinched and looked offended. Still, he was silent.

"Did whoever ordered the hit tell you I'm a US Marshal? Do you realize how much trouble you're in?"

This time, the man's eyes grew large, a sure indication of surprise and fear. They could see sweat roll down his forehead. Before the man could answer, they heard police sirens and a police car drove up.

Tigress got out of the car. "Wilton," he greeted.

Stephen nodded back at him.

"One shooter?" Tigress asked as he grabbed the man from Mak. His eyes scanned the parking garage. Another man got out of the police car and stood with his hand on his gun holster. He looked like he was ready to provide backup to his boss.

"One that we know of," Mak answered. She turned to the shooter. "Hey, are you working alone?"

The man said nothing. His jaw clenched.

Mak swiveled and leveled a look at the single police car and second officer. "That's how you provide backup? What if we'd been in a standoff?"

"I don't know you," Tigress said, ignoring Mak's challenge, as he looked Mak up and down. "I would remember if we'd met."

Mak rolled her eyes and shut her mouth, her lips in a tight line. She seemed to make a choice to overlook his comment. "You're right. We've never met. I'm Mak."

Tigress took the shooter from Mak. He put the shooter in the back of the police car. Then he came back to shake Mak's hand.

"I'm Chief Tigress," he said.

"Chief, huh? Either you're very hands-on or you're very shorthanded," Mak stated.

"All of the above, and training a new guy," Tigress tilted his head to the officer who was already back in the car and shutting the door. "What are you doing here in this building anyway?"

"We went to the last place where Selah and Maddox were seen. We interviewed Lizzie Taylor and her staff," Stephen answered.

"Dead end," Tigress snapped.

"How do you know?" Stephen asked. "I thought you weren't working on this case. Where we're from, we start at the last place the victims were seen and work our way backward."

"As you know," Tigress speared Stephen with his eyes, then swung them to Mak, "we dusted the hotel room. We also eliminated Ms. Taylor as a suspect."

Stephen stared at Tigress. Was he protecting Lizzie Taylor? The marshals had been given no such information. Before he could open his mouth to say so, Mak jumped in.

"I'm sure you'll understand why we decided to work the case from the beginning. In the meantime, this parking garage is giving me the heebie-jeebies. Can we just follow you to the station and take a real crack at getting this guy to talk?" Mak pointed to the suspect in the back of Tigress' police car.

"You can follow me anywhere, Marshal Mak," Tigress flirted.

"Are you a misogynist or are you really trying to hit on me?" Mak demanded. "Or do you think you're God's gift to women?

Stephen tried to hide his laughter. Tigress was in for it now.

"I apologize, I couldn't help myself." Tigress didn't look sorry.

"Well, get some control and get your mind out of your pants. Not only am I married, but I'm a colleague. If you don't mind, I'd like to get out of this parking garage in case he's got a friend coming."

"Yes, ma'am," Tigress saluted and got in the police car.

Mak found their rental and jumped in the driver's seat.

Stephen lost it. Laughter was rare for him. Perhaps the de-escalation of the situation plus Mak's reaction to Tigress was some release he needed.

Mak shot him a dirty look as she put the car in reverse. "I'm glad you find this situation so funny."

"Careful, you'll get your own nickname. Mak the Heart-breaker. Too-Married Mak. Mak the Ice Queen."

"I like the last one," Mak grudgingly smiled as she followed Tigress in his police car. "Keep your head in the game. That bullet was meant to take me out. Just like Booker. That man had no contingency plan. He didn't mean to miss me. I was just faster than him."

"Speaking of faster... Do you always run after people who shoot at you when you're not wearing a vest?" Stephen asked. "I mean, there was no thought. You just rushed after the guy."

"Yeah, that's a thing I do," Mak said. "I sort of follow my gut and rush in."

"But you didn't know if he had another gun," Stephen pressed.

"Well, I knew he dropped his and he didn't have time to reach for another one. Besides, I got him. He might be the guy who took out Booker. What's the problem?"

"Today, there isn't one," Stephen said. "I just like to pause to assess the danger for half a second before I make a move."

Mak bristled. "Sometimes a pause is the difference between life or death."

"Exactly," Stephen agreed but for a different reason.

Either his new partner was going to be very valuable, or she was going to get them both killed.

21

MAK

They pulled into the station and Mak was the first one out of the vehicle. Stephen wasn't far behind. Mak thought, not for the first time that day, *I wish he'd keep up*.

They fell in line with the officer-in-training and Tigress, who held the criminal, pushing him to walk at a steady pace. Tigress held up a finger to stop Mak and Stephen from following him further.

They watched from the hallway as he then opened an inter-rogation room, sat the criminal in a chair, and chained the man to the table. Then he shut the door and met Mak and Stephen in the hallway. They followed Tigress to his office.

"Here's how I like to play this," Tigress began. "I'd like to give him time to sit there and think. I like them to get good and nervous—"

"What?" Mak interrupted, not caring if she was rude. "And give him time to come up with excuses? If we strike while it's hot, he might talk to us without asking for a lawyer. If he has time to think it through, he'll defer to a lawyer."

Stephen took a deep breath. "This is the chief's station and if this works well in this city, maybe we should listen to him."

"With all due respect, guys," Mak said through gritted teeth. "The bullet whizzed by my head, and this guy might have killed Booker. We don't have time to sit around and wait until he has feelings."

Tigress stared at Mak, thinking through her words. Finally, he nodded slowly with a smirk on his face. "Okay, let's *strike while it's hot.*"

"I can hear your sarcasm," Mak said as she followed Tigress back to the interrogation room.

"Good. I mean, who says that anymore? *Strike while it's hot.*" Tigress grinned.

Mak caught the laughter in Stephen's eyes before he put his game face on.

"We ready?" she asked Tigress. Surely, Tigress would know she was asking if the recording was on.

Tigress nodded. "Yep. You lead."

Mak yanked open the door to the interrogation room. She walked in confidently and turned a chair around. She straddled the chair. Stephen sat normally in the remaining chair. Tigress stood against the wall, crossing his arms over his chest.

"What's your name?" Mak asked the man.

"Rich Landers," he answered. He looked Mak in the eyes now. There seemed to be something defiant about him.

There was no window in the interrogation room. Just one single light in the ceiling that cast a yellow hue over the room. It was minimalistic, like most interrogation rooms. The table was heavy steel with a galvanized tabletop. There were four chairs, two on each side of the table. There was a small camera hanging from the ceiling in the corner. A green light blinked, indicating the camera was on.

"Well, Rich, why did you shoot at me?" Mak asked. She studied the man in front of her. He was her height and thin. But now that she really had a chance to study his face, she noticed he had stubble on his face that didn't cover his light acne. His eyes were dark and his pupils dilated to make them look black. His salt and pepper hair was ruffled from running but otherwise cut short and well-kept. There was no emotion on his face. Instead, he sat practically frozen. He took his time to answer.

"It's nothing personal. Just a job," Rich finally answered with a touch of attitude. His tone of voice was quiet. "Can I get these things off of me?" he indicated to his cuffed hands.

No one seemed inclined to uncuff him.

"I see. And my partner, Booker. Was he *just a job*, too?" Mak seethed. Making a preconceived statement of guilt was an effective interrogation technique. But for Mak, the answer would determine how accommodating they would be.

Rich looked confused. "I don't know a Booker. Wasn't a target."

"How about Mrs. Lablanc, Selah Lablanc's mom? Was she the target?" Stephen broke in.

He was quiet for a minute, then shook his head. "You don't know what you're getting yourself into."

"Why don't you tell us. What are we getting ourselves into?" Mak pressured him.

"I told you. It's just a job for me," Rich said, an irritated edge in his voice.

"Who hired you?" Mak asked.

Rich shut his mouth and stared straight ahead.

"See, you shooting at me is attempted murder of a law enforcement officer. You admitted this is a for-hire job. That's attempted murder in the first degree. That's punishable up to life in prison. I think you killed my partner, Ethan Booker, too. Booker was another law enforcement agent." Mak swung around to Tigress. "Remind me, do they have the death penalty in New York?"

Tigress shrugged. "Jurors can recommend a death sentence." He didn't mention that this was rare. His words were effective enough.

"In case you have buddies on the inside you plan to hang with, you can forget it—"

"Fine, I want a deal," Rich said, breaking.

"A deal?" Mak spat. "No *deal* will bring my partner back—"

Stephen leaned forward and cut in. "To make a deal, you'd have to have information. You don't seem to know who hired you. I don't think you know anything. I got the make, model, and last three numbers of your license plates on the day you shot Ethan Booker. You're going down. No deal will save you."

"Wait, wait, wait," Rich's tone changed. "I've never actually met the person who hired me. It's a deep web contract. But I know a name. She calls herself *The Fan*. Mrs. Lablanc wasn't the target, your partner was. You were." Rich looked at Stephen, then he swung his gaze to Mak. "And you were. I didn't have your name though. Just *the female cop* and an address where to find you. It was a last-minute pick up. It was sloppy. A total fail."

"*The Fan*? That's all you got?" Mak laughed humorlessly. "We had that much. Do you have an address of where we can find *The Fan*?"

Rich shook his head, looking defeated.

"Can you give us anything else?" Mak asked sounding incredulous.

Rich shook his head again.

"What if..." Stephen seemed to be thinking through his words carefully. "Have you ever met her in person?"

"No," Rich shrugged. "The money just shows up as crypto when the job is done."

"What if we pose as Rich?" Stephen asked.

"What?" Mak was dubious.

"No, really. Pose as him." Stephen turned to Rich. "We'd need to get access to your account. Then we say the money never showed up and we need to meet."

"*The Fan* will never go for that," Rich said.

"No matter how we do it, we lure *The Fan* out and we get her to tell us where Selah and Maddox are," Stephen finished.

"Or no show and follow her back to where she's keeping them. This could work," Mak said excitedly.

"What do I get in exchange?" Rich asked.

Mak turned to look at Tigress.

Tigress groaned. "I hate negotiating with scumbags like him!"

"Scumbags?" Mak asked with a smirk and raised eyebrow. "Who says *scumbags* anymore?

"Yeah, scumbags," Tigress glared at Rich, then swung his angry gaze to Mak. "Let's take a break, work out a plan, and reconvene. I don't like the thought of this guy—this US Marshal killer—getting away with this."

"But—we had a deal," Rich sounded whiney and scared.

"Shut it." Tigress pushed off the wall and ushered Mak and Stephen out of the interrogation room. He stopped by the desk of one of his officers. "We're done with the interview. We need Rich Landers escorted to a cell. Only then can he get his hand-cuffs off."

The officer nodded and immediately jumped to his feet and turned toward the interrogation room where Rich was still sitting.

Tigress led Mak and Wilton into his office and shut the door. He stood behind his desk and faced them.

Mak glanced around, not surprised to find masculine décor. The desk was a deep brown mahogany. His office chair was a matching brown leather. The chairs in front of his desk were black, no-nonsense chairs with light padding. They were not chairs designed for sitting around and chatting. There was a big window behind Tigress' desk that showed the New York skyline.

"First of all, don't ever question my authority in front of a prisoner again," Tigress snapped at Mak.

"I—" Mak snapped her mouth shut realizing there was more. She felt her cheeks go pink. She'd really just been calling him on the use of his language, the same way he'd done to her.

"Secondly," Tigress turned to Stephen. "You do not have the right to make deals with prisoners in my precinct. That right belongs to me. I say he's a dead end. I don't want to put a *scumbag* like him—a for-hire cop killer—back out on the street. We need a different plan."

Mak nodded her agreement, still feeling humbled and a little embarrassed.

"Could we get a warrant for the laptop he uses to communicate? Maybe someone here knows a way around passwords and can access his deep web account without his help from his computer?" Stephen asked.

"If we have his laptop, a tech can probably trace his digital steps and find where he's been in the computer. Like a footprint —that's a thing, right?" Mak jumped in, feeling excited again.

"Now you're talking. I can get you a warrant based on what we have. But that's all I can do at the moment. I can text you, Wilton, and let you know when I have the warrant." Tigress tapped on his keyboard and stared at the computer. "This guy has priors and he's in the system. He's not going anywhere. Wilton, you said you have his car make, model, and license number?"

Stephen nodded and rattled off the three numbers he got from the license plate and the make and model of the vehicle that drove by Mrs. Lablanc's house after Booker was killed.

"Okay, yeah. It checks out. That is the last car registered to Rich Landers. He murdered your partner alright. He's not going anywhere. I have his address. I'll text it to you along with the *okay* when we have the warrant. I'd say you turned what could have been a bad situation—a shooting—into a lucky break. Regardless, you should never have been at that building," Tigress ended in a grumble.

"As we said before, it seemed like a good place to start," Stephen defended.

"Lizzie Taylor is a good person. You won't need to spend any more time with her." Tigress stood, clearly dismissing him.

Stephen's mouth opened and closed, like he wanted to say more but Mak jumped to her feet, cutting him off.

She hated apologizing. It didn't come naturally. She preferred to do it like ripping off a band aide. "I'm sorry, I—"

Tigress was curt. "Let's just call us even, shall we?"

"Yes, sir," Mak said and resisted the urge to salute him the way he had saluted her earlier.

Mak and Stephen left. They were quiet until they got back to the car. Mak slid behind the wheel of the car before she spoke again.

"That was stupid and unprofessional of me," Mak began apologetically.

"No," Stephen disagreed. "Why can he kid you about *striking while it's hot,* but you can't mess with him about the word *scumbag*? We haven't said that word since the nineties. There's something off about Tigress. I can't put my finger on it. But you most definitely weren't even. The reaction when he met you was unacceptable. Flirting with a fellow law enforcement officer with or without a wedding ring on is unprofessional. His reaction was designed to put you a step below him. Clearly, you're a US Marshal and an equal. Did he really think hitting on you was a good idea? What an idiot!"

Mak surprised herself when a short laugh escaped. "You're starting to sound like me, Wilton, and we've only been partners for a day."

"Yeah," Stephen switched the topic back to the case. "So, I guess that shoots our theory about Maddox. Since *The Fan* has been hiring Rich."

"I guess so," Mak said.

Stephen's phone vibrated. He looked at it. His eyes widened in surprise.

"What is it?" Mak asked, wondering if they already had the warrant.

"Lizzie Taylor just asked me out to dinner tonight."

"Business or pleasure?" Mak asked.

"Would it matter?" Stephen responded. His eyebrows knit together, looking concerned.

"Are you really asking my opinion?" Mak wondered aloud.

"Yes," Stephen admitted. "I have a habit of blurring lines and making cases emotional. I don't want to mess up this job—"

"Look, Wilton. Lizzie isn't a suspect. We went and talked to her today and she's clear. You two are consenting adults. Besides, maybe she will remember something she forgot to tell us today." Mak smiled and accelerated the car.

"You sure?" Stephen asked.

"It's not my place to decide for you. But if you want advice—"

"I do," Stephen said.

"Be clear about intentions. Why does she want to have dinner?"

"No clue, I'll ask," Stephen said. He responded to the text and got one back within minutes. He chuckled to himself. "She asked me what's the difference?"

Mak rolled her eyes. She backed the car out and drove away from the police station. "You really do make an impression with women, you know."

"How can you possibly know that?" Stephen's voice sounded frustrated.

"Well, my first clue was Alyah Smith. She cornered me before I left and asked me to keep an eye on you. Now, why would Alyah Smith, a woman I've talked to maybe twice since she's been a DA, make it a point to come and warn me about you if you hadn't gotten under her skin?"

"That's completely different," Stephen sighed. He was distracted as he texted Lizzie back and forth.

"How so?" Mak asked.

"Because I dated her sister. We were almost engaged. Her sister, Carley, broke it off with me, kidnapped my daughter, and faked a car accident so I would think they were dead. Little did we know she was living with my daughter, posing as her mother. She got involved with the wrong guy who ended up shooting her in the gut minutes before I showed up. I'd finally put it all together. I just got there minutes too late. Carley died. Alyah knows all that went down right after I got this job. I was off duty. But she assumes I was working some side case, I think. We didn't actually talk in-depth about it. She basically introduced herself and told me she doesn't trust me. She didn't want me to take this case."

"Woah," Mak said. "I wasn't aware that woman had emotions. I can see I was wrong. I'm sorry to hear about your ex-girlfriend." Mak navigated the terrible traffic.

"Thanks," Stephen said. "I got my daughter back that night. I feel thankful Anna was safe."

"Yeah, sounds like someone above was looking out for Anna," Mak said.

"Oh no, not you, too. You believe in that whole higher power thing?" Stephen asked.

"Well, I don't know about a higher power, but I believe in God," Mak said. "Trust me, Wilton. In this job, I see God come through all the time." Mak lapsed into a silence.

On the flip side of that, Mak couldn't explain why God hadn't saved the kid seven months ago. That's the thing she'd been wrestling through with her counselor. Still, she had to believe in God because she refused to give herself over to the darkness she saw so often in this job.

Mak sighed into the silence. It was okay if her new partner didn't agree with her. Just so long as he had her back.

"Let's go pay a visit to Selah's publicist," Stephen said by way of closing the conversation. "Apparently, I have dinner plans tonight."

22

MAK

Mak and Wilton walked into the lobby of the office where they would find Selah's publicist. This lobby was open, clean, and tastefully decorated. But it was much smaller than the other buildings they had been in. There was no desk with a receptionist. They wandered to the elevators and looked at the list of businesses on a wooden sign with the names engraved in gold.

Mak ran her finger down the list until she came to Lablanc Public Relations. "Bingo. Fourth floor."

Mak had just stepped inside the elevator when she heard a voice call out.

"Hold the elevator, please!"

Stephen took a step back and put his hand in front of the sensor to keep the elevator door open.

A woman ran in, her heals clicking on the tile. "Sorry," she said. "I'm late for a meeting."

"What floor?" Stephen, ever the gentleman, punched the number five for her when she named where she was going.

The woman watched as Stephen pushed the fourth floor. She smiled at Stephen and for a minute, Mak thought she was going to flirt with him.

"You're going to Lablanc?" The woman said sympathetically.

"Why?" Stephen seemed genuinely curious.

"She's a tough one, that Stacia," she said.

"We're actually going to see Emily Walters," Stephen said.

For once, Mak didn't feel put out with Stephen over telling their business. She watched the woman tilt her head and look confused. "Well, then, Emily is a doll. Can't figure out why she's stayed as long as she has. There's lots of turnover in that office. In fact, I think Stacia keeps scaring everyone off and is down to just one employee—Emily."

"We'll take note of that," Stephen said with a charming smile.

The woman smiled back.

The door to the fourth floor opened up and Mak rolled her eyes as she exited. Once in the hallway, Mak looked around, feeling confused. There was only one business here and it was Lablanc Public Relations. Mak could see before she opened the office door that the office suite beyond was small. She would have thought that someone in the business of promoting Selah Lablanc would have a bigger, fancier office.

Mak opened the door and let herself in, followed by Stephen.

What they found instead was a tiny waiting area with an administrative assistant sitting in front of a door that was closed behind her. There was one picture of the Statue of Liberty on the wall over a waiting area. There were no other decorations. Mak could see doors that opened into offices that connected with the office suite. Maybe those housed other Lablanc Public Relations executives at one time?

Mak made eye contact with the woman sitting at the desk outside a closed door.

"Hello, can I help you?" the woman smiled tentatively, though her eyes darted to the computer screen.

"Hi, I'm Mak Cunningham and this is my partner, Stephen

Wilton. We're with the US Marshal's office." Mak flipped her badge as did Stephen.

"Oh!" the woman exclaimed. Her eyes widened as she looked at the computer screen again. "Ms. Stacia is in a meeting for the next hour. She's not to be interrupted."

"That's okay," Mak said cheerfully. Though she made a note that it was odd the woman had jumped to the conclusion they were there to see Stacia. "We're really here to see Emily Walters, the publicist. Is that you?"

The girl's cheeks reddened, and she looked scared. "Yes, that's me. But what could you possibly want with me?"

Mak hesitated. Emily looked like an assistant. She acted like an assistant. Was it possible she was working two positions at one time until they could hire someone else? There was no way a publicist would have time to work both positions.

Mak plopped down in a chair that circled a makeshift lobby area. Stephen followed Mak's lead. Emily reluctantly rolled her chair over and crossed her legs. She primly interlocked her fingers on her lap.

"How can I help you?" she asked. Her dark blonde hair was cut off abruptly at her shoulders, and it swung around as she looked from Mak to Stephen. Her brown eyes held concern. She wore a long, conservative dress with brown suede booties.

"I understand you are the publicist for Selah Lablanc?" Mak asked.

"Yes," Emily agreed.

"Did I hear a rumor that you might also have been keeping Maddox on track as well?" Stephen asked.

"Well," Emily paused. "The truth is, Stacia is Selah's publicist—well, her business manager, really. She's the real talent behind Selah's popularity. Stacia books Selah on tours, interviews, and events. She makes the arrangements and makes sure Selah gets where she needs to go. I had watched Stacia for years and wanted more responsibility. So, I asked for more. Stacia put me in charge of Maddox when he was in town and attending functions with Selah. While I really am Stacia's assistant, we told Maddox I would be his publicist, which sometimes translates to personal assistant."

"Then you might have been the last person to have talked to Maddox and Selah," Mak sounded pleased.

Emily shrugged. "I don't know about that—"

"When did you last talk to them?" Mak cut in.

Emily's head turned in the direction of her computer screen.

"It's okay if you need to consult your calendar," Stephen gave her permission.

Emily nodded. She got up, went to her computer, and clicked a few times.

"It's been about four days now. It was shortly after *The Entertainment Today Show* interview. They were picked up by a hotel vehicle around..." Emily checked the screen again. "One-twenty that afternoon."

"That was the last time you talked to them?" Stephen asked.

Emily sighed and came to sit back down. "No."

"You seem like you have a story to tell, but you're reluctant to tell it," Mak surmised.

Emily's eyes widened, and her face flushed a deeper shade of red.

Stephen gave Mak a look. He fought the urge to jump in and save Emily.

Emily clasped her hands together again. She met Mak's eyes. "Maddox and Selah broke up. We had booked Selah's favorite spot at Casa Cipriani overlooking the East River. They wanted one last rendezvous—"

"Before...?" Mak asked.

"Maddox had practice for the big game, and Selah was going back on tour."

"So, you booked the room for the night?" Stephen asked.

"No, two nights, then they'd go their separate ways," Emily clarified.

"How do you know they broke up?" Stephen wondered.

"Maddox called me and asked for an extraction plan. We had to keep it a secret of course. No need to alert the media."

"If they broke up, wouldn't that mean your obligation to help Maddox was over?" Stephen asked.

Emily fidgeted. "I thought they were just fighting, and Maddox was being dramatic."

"Had he ever left early or asked for a way out before?" Mak asked.

"Once. They'd had a fight. I had to send a limo to pick him up and take him elsewhere."

"Where did he go?" Stephen asked.

"Then or now?" Emily asked.

"The first time?" Mak clarified.

"Home. Maddox wanted to go back home," Emily answered.

"And this time?" Mak followed up Stephen's line of questioning.

"Same. Maddox was ready to go back to Kansas City."

"But what made you think they broke up?" Mak asked.

"He told me they were through," Emily answered.

"Had he ever said that before?" Mak asked.

"No."

"Do you have feelings for Maddox?" Mak asked suddenly.

"What?" Emily sounded indignant and her face flushed a deeper shade of red. "No, of course not!"

"Why not?" Mak asked grinning. "He's great to look at, super fit, and have you seen his record this year?"

"No, absolutely not!" Emily repeated.

Mak shrugged and winked. "I would."

"Okay," Stephen stepped in to get the interview back on track. "Did the hotel car pick up Maddox?"

"No, we sent a limo."

"And where was he going?" Stephen asked.

"To the airport."

"A private jet or commercial?" Stephen wondered.

"Commercial," Emily shrugged. "We needed the jet for the tour. We didn't have time to gas it up, take Maddox to KC, then turn around and leave for the tour. Not to mention—"

"What?" Mak leaned forward.

"Stacia was mad that Maddox had just dumped her sister. She said even if the jet was available, she wouldn't have let him use it." Emily brushed her hands together like she was saying *good riddance.*

"Ah," Mak said with understanding. Stacia, the protective older sister. She shared a look with Stephen.

"So, the limo driver was the last person to see Maddox?" Stephen asked.

"No, he never saw Maddox," Emily stated.

"What?" Stephen looked confused.

"He told us Maddox never got in the limo," Emily restated.

"Huh. We're gonna need the limo driver's info," Mak requested.

Emily's hands moved restlessly. "I don't have it."

"You're the publicist. What do you mean you don't have it?" Mak shot back.

The door to the closed office swung open abruptly. A woman who resembled Selah with blonde hair cut in a straight line at her shoulders and fiery blue eyes emerged. Her face held a hard look, and her eyes were cold. She was thin and tall with a commanding presence. In her hand was a purple Post-it note.

"Emily doesn't have the limo info because I do. It's my contact." Stacia handed the Post-it note to Mak.

Mak took in Stacia's pleather pants, stiletto heels, and deep purple, flowy silk blouse as Stacia reached out a hand to her. Mak stood but found herself several inches shorter than Stacia.

Mak shook Stacia's hand.

Then Stephen reached over and shook her hand.

"Stacia Lablanc," Stacia said needlessly. "Are we about done with this interrogation?"

"We'd like to ask you some questions as well," Mak began.

"I need you to get back to work, Em. Please call my three-thirty appointment and let them know I'm going to be late," Stacia commanded. Then she turned back to Mak and Stephen. "I can hear everything from my office. I stand by everything Emily said."

"What are your thoughts on your mother getting shot at yesterday?" Stephen asked before Stacia could leave.

Stacia paused and turned around. Her eyes widened. "From what I understand, they were aiming for an agent. Is that not true? My condolences on the loss of your partner, by the way."

"That is true. However, we suspect the true target was your mother. You might be in danger, Stacia," Stephen told her. He was bluffing to see her reaction.

Stacia stepped closer and leveled Stephen with her icy eyes. "The only thing I'm in danger of is owing venues money for breaking contracts because my idiot sister decided to run off with her idiot boyfriend *after* trying to throw us off with a fake breakup. Now if you'll excuse me, I have to go fix the chaos that has resulted," Stacia spun on her heel and left the office without another word.

Mak's mouth was open, gaping at her sudden absence.

Stephen grinned. "Close your mouth. You, of all people, should respect a woman on a mission."

They left the office shortly after.

"I'm nothing like that," Mak defended herself in the elevator.

"You just keep telling yourself that," Stephen joked.

Mak pulled out her phone and called the number on the Post-it note. She left a message on the voicemail.

"See? Woman on a mission," Stephen grinned.

"Someone has to be," Mak stated.

"On a mission or a woman?" Stephen asked.

"Both," Mak grinned back, looking superior.

23

WILTON

Mak and Stephen were running. Actually, Mak was running while Stephen was trying to keep up. *Why is Mak in so much better shape than me?* he couldn't help but think as he picked up his speed.

When he hadn't answered his phone, they had decided to go pay a visit to the limo driver, Jason Jones, after they left Stacia's office less than a half hour ago. It hadn't taken any time to track down his shop, which was located just outside the city.

Mak and Stephen had arrived to find a near-empty garage. One man stood under the hood of a black limousine. He was large with a broad build and tubby stomach. He was tinkering with something under the engine.

Stephen had cleared his voice.

The man's hands stopped moving, and his body hovered over the engine as he paused what he was doing. His neck turned slightly so he could see them over his left shoulder.

"US Marshals Mak Cunningham and Stephen Wilton," Mak said in an authoritative voice. "Are you Jason Jones?"

The man had nodded slowly.

They both flipped their badges.

Mak began again. "We're here to ask you—"

The man had calmly put down the tool he'd held in his hand. He regarded them in silence for a few seconds. Then he took off in the opposite direction in a full-out sprint.

Mak had reacted quicker than Stephen, who seemed temporarily surprised. She took off after Jason.

He'll be no match for Mak, Stephen thought before he ran after them.

Now, Stephen was making up for lost time. Pushing himself to run faster. It was stupid for Jason to think he could outrun them. For one, they were running in the back lot of the man's business. They could see a tall privacy fence a mile off at the back of the lot. For two, Mak was clearly in much better shape than Jason was. That's why Stephen was surprised when it took Mak as long as it did to catch the man.

Stephen watched as Mak closed the gap and took a flying leap, the sheer force of her body mass throwing him off balance as she tackled the big man to the ground.

Stephen sprinted to the pair. He judged that though Mak was clearly in excellent shape, the man was large and would likely be stronger than Mak. He could easily throw her off his back. Though it also occurred to Stephen that he didn't really know anything about Mak's abilities or how she would handle herself in a fight.

Rather than wrestle the man to stay down, Mak jumped off Jason's back. She had pulled her gun at some point during the run, and she now kept it trained on him.

By the time Stephen reached them, Mak had let Jason stand back up. She had her gun pressed into his back. Jason was standing at the fence, holding his hands against it. Mak was reciting the Miranda rights to the man.

A cold breeze blew over the fence where the trees were rustling leaves that had just turned vibrant shades of yellow and copper. New York in the fall was chillier than Stephen had expected.

"I didn't do anything wrong!" Jason grunted.

Mak finished reciting the rights. "Yeah? Why did you run?"

"I dunno. I just reacted." Jason attempted to turn around.

Stephen reached out, took one of Jason's arms, and started the walk back with Mak, who grabbed Jason's other arm.

"Innocent people don't have that kind of reaction," Stephen stated.

They walked Jason back to the car. Mak suppressed a shudder. Stephen was beginning to wonder if it was cold enough to snow. He could almost smell the clean scent of winter weather in the air.

"Please tell me you have handcuffs in your gear?" Mak hissed quietly. "We took them back from when we cuffed Landers, right?"

"Are you guys real cops? If you were, you would cuff me—" the man whined.

"What part of, *Anything you say can and will be used against you in a court of law*, do you not understand?" Mak snapped. "I suggest you stop talking."

The limo driver and potential accomplice, Jason Jones, took Mak at her word. They found cuffs, cuffed him, and threw him in the back seat. The drive back to MCPD was made in silence. Jason had gotten the message to keep his mouth shut, and Stephen knew Mak didn't dare hold a private conversation in front of a potential criminal.

It made for almost forty-five minutes of silence, which Stephen coveted. He hadn't gotten any quiet time since Mak had become his partner. Stephen sent a quick text to Tigress that they had an incoming suspect to interrogate and were on their way. Just before Mak pulled into the parking garage, Stephen's phone buzzed. Thinking it was Tigress confirming there was an interrogation room open, he checked the text.

Lizzie: *Can't wait to see you tonight. Don't be late.*

Stephen: *Sounds good. Can I bring you anything?*

Lizzie: *Just yourself...* 😊

When they arrived, Mak and Stephen walked Jason Jones into the precinct. Tigress met them at the door and led them to an interrogation room. They deposited Jason Jones in the room, handcuffing him to the table, and shut the door. In the hallway, Stephen explained to Tigress how Jones was relevant to the investigation.

"This is Jason Jones, the limo driver who Stacia Lablanc's office called to pick up Maddox. Only their story is Jason never picked Maddox up. When we arrived at Jason's shop to ask him questions, he ran. So, we cuffed him and brought him in for questioning." Stephen shifted from foot to foot, suddenly realizing how weak this sounded coming out of his mouth.

"You are that sure he had something to do with this case?" Tigress asked, his eyebrows raised.

Stephen nodded.

"Well, let's go question him then," said Tigress.

After five minutes of questioning, Jason declared he wanted to talk to his lawyer. Stephen, Mak, and Tigress let themselves out of the interrogation room and walked back to Tigress' office.

Stephen handed Jason Jones' ID to Tigress, having confiscated everything in Jones' pockets shortly after cuffing him to the table. Tigress sat down at his desk and checked the criminal database on his computer.

"Ah," Tigress sounded pleased. "Jason Jones has a few priors and an outstanding warrant for arrest for theft. We can hold him until his lawyer gets here. Still, I think a lawyer can get him out of here pretty quick. What is it you need to know?"

"We need a way to know if Maddox Miller was in the back of that limo," Stephen stated.

"Hmm. We can get a warrant and go dust for prints but

who's to say he didn't wipe down the limo after Maddox arrived —if Maddox was indeed in the car to begin with? Don't limo drivers have some cleanliness protocols?" Tigress scratched his clean-shaven face.

"Most likely." Mak looked dejected.

"Well, we'll detain him until his lawyer gets here. I'm not sure we have grounds to get a warrant to search the limo, but I can try. You guys move on, and I'll let you know if we can get the warrant."

"Thanks," Mak said. "Speaking of warrants, any news on that warrant for Rich Landers' laptop?"

Tigress shook his head. "Not yet. You'll be the first to know when we get it. Keep your phones ready and waiting."

Stephen watched as Mak narrowed her eyes. They walked out the door and to the parking lot, where she mumbled grumpily, "How long does it take in New York to get a search warrant? It's been hours!"

"Over four hours," Stephen said after consulting his watch. "I was wondering the exact same thing."

"I just realized we skipped lunch. I'm hungry," Mak said.

Stephen grinned. "Are you hungry because you realized we skipped lunch?"

Mak rolled her eyes. "We've been too busy to think about food. Now that we're at a dead end for the day, I realize I'm hungry."

"Yeah, I could eat. But I do have dinner plans. So, I'll keep it light," Stephen said.

"Oh, that's right. What time is your date with the diva?" Mak grinned at Stephen as she wiggled her eyebrows.

"She's not a diva," Stephen defended. He settled into the passenger side seat and unlocked his phone. "Speaking of..."

Stephen didn't realize his eyes lit up when he read the text from Lizzie. Stephen was too focused on his response to the text to see Mak shake her head as she turned her focus back to driving.

"I hope you know what you're doing, Wilton," Mak mumbled.

Stephen looked up from the text with a smile. "That makes two of us."

24

WILTON

Stephen arrived in the lobby of Lizzie Taylor's penthouse apartment. He took in the white marble floors, the high chandeliers on the ceiling, and the crystal fixtures. The lobby was open with high-backed suede chairs sitting on a Persian rug in front of a black onyx fireplace. The artwork, candle centerpieces, and strategically placed greenery made the place pretty but did nothing to make the place feel warm.

"Going up?" A tall, broad man with a thick neck wore a staunch black suit and stood by the elevator. He looked like he was hiding some serious arm muscles under that suit. He appeared to be about ten years older than Stephen. Though Stephen had some doubts as to whether he could take him in a fight. "To see Ms. Taylor?"

It took Stephen a minute to realize the man planned to ride up with him. "Yes. Thank you. How did you know?"

"She said she was expecting someone. Name?" the elevator man asked.

"Stephen Wilton."

"Hi, Stephen, I'm Henry." The man pushed the button and when the doors opened, he got on the elevator with Stephen.

Once inside, he hit another button with an icon Stephen didn't recognize, which was apparently an intercom system.

"Yes?" Lizzie's voice sounded.

"I have a Stephen Wilton requesting to see you," the man said.

"Yes, send him up," Lizzie gave permission.

"Nice night," the man said pleasantly to Stephen as he pushed a keycode on the panel and then hit the button that said twenty-five. The penthouse apartment.

"Yes, it is," Stephen agreed. He'd never been on an elevator with a man whose job it was to ride the elevator up and down all day. He supposed it was probably some security measure. Judging by the look of the man, Stephen thought it must be effective. Stephen wouldn't willingly fight him.

The elevator opened right into the penthouse suite. Stephen wasn't prepared for the way he was suddenly in Lizzie's home. It was an open floor plan. From his vantage point at the door, Stephen could see the kitchen, dining room, and living room. It was classic and elegant. What drew Stephen's attention were the three arched windows with French doors that opened onto a terrace and showcased the New York skyline.

The elevator doors closed, and Stephen found himself in front of Lizzie.

"Wow," Stephen said.

"Me? Or my place?" Lizzie asked with a smile. Her lips were red. Her black hair was pulled back into a low ponytail. She wore a white, silky wrap-around dress with a short skirt and a fair amount of cleavage showing. She wore no shoes on her feet.

"You, of course," he came forward to kiss her cheek. "You look beautiful." If Stephen had any doubts about what kind of dinner this was, it had all become perfectly clear.

"Do you mind?" she asked. She pointed to Stephen's feet.

"Oh, sure," Stephen kicked off his shoes.

"You're not so bad yourself," Lizzie smiled and flirted back as she looked him up and down.

Stephen always traveled with a suit jacket and a nice pair of dress shoes. That combination dressed up his jeans and white button-down shirt. He'd put product in his hair after he'd gotten out of the shower earlier. His unruly blond curls had obeyed and waved in a way that flattered his handsome face.

Lizzie turned and led Stephen into the dining room. The twelve-foot modern table took up the length of the space. A beautiful flower centerpiece adorned the middle of the table. Candles were lit all around it. "I took the liberty of ordering dinner. I hope you like steak."

"I do, thank you." Stephen followed her to a liquor cabinet.

"What are you drinking?" she asked.

"Seven and seven," Stephen said.

"Whiskey? A man after my own heart," Lizzie purred.

Stephen watched her pour his drink and hand it to him. Then she poured lemon juice, simple syrup, and whiskey into a cocktail shaker, shook it up, and poured it into a glass. She took a sip of her whiskey sour.

Drinks in hand, they stepped to the table. Stephen pulled out a chair for Lizzie and sat opposite her where she had placed a second plate with a warmer lid over it. He took the lid off and inhaled the aroma of steak. He looked down at his plate to see a juicy steak with a melting pat of butter, sweet potatoes that looked too pretty to eat with caramel and marshmallow cream on top, and asparagus, which added color to the beautiful combination of food.

"So, tell me more about Maddox and Selah," Lizzie started. "Are they really missing? Did you find them yet?" She cut a bite of steak and shoved it in her mouth, chewing daintily.

Stephen hesitated, taking time to neatly cut his steak, thinking about his answer. "I really can't discuss the case. I'm sorry. I shouldn't have said as much as I did earlier."

Lizzie pouted. "Well, then what will we talk about?" She took a bite of her sweet potato and groaned, closing her eyes in pleasure.

"I want to talk about you," Stephen stated, interest in his eyes. The steak was cooked perfectly, but the sweet potato was, indeed, worth Lizzie's sexy moan when she put a bite in her mouth.

"Me?" Lizzie laughed, clearly caught off guard. "What about me?"

"What's your story? How did you get where you are today? First woman to sit in that CEO chair," Stephen flattered her. His food was rapidly disappearing off his plate. He hadn't had much to eat today, and this was hitting the spot.

"You sure you want to hear about that?" Lizzie asked. Her red lips turned into a frown. She looked unsure. Was that vulnerability that crossed her face? Stephen couldn't be too sure.

"Absolutely," Stephen gave her his full attention.

"Well, my dad was the CEO—"

"For the EBC network where you're the CEO now?" Stephen asked.

Lizzie's face flushed a little pink. "Yes, the same. When I was little, my mom would bring me to the city, and I'd go up to his office. I would go straight to the window and stare out at the view. I always loved the city in the daytime. But at night—wow, those lights were like Christmas to me."

"That explains your view here," Stephen interjected perceptively.

Lizzie nodded. "I would tell my dad, *When I grow up, I want to be you*. I want to work right here in this building. And I did." Lizzie came out of her daydream and smiled brightly at Stephen. She took a bite of steak with sweet potato. She swallowed and took a bite of asparagus. "How was your steak?"

"Fantastic!" Stephen answered feeling a little disappointed

he'd eaten his last bite. "But I think you skipped the part of the story where you worked your way into your position in that building."

"Oh," Lizzie's face got serious. "Well, that story doesn't have a happy ending. No one likes a Debbie Downer."

Stephen laughed but got serious. "No, really. I want to hear more about you and your rise to fame."

"Well, hardly to *fame*, but okay. Just remember, you asked for it," Lizzie looked into Stephen's eyes with warning, then shook her head and continued the story. "When I got old enough for my dad to take me seriously, I announced at dinner one night that I was going to get my MBA when I went to college. My dad laughed—he actually laughed at me—and said, *Why would you wanna do that? What could you possibly do with an MBA?* So, I said, *I'm gonna run your company someday.* He put down his fork and I still remember the look on his face when he spoke. He glared at me with strong emotion in his eyes. He said, *No, you won't. I got guys who have been with me from the beginning. Before you were even born. They've paid their dues. They will run this company until long after I'm dead—*"

"Wow," Stephen said sympathetically. "I'm guessing you like a good challenge."

"I do." Lizzie nodded. She took a big sip of her whiskey sour.

"So, what happened next?" Stephen asked.

"I got my MBA," Lizzie attempted to end the story again.

"And...?" Stephen rolled his hand to keep her talking.

She sighed. "My father had a heart attack. He had figured out those guys—the ones who'd been with him since before I was born—had been embezzling from him all along. He had been in the process of cleaning house when the stress killed him. He had a heart attack in the middle of it all. He'd had the foresight to change his will before that happened, which was a stroke of luck! I inherited the company after all. I had to walk in there and clean the rest of it up. Took years before I had the right people working for me who I could trust."

"That's terrible, but what a great outcome!" Stephen exclaimed. "I'm sorry to hear about your dad."

Lizzie nodded and blotted the corner of her eye. *Was that a tear?* Stephen wondered.

Stephen sat back in amazement. Lizzie seemed like a tough, in-charge woman at the office. Truth be told, he'd even felt a little intimidated by her. But she was just like everyone else. She was human and vulnerable.

Food half eaten, Lizzie pushed her plate away and downed her drink. She stood and made herself another one. Stephen finished off his food and then got up to join her.

"Would you like another one?" she asked.

"Please," Stephen said. He was close enough to smell her hair. A light lavender scent met his nose.

She turned with Stephen's drink in her hand.

Stephen took it but looked into her eyes. "Thanks for telling me your story. You're right, that was awful."

Lizzie laughed and wiped an eye again.

"But it means a lot that you told me." Stephen gently swiped a finger across her cheek.

"Come here," Lizzie grabbed his hand and led him to the living room and sat on a very comfortable off-white, bean-shaped sofa. She rubbed the seat next to her. "Sit."

Stephen did as he was ordered. This room was also bright with floor to ceiling windows. A large plush rug took up most of the room. Straight ahead was a large, boldly colored painting hanging over a white tiled fireplace in the corner of the room. A cozy fire glowed in the hearth. Stephen sipped his drink, staring into the fire for a moment.

"Your turn." Lizzie pulled her feet up under her and leaned closer to Stephen.

"For what?" Stephen asked.

"It's your turn to tell me something not many people know about you that's both sad and terrible." Lizzie's eyes sparked with challenge.

"This is a weird game," Stephen protested. He was starting to feel warm inside and the fire was making him a little sleepy. Was she trying to seduce him? Of course she was. It was working too.

You really do make an impression with women, you know, Mak's words came back to him. Really, it was women who made an impression on him.

"You can't weasel out of this. I told you mine, now you tell me yours," Lizzie giggled. Perhaps the alcohol and warm fire were getting to her as well.

"How about I *show* you mine?" Stephen responded, feeling uninhibited.

"Even better!" Lizzie's eyes widened ever so slightly.

Stephen unbuttoned his shirt.

"I like the way you play this game," Lizzie purred as she took in Stephen's ripped abs and light blond chest hair. Her eyes fell on a scar down the center of Stephen's chest.

"Oh!" she gasped. Lizzie reached her fingers out and trailed them lightly from the top of the scar to the bottom. "Does this hurt?"

"No," Stephen said. He didn't think he could hide the feeling that leapt into his blue eyes when she touched him.

"You're a little young for open heart surgery. But if you're going to make me guess, I'd say since you're in a dangerous line of work—"

"Shot in the chest. The bullet just missed my heart and punctured my lung. I hit my head on a doorframe on the way down, so I had brain trauma too. They put me into a medically induced comma to help me heal, but I didn't wake up for just over eleven months."

"Eleven months!" Lizzie gasped. "You lost a year of your life?"

"Yeah. When I woke up, I couldn't even remember my mother. The woman who'd been by my side the entire time."

"No loyal girlfriend to hold your hand while you were out?"

Stephen felt his jaw clench. He'd come a long way, but he still felt the emotion of abandonment when Paige, Anna's mom, had left him bleeding on the floor.

"Oh, I saw that." Lizzie softly stroked Stephen's jaw. She moved closer. "There's the real story. What happened with the girlfriend?"

"Who cares?" Stephen responded gently. The last thing he wanted to think about now was his first fail of falling in love with a woman who would never love him back. He turned his head, cupped Lizzie's chin, and drew her close to him, closing the gap between them.

Her lips were warm and sweet from the whiskey sour. She moved closer to him. He placed his hand just above her knee. He was aware that her dress had fallen open just enough that he could see the white lace of her panties.

He deepened the kiss. His tongue swept the inside of her mouth. She moaned in a way that made Stephen go hard. He broke away and kissed her neck slowly, making his way to her ear.

"I want you," he whispered.

Lizzie crawled up into his lap in response. Her lips found his with an urgency she hadn't had before. Breathlessly, frantically, she kissed him like her life depended on it.

Stephen kissed her back, his hand cupping her bottom.

Lizzie shifted her position and threw a leg over him, now straddling Stephen. She began to grind against the bulge in his pants. Her breasts pushed against his chest. Stephen brought his hands up and covered them. His thumbs gently caressed her nipples.

"Lizzie, you might want to slow down," Stephen warned her, trying to gain control of himself.

"Maybe you'd like to get more comfortable?" Lizzie invited. She stood up suddenly and held out a hand in invitation. She led Stephen through a door he could only assume was her bedroom and closed the door.

An hour later, when Stephen got up to leave, Lizzie stopped him.

"Please," Lizzie whispered, gently pulling him back down to bed. "Stay with me tonight. I don't like to be alone."

Stephen put an arm over her, pulled her tightly against him, and cuddled her until she fell asleep and he felt sleepy. Her back was pressed against the front of his body.

"I don't like to be alone either," Stephen whispered into her now still, sleeping form.

25

WILTON

Sunlight streamed into the apartment where Stephen found himself tangled up in the sheets. He wasn't sure when he actually fell asleep last night. He smiled, remembering that Lizzie had fallen to sleep quickly, and he had cuddled her until his mind finally relaxed and drifted to sleep.

"Lizzie?" Stephen asked. He lifted his head and looked around.

There was no answer.

Stephen reached for his phone. It was six-fifteen. He had several missed text messages. There was one from Mak asking if he needed back up.

"Ha, ha," he mumbled, knowing full-well Mak wasn't a fan of Lizzie Taylor. He checked the text from Lizzie.

Lizzie: *Hey! Sorry, I had to go in to work. I left you some coffee and scones. Help yourself. Last night was fun.* 😉

Stephen felt his heart sink. *Last night was fun?* He hated to admit, even to himself, that last night meant more to him than that. He'd thought they'd really connected. He liked Lizzie. He didn't believe for a minute she had a meeting this morning. Either she felt regret and was embarrassed, or it had just been a *fun* one-nighter for her. Either way, she'd skipped the awkward goodbye.

Her text told him everything he needed to know. Stephen got up, got dressed, and bypassed the coffee and scones. He hated how impersonal the text from Lizzie had been. In fact, it felt like a slap in the face. It was too easy these days to end things without looking someone in the eye by sending a text. He refused to do the exact same thing.

He looked around for a piece of paper. He found a notepad. He tore off the first sheet and scribbled a note, hoping Lizzie could read his handwriting.

Lizzie,
Last night was really special to me. I enjoyed getting to know you better. Maybe we could do this again sometime? ~ Stephen

He put the note on the table where he had been sitting last night. He wanted to be sure she saw it right when she walked into her dining room. He put the pen back down next to the pad of paper. There were six names written on the paper that had been underneath the one Stephen had ripped off.

1. ~~Roger Clamentine~~
2. ~~Jim Tallbott~~
3. ~~Tony Statten~~
4. Tray Walker
5. ~~Trevor Kaites~~
6. Logan Pierce

Four names were crossed out. Stephen thought he recognized one of the names. He took out his phone to take a picture. He hesitated. If Lizzie saw this pad of paper left out and this was information Stephen wasn't supposed to see, Lizzie would likely get mad. Instead, Stephen impulsively tore off the names and put the paper in his pocket. He threw the pad of paper back in a drawer.

He started to leave when he heard his stomach rumble.

"On second thought," he mumbled. He picked up a scone and took a bite as he pushed the elevator door.

"Good morning," Henry, the doorman, greeted cheerfully. "She left bright and early today."

"Hi. Did you stay here all night?" Stephen wondered, in awe of his chipper attitude.

Henry laughed. "No, I left about an hour after you arrived. My replacement hung out here all night. I came back an hour ago."

Stephen nodded. "Hey, I'm curious. What happens if someone who isn't approved tries to come up to see Lizzie ?"

Henry laughed. "I'm trained to take care of it."

"Trained how?" Stephen asked. He wondered why the elevator even went straight to the penthouse. It seemed dangerous.

"I'm not just an elevator attendant, you know." He grinned at Stephen.

Stephen took in the bulk of the man's body. "So, you're like a bodyguard?"

"Exactly."

"Who else lives here? Are you bodyguard to all of them?"

"Well, Ms. Taylor owns the building—"

"Of course she does," Stephen said, not feeling surprised. "So, this is an apartment building."

"She rents to a handful of elite people. We keep an eye on all of them."

"I see," Stephen said. "We?"

"There are three of us. We split shifts," Henry grinned.

Stephen was normally cheerful in the mornings as well, but

this one had him in a funk. "Have a great day, Henry." Stephen stepped off the elevator when it stopped.

"Don't work too hard today," Henry responded.

Stephen finished his scone and hailed a cab. He couldn't promise not to work too hard. It was what he did best. But as he got into the New York traffic, he couldn't help but feel like he couldn't wait for this particular case to be done so he could get back home. Maybe he was tired. Maybe his feelings were hurt. Whatever the reason, he felt like he just wanted to crawl in bed and sleep for a week.

26

SELAH

Selah was throwing up again. She honestly couldn't tell if it was from anxiety or if it was her pregnancy. She wasn't sleeping much because the ground was cold and hard. There were no blankets or pillows so most nights, Selah wrapped her arms deeper into her sweater, hoping to stay warm. When she did finally fall asleep, she jerked awake with the realization that what she was living was the actual nightmare. Her whole body hurt. Not to mention, the food they had been eating was not enough to sustain them. A bowl of oatmeal and a cup of soup for two meals a day was not enough. It certainly wasn't enough for the baby growing inside her. Selah felt so weak.

"Sey?" Maddox waited until she finished throwing up and walked up to her. "You okay?"

"Does it look like I'm okay?" Selah asked. She closed her eyes to try to stop the spinning and dizziness that usually accompanied her throwing up.

Maddox handed her a bottled water he hadn't finished so she could rinse out her mouth. "It's just that you've been sick a lot. I'm really worried about you."

Selah took a big drink and wiped water droplets from her mouth. She stared at him. "You are?"

"Yeah, I am." He reached out and pulled her into his arms. He put a hand up to her forehead. "Do you have any other symptoms?"

Selah sighed and stepped back just out of reach, feeling instantly cold. Maddox dropped his arms by his side.

"Do you remember when we met?" Selah asked abruptly. She rubbed her arms, thinking again about how cold it was down here in this basement. She tried not to think about the fact that each time she rubbed her arms, she was likely removing a layer of dirt. There was no way to tell how long they'd been down there—Selah thought a couple days—but Selah was starting to feel as disgusting as she knew she smelled. To be honest, she wasn't sure if the body odor was coming from her or Maddox or both of them. If whoever had taken them had wanted to torture them, they had already succeeded. Selah had never felt so uncomfortable in her life.

"Yeah, of course." Maddox looked confused. "We were at that party. You were wearing that smoking hot cocktail dress that showed off your legs and the top came down low—"

"Yeah," Selah interrupted. "See, I remember thinking you were the hottest guy in the room, too. But I misjudged you. I wasn't interested in you until you approached me, and you said—"

"What's a musical genius like you doing over here by your-self in the corner," Maddox smiled at the memory.

"Right, you complimented my talent. You didn't mention my legs or body. I was so tired of shallow guys who only cared about how good we'd look together. But that's what we eventually became."

"What? No, we were great together. Everything was going great until the *incident*." Maddox looked angry again for a fleeting second.

"See, that's what I need to talk to you about." Selah sat down on the cold, hard ground and Maddox did the same. "I need to talk to you about that *incident* you keep referring to. That incident was really important to me."

"You didn't have to play games. I was yours. All yours." A flash of anger passed in Maddox's eyes.

"Maddox, stop talking. Stop making assumptions. I'm trying to tell you something. I really was pregnant. But I hated your reaction. So, I lied to you and told you I'd lost the baby. I'd decided if I had to choose between you and the baby, I'd choose the baby."

"Gee, thanks." Maddox crossed his arms over his chest. "Wait, you lied? What did you lie about?"

"I didn't lose the baby, Maddox. I'm still pregnant. And right now, I'm scared. I haven't had time to go see a doctor. None of this can be good for the baby. But if we don't make it out of here alive, at least you'll know the truth."

"Jesus, Sey. We're going to make it out of here. Why didn't you just tell me that? You let me believe you were a horrible person."

"You scared me. Your reaction was not good."

Maddox stared at her. "Literally? Were you actually scared of me?"

Selah nodded and wiped a tear.

"Wow, so I was the horrible person all along," Maddox self-discovered.

Tears were now streaming down Selah's face and down her chin.

"Hey, don't cry. Okay? We'll figure this out." Maddox pulled her into his arms again. This time, Selah allowed herself to relax into him.

The sound of sudden, abrupt walking sounded from the top of the stairs.

Selah stiffened.

Maddox hugged her closer.

Elle was back. That crazy lady kidnapper. Other than leaving food at the top of the stairs or occasionally cleaning out the bucket, they had not seen her and when they had, she didn't speak to them. They watched as she took each stair one at a time. Elle peered at them with happy, crazy eyes.

Selah forgot to breathe.

"Congratulations, you two! This is such great news. You're going to be parents. America will love this!" Elle squealed.

"How could you possibly know that?" Maddox asked.

"I have my ways," Elle brushed off his question.

"Great, does that mean you're going to let us go?" Selah asked.

Maddox scanned the basement. Selah thought he was looking for a camera they both knew must be somewhere.

"This is a very private moment. What is this? You turn in some secret video of us and get paid a million dollars? Is that what this is about?" Maddox snapped.

Elle burst into manic laughter. Her ponytail was lopsided and frizzy pieces of hair stuck out. Her pupils were dilated, making her eye color seem black. She was tall and thin. Not for the first time, Selah thought she could take her if only Elle wasn't carrying that gun.

"If only it were that simple," Elle sang out. "No, we have a proposal for you. *The Boss* is coming in tonight. She wants to make a deal with you. Mostly, you, Maddox. She wants control of the NFL. Your team is hot right now. Without you, they are nothing."

"Control the NFL? How does someone *control the NFL?*" Selah said, looking baffled.

"She just needs you to throw a few games here and there—"

"Do you mean lose on purpose?" Selah was feeling naïve. She hadn't known much about football before she met Maddox. "Like purposely drop the ball and not make the touchdowns?"

"No way!" Maddox jumped to his feet.

"I'd slow my movements if I were you." Elle waved her gun back and forth, her eyes narrowing dangerously, looking unhinged.

"Selah, we just want you to be at our beck and call. Influence marketing deals... You know, endorse whatever products or services we need you to. It's kind of like you'd work for us."

"Us?" Selah asked.

"*The Boss* and me," Elle clarified. "Even powerful business-people need star power. With your endorsements of our products, we'll profit off everything we touch. It'll all turn to pure gold."

"That doesn't sound so bad. You'll let us go if we work for you and do what you tell us to do?" Selah asked.

The crazy woman nodded.

"I'm not throwing games, Selah," Maddox responded angrily. "It's illegal. People bet on these games and if it looks like I'm losing on purpose, it'll make me look like I'm conspiring with them."

"Not if you don't get caught," Selah whispered to Maddox with tears in her eyes. She had to get out of here. She had to think about the baby.

"Ah, ah, ah, Maddox. Watch that temper. You don't want to *scare* anyone," Elle used the exact words from Selah and Maddox's private conversation earlier.

Now Selah scanned the basement for cameras. There were definitely cameras down here.

"I have way more to lose here. I can't tamper with games. That's possible jail time if I'm caught." Maddox clenched his jaw.

"Then don't get caught," Selah now argued, feeling frustrated he wouldn't just agree. They could say *yes* and find a way out later.

"It's not easy to get away with. They do Netflix documentaries from jail with people who tried it and got busted," Maddox protested.

"We need to get out of here," Selah said weakly.

Maddox clamped his mouth shut. He stared at Selah. His frustration was evident.

"I'll give you a little time to think about it. Ticktock though, Maddox. The big game is coming up," the woman stated as she went back to the stairs. "Selah, I'd think about what's best for the baby right now if I were you. You probably need to get to a doctor soon."

They waited until the door shut. Maddox stared at Selah obstinately, saying nothing. Selah pleaded with him with her eyes. She wondered if she agreed if they would at least let *her* go free. Maybe she could choose for herself and her baby.

But then she looked into Maddox's eyes, and she knew. She really did love him. Even if she was still mad at him. She knew him and on their good days, they really were great together. With a sinking heart, she acknowledged to herself that she couldn't take the easy way out. They were in this together.

This one decision would determine the rest of their lives. Starting a new life with a baby should be joyful. Adding in the stress of a father who was committing criminal acts didn't seem like a good way to keep her and the baby protected. Selah realized, with a start, that she was being the selfish one. Not only did she need to protect the baby, but she also needed to protect the baby's father. This was so dangerous for Maddox. How had she entertained it, even for half a second?

They had to make this decision together. Forget whether they had a future together. This would determine whether they lived through today.

27

MAK

Mak was up bright and early. She started fretting when she noticed Stephen never made it back from his date. Mak hoped her advice to him hadn't been wrong. While it was true that Wilton was free to do what he wanted on his own free time, and Lizzie wasn't a suspect, Mak sure wasn't a fan of hers. She couldn't help but feel there was something off with that one.

She was making coffee when Stephen walked in. Mrs. Lablanc was still asleep. Mak was giving Jonas a chance to get some sleep before she and Stephen went back out.

"Well, someone had a good night," Mak greeted him. She poured a cup of coffee and watched him do the same. "I'm seeing how this *Love 'Em and Leave 'Em* thing works firsthand."

Stephen rubbed the back of his neck. Was it getting red? "It's not like that. She's not what we thought. It was—" Stephen stopped to search for the right word. "Unexpected."

"Oh!" Mak said in surprise. "You like her. Like, really like her."

"Yeah, she was kinda great," Stephen said. "And you should probably know I'm not actually the one who does the leaving."

"What do you mean?" Mak asked. She was still standing in the kitchen, leaning against the refrigerator.

"I mean, women leave me. Okay? I hate the nickname, but I don't exactly want the office to catch wind that I can't keep a girlfriend either. No clue what I do wrong. They just lose interest and leave after a while."

"Lose interest?" Mak couldn't believe what she was hearing.

"Yeah. Okay, look. I want the whole wife, white house, picket fence, two-point-five kids thing, but when the women I date figure that out, they leave. I'm sort of unlovable."

"White house, picket fence... what, are you from the fifties, Wilton?" Mak asked. "Do you lead with that? Forget being unlovable. That would scare the bejesus outta me back in the day, too."

"No. I don't lead with that," Stephen huffed.

"Well, what happened with your last girlfriend?" Mak asked.

"Kristie. She said I was moving too fast. She got mad because I have a framed picture of my daughter with her mom on my beside table—"

"What?" Mak laughed but looked horrified. "Please tell me you put that away after you two got together?"

Stephen shook his head, looking miserable. "It gets worse. She found the ring I had bought for Carley, my ex-girlfriend, and assumed it was for her."

"No way." Mak's mouth hung open. "You've got to be doing this on a subconscious level, right? You're a detailed guy. There's no way you missed these things. You don't want to be with this woman so you did everything you could on a conscious or subconscious level to scare her off."

"Thank you, Dr. Phil," Stephen said, walking into the living room. He sat on the couch feeling grumpy or maybe just a little tired. Stephen didn't sleep well in unfamiliar places, or in general.

"Come on," Mak followed Stephen out and plopped on the

other couch. "You're young. Just live your life and let things happen organically. Why do you want to be married anyway? It's a tough balance with this job."

"You seem to do just fine," Stephen said.

"Yes, but I'm the exception. I know how to balance. Not to mention, when I met my husband, I was already a US Marshal. He knew what he was getting into. He stays home with Harper. He does some consulting work here and there. But everyone in the house knows mommy's off fighting bad guys. You're not unlovable. You just haven't found the right match."

Stephen thought through her words and tried to picture what his life would be like if he fell for a US Marshal. Was he trying too hard to fit these women in his perfect future picture? What if he met them where they were and formed a life that he and a partner could excel in?

"How did you leave it with Lizzie Taylor?" Mak wiggled her eyebrows.

"She already left me," Stephen frowned.

Mak could tell this was hard to admit. "What? It's too soon—"

"No, really. She was gone by six this morning. She sent me a text. It said, *Last night was fun, help yourself to some scones on the way out.*"

"Ouch!" Mak said, flinching. "You're right, that doesn't seem promising. Who leaves that early for work?"

"You were up. You texted me before she did." Stephen flashed his phone at Mak for proof.

"Well, that's different. I'm a morning person and I get jittery if I sit in one place too long. I was up and ready with no place to go."

Stephen's phone buzzed.

"Lizzie?" Mak asked.

Stephen looked at the phone. "Hardly," he scoffed. "They got the warrant to search Rich Landers' apartment. Let's go get us a laptop."

Mak jumped up. "Took them long enough. Let me go wake Jonas."

"Yeah, let me go change my clothes and brush my teeth. Be out in a minute."

Mak watched his movements and shook her head at her own misjudgment. Stephen wasn't what she expected at all. She went to wake up Jonas, barely containing her excitement. Maybe they would catch a bad guy today.

"Jonas, time to get up. We're off to catch some bad guys!" Mak knocked and yelled through the closed door with an obnoxious cheerfulness in her tone.

"Good morning." Jonas blinked owlishly at Mak as he walked into the room. He immediately turned on the TV. Mak found a mug with a lid and filled it with coffee. Though the TV volume was low, Mak heard a reporter's voice mention the words, *"Selah and Maddox."* She nearly spilled her coffee.

"Hey, can you turn that up?" Mak asked.

"Yeah," Jonas complied. "They just announced Selah Lablanc and Maddox Miller are missing."

"Shit!" Mak swore, knowing exactly who had leaked that information.

Stephen came back into the room with coffee, looking fresher, more alert, and ready to go. He turned his head toward the television, which was showing a popular photo of Selah and Maddox, hand in hand, walking toward a restaurant.

"Less than twelve hours ago, an unnamed source confirmed that Selah Lablanc and Maddox Miller are currently missing, and the search is underway. It is rumored that Selah Lablanc is pregnant. If you have any knowledge of their whereabouts, please call the number on the screen…" the reporter continued on to another story.

Mak put her hands on her hips and turned to Stephen. "Well

now we know where your girlfriend rushed off to this morning."

"Not my girlfriend," Stephen protested.

"What did you two talk about last night?" Mak demanded, feeling beyond peeved.

"Not that. She asked for information, and I refused to give her any. If you recall, I spilled some of that information when we went to talk to her yesterday at her office."

"Oh right," Mak grumbled. "This is going to make our investigation a circus."

"Or maybe we'll get a lead," Stephen argued optimistically.

"We've already got one," Mak said, pointing to Stephen's phone. "Let's go get Rich Landers' laptop and pray we can track down *The Fan*. Find *The Fan*—"

"We find Maddox and Selah," Stephen finished. He knew better than to believe it would be that easy.

28

MAK

When Mak stopped the car where the GPS directed her, she hesitated to get out of the SUV. Stephen waited, his eyes watching her. She knew why. It was because Mak never hesitated. But this was Chinatown, and the neighborhood was rough. She was debating the safety of leaving a vehicle here. But there was something else. Something that made her stomach turn.

This is ridiculous, Mak thought, putting the feelings aside and throwing open the door to the vehicle. She got out and led the way up a creaky, dark staircase that led to Rich Landers' apartment. She could smell the musty carpet under her feet. Like it had been wet, had dried, and then been run over by a league of smelly feet. Mak felt downright queasy now.

Mak paused at the top of the stairs. The long hallway was dimly lit and one of the fluorescent lights overhead buzzed. This felt familiar somehow, but the connection eluded her. Dismissing it, she charged ahead.

Stephen read the number on the door aloud and shook his head as they walked down the hallway. They paused outside an apartment.

"This is it." Stephen pointed.

Mak paused at the door of the apartment. Mak pulled her gun and made eye contact with Stephen, who also pulled his gun. He waited until she nodded. Not wanting to delay any longer, Mak leaned forward and knocked on the door.

They had both agreed during the drive over to assume the apartment of a contract killer would be booby trapped. While Rich Landers was still sitting in a jail cell, they had to prepare for the possibility of another person or two sitting inside his apartment waiting for them.

No one came to the door. There was no sound inside.

Mak knocked again. "US Marshals, open up or we're coming in." Mak waited one minute, then kicked the door jam. It splintered and broke. Mak kicked again, and the door popped open, gaining them entrance. The front room was empty. But Mak's mind flashed back and she cringed.

Three men had sat on the other side of the door. Their faces were familiar. They were the criminals she'd been after. Each of them leered at her. Then one of them had stepped to the side with smug hatred in his eyes. Mak had gasped, feeling all the air leave her as this movement revealed the body of a lifeless little boy.

"Nicely done!" Stephen complimented his partner. But then he got serious as he followed Mak through the door.

The apartment was small. They could see a kitchen and living area in one big, open room. Mak opened a closed door. She peeked into the bedroom, her hands straight in front of her holding her gun. Then she stepped inside. She checked behind the door, in the closet, and under the bed.

"Bedroom," she called out. "Clear!"

Mak took a deep breath in. She looked slowly around the room again. She was missing something. Then she saw it. Her heart sped up. The laptop sat in the windowsill.

Stephen had found another room. The place was small. Mak could hear him in the next room that was separated from her by a wall. She heard him slowly move what sounded like a shower curtain to the side.

"Bathroom clear!" he called out.

"Okay," Mak responded. "Located the laptop."

"Good job," Stephen said. He was scanning the main room and living room when Mak reappeared by his side. She wanted to get out of there as quickly as possible. This place made her feel uncomfortable.

"What are you doing? You ready to go?" Mak asked. She had emerged holding the laptop with gloved hands. She'd placed the laptop in a clear plastic evidence bag she'd stuffed in her back pocket before they had left.

"Just looking around to see if there's anything else here we might be overlooking," Stephen said, looking a little disappointed. "Everything seems to be in place. Look how clean and tidy Rich's apartment is. Don't you think that's weird?"

Mak waited with ill-concealed impatience. "He's a meticulous sharpshooter."

"Okay. Good to go," Stephen decided. He followed Mak out of the tiny apartment. Mak was thrilled to find their vehicle, along with the tires and wheels, still intact. They got in and drove back toward the station.

Mak felt relieved as she drove away from that apartment. She started to feel excited. They had his laptop. They had to be one step closer to finding this kidnapper. She pulled into the station and hopped out of the car.

Three hours and twentyish minutes later, Mak and Wilton were still waiting at the station in a conference room that had a great view of the city. They'd immediately turned the laptop over to the computer geniuses who believed they could get in without Rich's passwords. The plan, once they did that, was to set up a time to meet *The Fan* via Rich's account on the deep web.

"Another tip on Selah and Maddox, boss. Line one," the

Chief's office assistant called out to him. Her hand was covering the phone receiver.

"Damn it," Tigress muttered as he walked by Stephen and Mak. They watched him stalk over to the phone and place it on hold. He addressed the assistant. "How quick could you hire a temporary person to man the phones and sift through the tips coming in? We're still on the CEO killer case. I don't have time for this. Either assign a rookie to take these calls or a temp. I'm sorry, I just can't today."

"Got it," the woman agreed. She looked around the room and found the rookie, who they recognized as the officer in training Tigress had toted around the day they'd picked Rich up. She approached him and started a quiet conversation. The muscular man towered over the woman and had to bend a little to hear her words. Then he looked up and nodded, dark hair, longer than was typical for a cop, flopping with the movement.

"You two, come with me," Tigress ordered them as he kept walking.

Mak got up first and Stephen followed.

"Did you find *The Fan*? Are we able to start a conversation?" Mak asked eagerly.

"Let's go check. I've got the best tech team in the area." Tigress smiled unexpectedly. "Let's see if they were able to locate her."

Mak tried not to get her hopes up.

They walked into a room where several people were working on computers, laptops, cell phones, and tablets.

"Cool," Stephen breathed, looking around.

A tall, thin man wearing wire-frame glasses turned to them. He had Rich's laptop open in front of him. His face was serious, and he looked resigned to what he had to tell them. He turned the screen to show them.

The man pointed to the computer screen. "This is Landers' login—way into the deep web. As you know, the deep web is known for untraceable transactions. We can find *The Fan* and request a meetup, but we cannot find any evidence of prior contracts between Landers and *The Fan*."

Mak exhaled with irritation. "So, getting his laptop was all for nothing?"

"No. Not for nothing," the wire-framed computer guy protested. "The original plan was to use Landers' laptop to get us in where he receives his contracts. We can watch for another message with a request to come through and cross our fingers it will be *The Fan*—"

"That'll take too long." Mak threw her hand dismissively up in the air. "Other options?"

"Go back to the original plan and try to coax *The Fan* out of hiding with a meetup. That's tricky too, though. If that veers from her pattern, she might smell a setup." The computer guy was shooting down all their hope.

"What about Jason Jones, the limo driver?" Stephen said suddenly.

Mak whirled around and looked at him like he was crazy. "What about him?"

"Do you still have him in custody?" Stephen asked Tigress.

"Yes," Tigress answered. He crossed his arms over his muscular chest. "We got him on grand theft auto. His lawyer couldn't get him out of that. He's waiting out his bail hearing in a jail cell."

"Grand theft auto? That's it?" Stephen asked.

"Wilton, that's a felony and he deserves to be behind bars—"

"No, I get what you're saying, Wilton," Mak jumped in excitedly. "If his worst crime—prior to this alleged kidnapping—is stealing cars, we can make a deal with him. He gives us the correct location of where he dropped off Maddox Miller, and we wipe his record?"

Tigress bristled. "I don't like making deals with criminals."

"Right," Stephen agreed with a curt nod.

Mak narrowed her eyes. Maybe Tigress was just reacting to Mak's blunt approach. Mak and Wilton were well within their rights to make the deal, but they were really working to stay on good terms with local law enforcement.

"I completely see why you wouldn't make a deal with Rich Landers, a contract killer for hire. He killed one of our own, which is unforgivable," Stephen continued. "But if Jason Jones has information that could help us find Selah and Maddox, wouldn't it be worth it to wipe his record clean? Besides, it's probably a matter of time before he steals again, and he's on your radar now."

Tigress seemed to be thinking this through. "Might work. But if I find out he hurt anyone, or if those two end up dead and he was involved, the deal is off."

"Makes sense," Mak agreed easily. "Might be worth it to put it in writing so there's no questions later."

Tigress nodded and left the room in a rush.

"Well, that's a different solution," Mak said with a hint of admiration.

"Excuse me," the computer man interrupted. The laptop had been sitting on his desk open in front of him as he listened to the conversation. "Should I keep looking for a way to contact *The Fan*?"

Mak nodded. "Yes, please. It can be our new plan B."

Mak and Wilton caught sight of Tigress who called them over.

"Jones is on his way here. I'll let you know when we're ready for a second interrogation. Let's just hope we can get him to take the deal without waiting for his lawyer to arrive."

Mak nodded. They had already wasted half the day waiting around.

Stephen agreed. "Let's hope he has what we're looking for."

29

WILTON

They were in front of Jason Jones again in an interrogation room. This time, the large man looked tired and defeated. His dark eyes were weary, but there was a humility that made Stephen think Jason was going to talk this time.

Tigress offered him the deal. Instead of waiting for Jason to demand it in writing, Tigress slid the piece of paper in front of him.

Mak and Wilton waited while Jason read every last word on the page. Finally, he looked up.

"I want to be clear about what I'm reading," Jason said. His eyes flit from Tigress to Mak and settled on Wilton. "I tell you an address where *The Fan* is—no questions asked on how I know —you drop all past theft allegations and felonies and I'm not implicated in this case?"

"Correct," Tigress stated. "But if we get to that address and we find two dead celebrities, the deal is off."

"Listen, man." Jason put his palms in the air. "I didn't hurt nobody. All I did was drop them off—"

"You admit you had *them*—as in Maddox *and* Selah in your limo?" Mak interrupted excitedly.

Jason clamped his mouth shut.

Stephen was sure his eyes showed what he felt. Triumphant. Jason Jones had pretty much admitted he'd taken the stars for a ride. There was no way around him taking this deal now.

The realization that he'd implicated himself must have been dawning because Jason slowly nodded his head. He picked up the pen and signed the paper. He also wrote an address on the upper right corner of the paper.

"I don't know what's happened since I dropped them," he stated. "I haven't seen them since, and I don't know what kind of condition they're in. You can't hold me responsible if—"

"Save it, Jones," Tigress snapped. He grabbed the pen and paper. "You better hope they're alive when we get there. If not, you'll have a grand jury to convince, not us. In the meantime, you're going back to your cell. We'll let you out if you've held up your end of the bargain and this address is real."

"Suit up!" Tigress called loudly to the main room as he walked out of the interrogation room, Mak and Wilton on his heels. Tigress pointed to two officers. "We're going to save some kidnapped celebrities!"

30

SELAH

The sound of sudden pounding, running feet overhead grabbed Selah's attention. Her heart began to race. The feeling of ice and heat flushed into her veins. For a moment, her terror held her frozen.

"Did you hear that?" Selah asked as she quickly got to her feet. There were no windows in the room so she couldn't look outside. She supposed the light their kidnapper kept on during the day was a small thing to be thankful for. Otherwise, they would have been sitting down in the dark this whole time.

"Yeah, it's pretty loud," Maddox agreed with sarcasm lining his tone but followed her actions. They stood together, shoulder to shoulder, backed into a corner, eyes glued to the staircase, trying to mentally prepare for what was coming for them.

The basement door flew open.

Selah gasped. She felt Maddox tense beside her.

The door slammed against the wall and seemed to bounce there. *Tap. Tap. Tap.* Then they had heard what sounded like a gunshot. Maddox wrapped his arms around Selah. They clung to each other. Selah forgot to breathe.

"You think *The Boss* is here?" Selah whispered, feeling panicked. They hadn't made a decision yet.

Maddox didn't have time to answer.

Something hard hit the stairs. It thunked loudly and then rolled down loud and fast. When it came into view, Selah screamed and buried her face in Maddox's chest.

It was Elle, their kidnapper. Her body had rolled down the stairs with a trail of blood soaking each step as it hit. When she had stopped rolling, Selah and Maddox could clearly see that there was a bullet wound in the middle of her forehead. Blood poured from her wound. Her glossy eyes stared ahead at nothing.

Selah sobbed into Maddox.

Maddox put his arm around her. "It's okay, Sey. This is great news. She's dead. Our kidnapper is dead. We can leave now."

"No, no, no. It's a trap. What if it's *The Boss*? She's done with Elle, and she's done with us. What if we're next? What if she's up there right now. Someone killed Elle. We're next."

Maddox considered her words. He looked up the stairs. He seemed to be considering his next move. "I'll do it."

"Do what?" Selah asked, wiping her hysterical tears with shaking hands.

"I'll agree to the terms. You're right, I need to get you out of here. We're more valuable to them alive than we are dead. As long as we agree to the terms." Maddox nodded his head for emphasis as if he was trying to convince himself he was doing the right thing.

"No, Maddox. You were right. There are way bigger consequences for you than me in all this. I don't think we should—"

"Shh, someone's coming," Maddox interrupted.

Selah stopped talking, but she could not control the way her body shook from head to toe. What if this was their last moment together?

"Maddox," she whispered urgently. "I love you. I always have. I never stopped."

"I know, Sey. I love you, too." Maddox kissed the top of her head.

Selah felt the way his muscles tensed up as he pushed her behind him protectively. He put his hands up in fists to defend them from whatever was coming.

31

MAK

Bullet proof vests, loaded guns, and a van full of cops along with a police car that followed had Mak's adrenaline pumping.

"You ready?" Mak grinned excitedly as she glanced at Stephen for the tenth time since they'd left the station.

"Yeah." Stephen's expression was stoic, his eyes were void, his body was tense.

Mak shook her head. The two of them could not be more different. Mak lived for the thrill of the chase.

Stephen, on the other hand, appeared to be mentally prepping.

They watched as the city flew by and got more rural by the second. Trees lined the road and the houses got fewer and farther between.

Tigress turned on loud alternative rock so suddenly, Mak jumped a little. Stephen protested but Tigress, who was driving, grinned over his shoulder.

"Driver's choice. Gets the adrenaline flowing." Tigress turned back to the road.

After what was close to an hour, Tigress slowed the vehicle and cut the music as suddenly as he had punched it on. A small home came into view. They were just outside the city limits. The home looked like a little farmhouse with old grey shingles in bad need of repair, and it sat on acres of land. There wasn't another home in sight. It almost looked Midwestern. Mak noted there was one car on the side of the house. It was black, but she couldn't see the make and model. It looked like there was a storm cellar close to the car. Or was it an entrance into a basement?

"How do we play this?" Stephen asked the minute the music shut off.

"Try not to get shot," Tigress threw over his shoulder. "Catch the bad guy. Save the victims." Tigress slowed to a stop. He turned off the car. He quickly double checked his bullet proof vest, racked his Glock, making sure it was hot and ready to shoot. He held it toward the sky as he jumped out of the SUV.

"That's it?" Stephen's voice was incredulous. He looked at Mak who was double checking her own equipment. She placed a backup gun in her holster, her other weapon already drawn. She stuffed a pair of handcuffs in a pocket of her vest. Stephen mimicked Mak's routine.

"I agree with him on this one, partner. There's no plan for the unknown." Mak jumped out of the car without a backwards glance. There was no way to know how many people would be inside. She was ready for battle.

Weapon's drawn, Stephen followed Mak out of the van. Behind them, two more cops, whose names Mak hadn't even tried to remember, got out of the car and followed them.

"There's a cellar that looks like it connects to a basement. We need a body there and to cover any other doors," Mak hissed in a whisper.

"Ericks, cover the cellar. Bon, check the house for another opening." Tigress sent his officers off.

Within minutes, Bon returned to meet them at the front door. "No other doors," he reported.

The four of them walked to the front door on high alert. The afternoon was overcast. It looked like rain and Mak could smell it in the air.

Before they walked through, Stephen growled, "Wait!" He pointed to the small hole in the window next to the front door and the crack around it. He immediately turned to find a patch of trees behind them. "Sharpshooter?" Stephen asked.

"Or it came from inside," Mak countered.

"Eyes up, everyone!" Tigress commanded in a low voice. "Bon, be on the lookout for a shooter in the trees." Then he turned to the door and pulled it open. The door wasn't locked. "MCPD! Nobody move!"

The officers filed into the home, guns pointed defensively. They spread out and began to check the home.

Tigress peeled off toward a living room. After a moment, he called out, "Living room, closets, and bathroom, clear!"

Stephen went toward a bedroom at the back of the house. "Bedroom and bathroom, clear!"

"There!" Mak cried. She spotted a basement door that was flung open. She groaned as she spotted a smear of blood on the white door. "Got something," she called. She could hear the buzzing of a fluorescent light leading down to the basement. Her stomach turned.

Stephen was at her elbow. "This door lines up perfectly with the bullet hole in the window."

Mak glanced behind her and shuddered. She hated turning her back to the door. She felt an overwhelming sense of anxiety. She stood still as Stephen went down the stairs ahead of her.

"Covering the door and outside entrance," Bon called out.

Mak turned her focus back to the blood in the basement.

"We've got a body!" Stephen yelled, his eyes looking down the stairs.

Mak forgot to breathe. Her mind flashed back. She flinched.

The door flew open, revealing the body of a lifeless little boy.

"We've got a body!" a deep, masculine voice had shouted into the comm system while Mak had stood frozen. She couldn't remove her eyes from the little boy's body.

"Freeze! You're under arrest…" the officer beside her shouted. Words faded out as more officers moved into the room to detain the three men— the killers. Mak could hear nothing but her blood rushing into her ears. Her eyes glued to the little boy, denial filling her brain.

"What if he's not dead?" Mak whispered.

"What?" the officer nearest Mak turned, tightly holding his cuffed victim.

Mak sprinted to the boy, carefully avoiding the puddle of blood on the floor under him. She reached across his body and felt for a pulse. There was none. Anguish filled her whole body and for one horrible moment, Mak thought she might burst into tears right there in the room full of men. She took a deep breath. She fought for composure. She looked up to find the room had filled with stunned silence. Every eye had fallen on Mak.

There was no time for this. Mak took a deep breath in. She could hear her counselor's voice guiding her. *Take a deep breath in, hold it at the top, and exhale out.* She needed to move. She shoved forward in front of Stephen and peered down the stairs where she could see a victim.

Mak heard Tigress call out to Stephen.

"There's a body at the bottom of the basement stairs," Stephen answered, repeating himself.

"Bon! Call it in. We need an ambulance here as soon as possible!" Tigress yelled out at the top of the stairs to the officer still watching for a shooter. Tigress appeared and followed Mak and Stephen down the stairs.

"Hello?" Mak called out, both hands on the gun she was holding straight out in front of her. "Anyone down here?" They couldn't assume anything. If they cornered a murderer, she bet the criminal would come out shooting.

There was no answer. Still, Mak proceeded with caution. Mak reached the woman at the bottom of the stairs first and felt for a pulse. "No!" she cried out in despair, having found no pulse. "We needed her alive to answer questions!"

That's when Mak heard the sound of someone crying. She looked up just as she stepped over the body, working hard to avoid the blood on the stairs. The last thing she wanted to do was contaminate a crime scene. She was surprised to see Selah Lablanc hiding behind Maddox Miller, who was standing in a fighting stance. Their bodies were visibly shaking.

"Hi," Mak said quietly. She could have been annoyed that they hadn't answered her when she shouted down. Instead, she slowly grabbed her badge and showed it to the scared, shaking stars. "I'm Mak. I'm a US Marshal and this is my partner, Stephen Wilton—"

"I'm Chief Tigress," Tigress announced, having made it down himself. "I'm heading up this investigation. MCPD Chief of Police." He flashed his badge. "We're here to rescue you."

"Thank God!" Selah's tears fell faster. Her face was red and she wiped snot from her nose.

"You'll have to excuse her," Maddox shielded Selah protectively. "She's—"

"Pregnant, we know. In fact, you should be aware that all of America now knows," Mak warned. "But I'm betting she'd be crying even if she weren't pregnant. PTSD is a real thing, and it has nothing to do with hormones. You two have been through a lot."

Maddox nodded.

"Are you hurt?" Stephen asked.

Maddox shook his head in the negative.

Selah hesitated and then said, "No."

"Let's get you out of here," Mak said. She turned to Stephen and pointed to the body on the stairs. "You think that's *The Fan?*"

"What gave it away?" Stephen asked dryly.

Mak smiled. "Logic in reverse. Find Selah and Maddox—"

"Find *The Fan*," Stephen grinned back.

"That's her, all right," Tigress agreed. "We've got a nice mugshot of her at the station."

They waited until the ambulance showed up to check Selah and Maddox. The EMT gave the okay that Maddox and Selah were physically unharmed.

Bon and Ericks had met them at the EMT.

"Call a coroner and stay behind to wait with the body," Tigress ordered the two officers.

Mak approached Selah. "You can ride back in the ambulance if you would like or—"

Selah shuddered. "You'll understand if I have trouble trusting anyone who doesn't have a police badge right now."

Beside her, Maddox nodded his silent agreement.

"Right," Mak nodded. She helped the two victims walk to the police SUV. Mak opened the door for Selah and Maddox and helped them into the vehicle.

The five of them started the long drive back to the city.

Mak knew she needed to deal with what happened on the staircase. Come to think of it, this was the second time she'd experienced those feelings. Maybe she'd visit her counselor when she got back home.

In the meantime, Mak felt that familiar sense of satisfaction over a job well-done, but she couldn't help but feel frustrated that they couldn't prosecute *The Fan* or even ask her questions. At least it was officially over.

Now Mak and Stephen could go back home and focus on what was coming up in three days—Booker's funeral.

32

WILTON

Stephen strode through the airport feeling like a weight had been lifted. He could tell Mak felt the same way. They had taken Mrs. Lablanc home safely before driving to the airport to catch a flight home. Jonas had offered to stay with Mrs. Lablanc until she felt settled in and safe. Either the two of them had become friends or Jonas was waiting around for his chance to meet Selah Lablanc.

Having already gone through the security checkpoint and settled in at the terminal, Mak and Stephen were awaiting their flight. Stephen's eyes strayed to a TV where Selah Lablanc and Maddox Miller were holding a press junket. He nudged Mak and pointed to the TV. Mak looked up from a magazine she'd been reading and grinned at Stephen, turning her full attention to the Q & A session.

"As you all may have heard," Selah smiled widely. "Maddox and I are expecting."

Pandemonium exploded in the press room.

Maddox held up a hand. "One at a time, please."

A pretty reporter stood up. "How long were you held hostage?"

"Five days, I think? Someone told us it was five days. We didn't exactly have access to watches, cell phones, or clocks there." Maddox smiled a charming smile.

The room broke out in laughter.

Another reporter stood. "Did the pregnancy have anything to do with the kidnapping?"

Selah answered. "We don't think anyone knew before we were taken."

"Did the kidnapper tell you why she took you?" Another reporter shouted.

"She had a record. She went by the nickname *The Fan*. We're told she had tried crazy stunts like this before…"

The interview continued, but Stephen stared off into space.

"Earth to Wilton." Mak elbowed Stephen. "They're starting to board."

"How do you think the press got wind of Selah's pregnancy?" Stephen said in a quiet voice.

Mak rolled her eyes. "You kept telling Lizzie Taylor things you shouldn't have, remember?" She stood, preparing to get in line.

"No, I never told her that. I only confirmed that Selah and Maddox were missing. I never mentioned the pregnancy."

"You sure? Didn't you drink with her that night? Did you let something slip?" Mak asked.

"No, I remember the whole night. Believe me, I remember the whole night—"

"Spare me," Mak said. "Who knows, maybe Mrs. Lablanc told her best friend who leaked it."

"Or Jonas," Stephen said.

"What about him? He would know better than to go to the press. Details of an investigation are highly confidential. He knows the drill," Mak dismissed.

"Still." That wasn't the only thing that bothered Stephen.

"What now?" Mak asked. She seemed to be picking up on Stephen's hesitation.

"We never found the shooter. We don't know who shot *The Fan* or why they did it. It wasn't one of our people. The other shooter, Rich Landers, is heading to prison—"

"Where he'll live the rest of his life," Mak interjected cheerfully. Still, Stephen could see the doubt in her eyes.

"What if someone was trying to shut *The Fan* up? Any chance someone knew we were on the way to rescue Selah and Maddox?"

"Wilton! Would you stop? Do you ever rest that mind of yours? Take the win. We did it. We rescued Selah and Maddox. We found *The Fan*. We even got the guy who killed Booker. Case closed."

"I think it bothers you too." Stephen stood firm. "I know you move fast and like to solve cases fast, but you know there are loose ends, and it bothers you as much as it bothers me. I can see it in your eyes."

Mak opened her mouth to protest but shut it again. She shook her head and looked skyward. "Okay." Mak looked back at Stephen. "Of course it bothers me. But the Attorney General gave us one job. Find Selah and Maddox and bring them home. We did that. The person who took them is dead. They're alive. We did our job."

They heard their section called and Mak moved toward the line.

Stephen followed slowly. His gut was churning. It had been too easy in the end. They had missed something important. Something that would change everything. He could feel it.

"Come on," Mak encouraged with a sad look on her face. "Let's go bury our friend."

33

WILTON

The day of Booker's funeral had turned out to be a nice, sunny, and mild day for mid-November. Stephen's dress jacket was enough to keep him warm. Deputy Sikes had asked him to be a pallbearer. Stephen had been honored to help. He knew Mak had been asked as well but she'd turned it down. She reasoned she needed to just be there to grieve and honor her former partner.

Now, Stephen held his corner of the casket, following the color guard who escorted the family under the canopy. Stephen lowered the casket to the staging area and the ceremony began.

Stephen stood at attention as the color guard presented the colors. He swallowed the lump in his throat, feeling emotional as the American flag that decorated the top of Booker's coffin was folded up and presented to Booker's mom, dad, and sister. The family cried, unafraid to show their emotion.

Around the cemetery, flags waved in the gentle breeze at half-mast. Stephen was looking out over a sea of hundreds of uniformed officers. Beyond that, the cemetery was filled with civilians who had lined the streets to show their respect for the fallen officer. They had moved inside the cemetery and now listened in respectful silence to the invocation prayer.

Is this how it would end for Stephen someday as well? Stephen couldn't help but wonder if he would have the same kind of turnout at his funeral. Would they present a flag to his own parents and his daughter as the only surviving members of his family?

His eyes connected with Mak Cunningham. Tears streamed unchecked down his new partner's cheeks. Her hair was pulled back into a tidy bun, and she wore a black dress and high-heeled leather boots. A broad, muscular, and very tall man Stephen assumed was her husband, John, stood next to her. John's shoulders were back, and he seemed to stand at attention. Pride and sadness etched his face. Stephen knew he had likely known Booker as well. Stephen could only assume John was thinking about his wife's eventual outcome. Stephen remembered Mak's assessment of her husband. *John knew what he got himself into when he married me,* she'd said. They had made it work.

After a few speeches from people of notoriety such as the mayor, the Attorney General, Deputy Sikes, and a pastor, the ceremony concluded with the 21-bell ceremony. Stephen couldn't keep a tear or two from falling, though he tried to be stoic.

Ethan Booker had been Stephen's first partner since joining the US Marshals. He had respected Booker and would have even called him a friend in the short period of time he'd been there.

He followed the crowd as they filed out to the words of "Amazing Grace." Stephen glanced back at Mak, who was walking out with her husband by her side. He realized he was beginning to feel the same way about her that he'd felt about Booker. He'd only worked with Mak a week but in that short time, he'd begun to trust her as his partner and was on his way to calling her a friend.

He found his car and clicked the unlock button on the key fob. Stephen felt surprised when he saw, out of the corner of his eye, a man in his late twenties jogging up to him. Stephen turned, instantly on-guard, and watched him approach. There was something about this man. Something familiar that reminded Stephen of his past. He was shorter than Stephen, but he remembered him being taller. He seemed to have put weight on over the years. Despite these flashes of memory, Stephen could not place the man.

"Stephen Wilton?" he gasped, seeming out of air.

Stephen quickly scanned his surroundings, a habit he had formed when he became a marshal. Several people, mostly family and close friends, still huddled together at the casket, twenty feet from him, down the sloping hill. Graves lined the field behind them. Few people milled together at their vehicles in hushed conversations, giving hugs and compassionate back slaps. The air was filled with sounds of car doors opening and slamming shut, cars starting up, and gravel crunching in the parking lot with the weight of the cars driving away.

"Yes?" Stephen stopped and gave the man his attention. It was then that he noticed a letter-size manilla envelope in the man's hand. The man held it out to Stephen. At closer glance, Stephen realized the man was older than he'd originally assumed. Maybe he was a little older than Stephen.

"Man are you hard to catch!" the man stated, his hand reaching out to give Stephen the package. The envelope froze midair in the man's hand.

Stephen made no move to take the envelope. Rather, Stephen lifted both of his hands in a move to refuse it. "What is this? A subpoena for something? Are you trying to serve me at my fallen partner's funeral?"

"You seem angry and a bit paranoid, but I assure you, it's nothing like that. Trust me, you're going to want to see what's inside this envelope." The man shoved it at Stephen again.

"Not a chance until you tell me who you are and what this is," Stephen argued.

"I'm just the messenger. You know what they say about the messenger, right?" the man tried to joke. "Don't shoot—"

"What's your name?" Stephen interrupted, peering harder into the man's face. He looked familiar.

The man hesitated. "Trevan Collins."

"Trevan Collins," Stephen repeated. He knew that name. He tried to go back through his memory, but it was alluding him. The man was familiar. The name was familiar. But Stephen couldn't place him.

"I was friends with your brother. The night it happened. It never sat right with me, how it all ended for him." Trevan shrugged. "I've wrestled with this for over a decade. You need to see what's in the envelope. You also need to forget it came from me."

Stephen reluctantly, if not curiously, took the envelope. "How it all ended? My brother was shot in the face for mouthing off to a guy who was a bigger bully than he was. We can't rewind time. It ended how it ended. Case closed." His words reminded him of Mak's words in the airport when she tried to cling to denial over how their case had ended.

"You need to see what's in that envelope," Trevan repeated. He abruptly turned and jogged away.

Stephen got in his car and threw the envelope in the seat next to him, feeling irritated by the man who dared to open a door to a part of Stephen's past that he had grieved and made his peace with, then shut tightly behind him.

He started his car and followed Trevan with his eyes until he got a distance away. He pulled out and drove by as Trevan got into his car. Stephen memorized Trevan's license plates. At a stop sign, he jotted the numbers on the envelope in his seat.

He pulled out onto the main road and drove to Peak's Place Bar where they were holding Booker's after-funeral reception.

He put the envelope out of his mind as he got out of the car and
went into the bar.

34

WILTON

The reception was in full swing when Stephen got in line for the buffet. When he had a plate full of food, he felt a tap on his shoulder and turned to find Mak standing behind him with her husband, John, beside her.

"Hey," Mak said. "I wanted to introduce you to my husband, John."

Stephen immediately put out a hand. "I'm Stephen. Nice to meet you. I've heard great things about you."

"Thanks," John said. "Same here."

"What?" Stephen smiled with surprise. "Mak saying nice things about me? Never would I have expected—"

"Shush." Mak punched him in the arm. "Come on, we're sitting over here."

Stephen's smile stayed where it was as he followed Mak without question. She sure was bossy, but at the moment, Stephen could use a little direction. He was aware that he only knew about twenty-five percent of the people in this room. He put his food down and noticed everyone else had drinks.

"I'll be right back," Stephen said. He went and stood in line at the bar.

It took him a minute to notice he was standing behind a petite woman. She had long, waving hair, tight black pants that accentuated her curvy backside, and a silky white blouse over a black lacy camisole. She was still short despite her three and a half inch stilettos.

The smell of her hair drifted to him—orchids. She smelled expensive. That, coupled with her light, floral perfume, met his nose. That was when he realized he was standing a little too close.

The woman whirled around, and Stephen found himself face to face with Alyah Smith. Without thinking about it, Stephen took a step back.

"Oh, Stephen!" she exclaimed. She was likely the only person in the office who called him by his first name. He tried not to think about how her musical voice warmed his chest. Instead, he reminded himself that this woman disliked him enough to warn Mak, his new partner, about him before he'd even met her.

"Alyah," Stephen nodded his head professionally.

"Congratulations, Stephen. You did it. Helluva win for our office. And for you—Rookie," Alyah smiled, almost shyly.

Stephen bent down a little to hear her better over the noise level of the bar. "I thought you hated me," Stephen blurted the first thing in his mind and felt instant regret. He remembered Mak's words a few days ago after the case closed.

Take the win, Wilton.

"I don't hate you," Alyah smiled.

Stephen was mesmerized by the way her smile lit up her face.

"I just didn't know you, and this was a really big case. But you did it. You delivered and made us all look good," she tilted a little on her heels as she looked up at him.

"Woah," Stephen said as he reached out a hand to steady her. Was she drunk?

"Sorry," she laughed lightly. "I'm not really good at funerals."

Stephen smiled. "Is anyone really good at funerals?"

"No, I guess not," she said. The line had moved, and Alyah spun around to the bar. "Moscato, please. You?"

Stephen stepped up and ordered a seven and seven. "Alyah, I need to get back to my table. I'm over there with Mak and her husband."

"Sure," Alyah said as she grabbed her drink. "I'll catch you later."

Stephen walked away, processing how differently that conversation had gone from the first one.

"Your food is probably cold," Mak teased as Stephen sat down.

Stephen suddenly wasn't very hungry.

"So, that was inspiring," Mak said.

"What?" Stephen asked, pretending he didn't know what she was referring to.

"I told you Alyah likes you. You really do have a way with women."

"I think she's just been drinking," Stephen mumbled quietly. He started eating, hoping Mak would take the hint.

"What's next for you two?" John asked Mak and Stephen.

"There's always a new case tomorrow," Stephen said but his mind went back to the end of the last case. He tried not to think about how uncomfortable he was with the way it all had ended.

Jonas Petry found his way to their table and sat in the empty chair between Stephen and Mak.

"Hey, Jonas!" Mak greeted. She gave him a high-five. "Great job keeping Mrs. Lablanc safe. Did you get to meet Selah?"

Jonas smiled but made a sad face when she mentioned Selah. "No, I didn't. I guess now that she's pregnant, it's official she and Maddox will be announcing wedding plans any day."

"Not necessarily," Mak protested.

"Speaking of her being pregnant," Stephen jumped at the opportunity. "Did you ever mention that to anyone while we were working the case?"

Mak's eyes got big, and she mouthed, *Let it go.*

"No way," Jonas said. "Mrs. Lablanc asked us to keep it a secret. Not to mention, I don't talk to anyone outside those walls while I'm on protective duty."

"Okay," Stephen said. "I just thought I'd check. Someone leaked that piece of info to the media. I just wasn't sure who. It's like this one thing I can't seem to explain—"

"What about Stacia?" Mak said suddenly. "Did she know? Maybe she knew and word leaked out through her somehow."

"I guess that's possible," Stephen said, feeling lighter. Stacia did work with Selah after all. Even if Stacia mentioned it to another person, or a few people, anyone could have gone to the media.

"Well, it's been a long day, and we need to get back to Harper," Mak said as she and John stood.

"Wait, are you even done eating yet?" Stephen looked at their plates in astonishment.

Mak smiled. "We were here before you got here, Stephen. Then you spent an hour in the drink line."

Stephen felt his cheeks redden. "It wasn't an hour," he said sheepishly.

John reached over and shook Stephen's hand again. "It was nice to meet you."

"You, too." Stephen grasped his hand, feeling jealous of the obvious closeness of John and Mak's marriage. If nothing else, she was modeling what he could have one day. He watched John put an arm around Mak as they walked out the door.

"So, how did it go with Mrs. Lablanc after we left?" Stephen asked. "Did she get settled back in and all is well?"

"Yeah," Jonas nodded. "I really liked her. She reminds me of my grandmother."

"Really? Where does your grandmother live?" Stephen asked.

"Well, she passed a few years ago," Jonas answered.

"Sorry to hear that," Stephen said. "Mine did too." He ate a few more bites in silence. Stephen was silent so long, he noticed Jonas had started a conversation with a friend on his other side. Not wanting to intrude, Stephen quietly finished his food.

His eyes strayed over the noisy venue. He saw Alyah sitting by herself at the bar. She looked sad and alone. "Hey Jonas, I'll catch up with you later."

"Sure. See ya," Jonas called as Stephen moved away.

Stephen approached Alyah and sat next to her. "Hello again."

"Hi," she smiled sadly.

"Another drink?" Stephen asked pointing to her empty wine glass.

"No, thank you," Alyah said. "I'm at my limit."

"Did you eat?" he asked. He couldn't figure out why he suddenly had the feeling that he wanted to take care of her. Maybe he just wanted to cheer her up. Or maybe, he didn't want to connect that he felt exactly the way she looked.

"Yeah, I had enough," she said.

"You wanna get out of here?" Stephen asked. He found himself having to yell and it was making his head hurt.

"Yeah, I do," Alyah said. She left some money on the bar and grabbed her purse.

Once out the door, Stephen was aware of two things. The silence outside in contrast to the bar was deafening. And there were big, dark storm clouds rolling in, casting the afternoon darker than before.

Alyah took her spiky heels off once her feet hit the parking lot pavement.

"Where to?" Stephen asked.

Alyah looked up at the sky and listened to the thunder. "How 'bout we just walk."

"Alyah, I think it's going to rain," Stephen tried to protest.

"So what? A little rain never hurt anyone." Alyah took off walking and Stephen followed her, feeling a little mystified. This was not the Alyah he had first met at the office. Drinking really must lower her inhibitions. He'd have to keep a safe distance. But for now, he wanted to make sure she didn't do something she would regret tomorrow.

They found a park a few blocks down the street. Alyah walked slowly, her bare feet disappearing into the uncut grass. "Do you know what this funeral made me think about?"

"No," Stephen answered.

"The memorial service we had for Carley."

"Ah," Stephen understood now. He remembered the range of emotions he had experienced after he'd lost Carley. But now, remembering his interaction with Trevan Collins, his mind strayed to the loss of his brother.

Alyah stopped walking and looked up at Stephen. "I don't understand what happened. My mom called me and said Carley had been in a fatal car accident. We buried her—at least we thought we did. We had a ceremony. Months later, we get a call saying she hadn't died in that accident, that she had been murdered. Only, she had faked the car accident before, got mixed up with the wrong people, and was now officially dead. Then they asked where could they send the body. They couldn't answer our questions because it was part of an—"

"Ongoing investigation," Stephen finished, his mind going to Demitri Abbott. "God, Alyah," Stephen shuddered, reliving that night. The night Carley had died in his arms. "That's truly terrible. I'll tell you what I know."

They walked to the middle of the park. With the clouds rolling in, the park had emptied out. They were alone on the playground, blocks from a crowded bar, where co-workers toasted to a fallen brother. Where they could feel the sadness of the death that surrounded them—past, present, and future. The swings swayed as an indication that stronger weather was on its way.

Stephen guided Alyah to a bench in the park where they both sat down. Stephen noticed that Alyah sat, then scooted closer to him, closing the gap so that their shoulders, hips, and legs touched. Stephen could feel the electricity the closeness of her body elicited.

"I loved your sister. But Carley kept telling me she was getting too domestic. She didn't want to be like—" Stephen stopped talking abruptly, not meaning to be offensive.

"Our mother. Right. That would have been Carley's worst fear. At least, that's what she said a lot growing up. I hadn't talked to her in years."

"Yeah, but she lived with me for about a year and helped me raise my daughter, Anna. I'd found myself a single dad of a toddler. I guess she fell in love with Anna but not me. So, she kidnapped Anna and staged the car accident. She wanted all of us to think they had died so she and Anna could go live happily ever after."

"That's really terrible. Did you buy it? Did you believe your daughter was dead?" Alyah asked. She wiped tears from her eyes.

"At first, yes. But there was a point where her mother insisted Anna was alive and had a theory that Carley had taken Anna. I didn't believe it. No way would Carley go that far—"

"Yep, that sounds like Carley to me. Too selfish to care who she hurt in the process of getting her way. So, you were looking for Anna the night you found Carley?"

"Yeah. After I became a US Marshal, I was assigned to make friends with your uncle—Scott Milternett—"

"Who wasn't really our uncle at all, just mom's ex-boyfriend. Only he tried to take care of me and Carley after they broke up. Carley was closer to him than I ever was. I was quite a bit younger when he left."

"Well, Anna's mom would say that assignment was a 'higher power moment.' Scott was hiding Carley and Anna. I suspected it. But I investigated in my personal time. I was on a stakeout when Scott Milternett called me. He was frantic and told me someone was after Carley. That's when he confirmed Carley had Anna."

"So you went to find them?" Alyah asked.

"Yes, but I was too late," Stephen's eyes now filled with tears. "I couldn't save Carley. A man named Demitri Abbott got there first and shot her in the gut. She died in my arms."

"I'm sorry, Stephen," Alyah said. "That must have been awful for you."

"Yes, but the silver lining is, I found Anna."

"What a relief that my sister didn't ruin the most important thing in your life," Alyah rubbed Stephen's arm. "How old is your daughter?"

"She's four and a half," Stephen grinned.

The sky had grown dark and thunder rumbled in the distance.

"I'm happy you found her, and I'm sorry I misjudged you," Alyah said but looked sad.

"We should get back," Stephen said, trying not to acknowledge how much her words warmed his heart. He glanced at the time on his cell phone. It would get dark soon.

Alyah got up from the bench and began walking back toward the parking lot.

Without warning, the sky opened up and rain poured down on them. Big raindrops pummeled them mercilessly. The rain hit the pavement and formed puddles, hitting and splashing water back up with each drop.

They ran, but it was too late. They were both drenched by the time they reached the parking lot. Alyah's white silk blouse had become completely transparent. Stephen tried not to notice the way it clung to her and showed the thin, lacy black camisole under her shirt.

Stephen could only assume she was still tipsy. "Alyah, can I give you a ride home?"

Alyah nodded and tried to wipe the water pouring out of the sky out of her eyes. "I think that would be good."

Stephen opened the door to his Tahoe for her and waited until she was in before he shut it and got in on the driver's side. He paused when he found Alyah holding the manilla envelope he'd thrown on his seat before driving away from the funeral. The envelope that Trevan had hinted held information about his brother.

"I almost sat on this," Alyah said. "Is this important?"

"Thanks," he grabbed it and threw it in the back seat. "I'm not sure."

"You haven't opened it?" Alyah asked.

Stephen didn't take her for the nosy type, but he supposed she had been open with him. "Truth is, some random guy at the funeral handed me the envelope and told me I needed to see what was in it."

"And you haven't looked? Aren't you curious?" Alyah asked.

"I'm going to guess you know what all your Christmas presents are before you open them," Stephen laughed.

"Maybe. But you're trying to change the subject," she said bluntly.

"Yes, I am. The man was familiar to me. I want to figure out why and who he is before I open a package that *I need to see what's inside.*"

"Okay, your call," she said, letting it go.

He drove in silence. Alyah looked like she wanted to ask more but didn't. Instead, she stared out the window, seeming lost in a world of past memories. Her sadness filled the car.

Stephen let her have the moment.

35

WILTON

Stephen pulled his car into a home that Alyah had directed him to. It was a modern classic gray home with white shutters and brown trim. Stairs led up to a porch. Two wicker chairs sat on the porch on either side of the door. A cobblestone retaining wall gave the home its charm.

Stephen walked her to the door. He told himself he wanted to make sure she got inside okay.

Alyah fumbled with her keys until she finally got her door open.

Stephen waited patiently.

She paused and turned to Stephen. "Well?" Alyah asked. "Are you coming in?"

"Alyah, I don't think I should—"

"Why not?" she had taken the steps up and into the house and grabbed one of his hands to pull him along.

Stephen could feel the warmth that rushed through him at her touch. He reluctantly stood his ground. "You're a little drunk."

Alyah leaned forward when Stephen hesitated, closing the

gap between them. "I'm not that drunk," she whispered and winked. Alyah smiled shyly, still holding Stephen's hand.

"Really?" Stephen asked as his eyes searched hers for the truth.

"Really," she confirmed.

"You aren't bothered by my relationship with your sister?" Stephen asked, aware that this might not be the best time to ask.

"No, Stephen," she answered quietly. "That doesn't bother me." She gave his hand a tug. Stephen allowed himself to be pulled into her living room.

"I'm sorry I was so horrible to you when we first met. I judged you unfairly. Then I heard about your nickname, *Love 'Em and Leave 'Em*. But I don't think that's really you, is it?" Now it was Alyah's turn to search his eyes.

Stephen shook his head back and forth. He felt like he was becoming hypnotized as he stared into the depths of her soul through her mesmerizing deep green eyes. Without thinking, he drew closer.

When he paused, Alyah met him. Their lips connected in a powerful explosion of emotions and deep feelings that Stephen was sure he'd never experienced before. He could see a future. He could see kids that looked like her. He could see them together. He could spend the rest of his life making this beautiful, smart, powerful woman happy. Starting right now. He didn't care that this is exactly what Booker had once warned him about—moving too fast.

"Stephen?" she whispered, her lips still on his.

He opened his eyes.

"I'm cold and wet. I'd like to take a shower."

Stephen nodded, feeling bereft as she moved away from him. He watched in shock as she unbuttoned her see-through, white silky blouse and let it fall to the floor. The camisole, which was plastered to her full, round breasts was the next article of clothing to go. She peeled it off, revealing a lacy black bra. Next, she took off her pants. She walked out of them, revealing a lacy black thong that matched her bra.

Stephen was afraid to blink.

"Well?" she looked back at him. "Are you coming?"

Surprised by the invitation, Stephen shed his wet clothes quickly and followed her as she stepped into the bathroom and turned the shower water to hot.

Stephen kissed Alyah and reached behind her back to unclasp her bra. She wiggled out of her panties.

"You are beautiful," he said, pausing to give her a once over.

She smiled. "Thanks, so are you." She ran her fingers over his ripped abs. She hesitated when she got to the scar on his chest. She looked at him in question.

"I was shot in the chest," he explained.

Alyah gasped. "How did you—"

"A story for another time," Stephen said, kissing her softly, then with more urgency.

Steam filled the bathroom. Stephen picked up Alyah's petite body, walked into the shower, and pushed her against the wall. She wrapped her legs around him and moaned softly. Stephen closed the shower curtain.

36

WILTON

Stephen woke to the sunlight streaming in through a window in a room that wasn't his. The sound of his phone ringing woke him. For a minute, he felt afraid that he had been left again. But the sun picked up reddish brown hues in Alyah's hair as it fanned out on the pillow beside him.

The phone rang again. It was Paige's number, but he knew it was Anna calling.

"What time is it?" Alyah gasped awake suddenly. "I'm due in court."

"It's seven," Stephen smiled at her and kissed her cheek. "We'll make it in time. I have to get this."

Stephen got up off the bed and took his phone into the other room.

"Daddy?" Anna asked. Her voice sounded sad.

"Anna? Hey, kiddo. What's wrong?" he asked. Guilt hit his chest like a sledgehammer. He was back but he hadn't been able to go see her yet. He supposed he could have run down and back in one day. It would have been tough with all the debriefing meetings and last-minute preparations for the funeral, but Anna was worth that.

"I just miss you, daddy," Anna said. Sometimes Anna still had nightmares. Stephen and Paige had hoped Anna hadn't seen anything when Carley was killed. A child therapist had uncovered that Anna had seen it all and somehow, though she had barely been four years old, Anna could not seem to forget the images.

"I miss you too, Anna," Stephen sighed, thinking about his quirky little girl who looked most like him with her blonde curly hair and bright blue eyes. "What have you been doing since I've been gone?"

"Nothing," Anna's voice held a pout. "Just karate. Oh, and I taught Molly a new trick."

"That's fantastic. What's the trick?" Stephen asked.

"She shakes," Anna said, proud of her dog.

"And how's karate going?" Stephen asked.

"It's boring," Anna complained.

"No way!" Stephen protested. "Karate is important, Anna. I thought you were excited about the tournament."

"No, I want to go to dance class. Hip hop!" she announced excitedly.

"What?" Stephen laughed.

"Hip hop! I'll show you how to do it when you come," Anna promised.

"You're going to teach me how to dance hip hop?" he asked, still laughing.

"Yes. Can I dance, daddy?" she asked. "Please?"

"Always," Stephen agreed.

"Instead of karate?" Anna asked.

"Ah," said Stephen. There was the strong-willed, opinionated daughter he knew. "No, sorry. Karate is important."

"Ohhhh!" Anna whined with protest.

Stephen could see Alyah frantically running around her room trying to get ready in a hurry. He checked his watch. She must like to get to work early. Not to mention he had to take her back to her car.

"Anna, let's talk about it when I come home." Stephen found the laundry room and pulled his clothes from yesterday out of the dryer. Alyah had washed them for him.

"It's my tournament in ten days!" Anna said.

"I know! I can't wait to see you, kiddo," Stephen said.

"Love you, daddy."

"Love you, too."

He hung up the phone.

Alyah walked out of the bedroom in a red dress that fit a little too well and red high heels. She held a black cardigan in her hand. She paused to kiss Stephen as she walked by. He had just buttoned his pants. He pulled her into him, and his hands lingered at her waist while he enjoyed the feel of her curves under his hands.

Stephen was surprised how right kissing her felt.

"We're gonna be late." Alyah broke away and walked to the kitchen.

Stephen could hear the Keurig gurgling as it made the first coffee of the day. He finished dressing and found her in the kitchen. He leaned against the doorway, watching as she moved quickly, clearly in a routine she practiced every morning.

"I could get used to you standing there, Stephen," Alyah sighed as she poured her coffee into a travel mug she'd already filled a quarter of the way up with French vanilla creamer.

She got a second mug down. "Grab a cup if you want one. We've got to be out the door in two minutes."

Stephen made his coffee, leaving it black.

"Gross," Alyah commented.

"Speaking of gross," Stephen said. "Do you have an extra toothbrush?"

"Oh! Of course," Alyah said. "Follow me." She took Stephen

to the bathroom and rummaged around in a drawer until she found a toothbrush still in the package.

"I'll be ready in two minutes," Stephen smiled at her.

True to his word, Stephen was ready quick, grabbed his coffee mug, and raced out the door with Alyah.

They were quiet as Stephen drove. Hating the silence, Stephen turned on the radio.

"Stephen," Alyah finally broke their silence. "Last night was…" she seemed to be searching for the right word.

Stephen held his breath. *Please don't say fun,* he thought. He braced himself for the hit.

"Amazing. Unexpected. You should know I'm not usually impulsive," she said. She looked worried.

Uh-oh, here it comes, Stephen thought. He said nothing.

"It meant a lot to me. I don't want you to think I'm the kind of person who—"

"I don't. Thank you for saying that. It meant a lot to me too," Stephen agreed. He rubbed her knee affectionately. His heart resumed beating at a regular pace when there didn't seem to be a *but* after her words.

After a brief silence again, this one more comfortable than the last, the words from the morning news on the radio drifted to Stephen.

"In other news, Trevor Kaites, the CEO of the DBC Network in New York, has passed away at age sixty-two. The nation will mourn the loss of this great man…"

"Trevor Kaites…" Stephen repeated. Why did that name sound familiar?

"What?" Alyah asked.

"Did you hear the news?" Stephen asked.

"No, I'm sorry, I wasn't paying attention," she admitted, her eyes full of question.

"The reason we were called in to help with the kidnapping

case is because both the FBI and the MCPD are in the middle of investigating a CEO serial killer case."

"Right, I remember," Alyah said.

"Well, they just found another one dead. His name was Trevor Kaites, and I can't remember why that name sounds familiar to me."

"Leave that one to the FBI, Stephen. We accomplished our goal," Alyah's words echoed Mak's.

Stephen nodded, feeling distracted.

When they got to Alyah's car, she leaned over. Her eyes went to that manilla envelope in the back seat. "Open that envelope, Stephen." She kissed him slowly and with passion. Then she got out of the car.

"Way to turn me on and leave me hanging," Stephen called after her.

"There's more where that came from," Alyah called. "Dinner tonight? My place?"

"I'll be there," Stephen said. Then he turned up the radio. But he was too late, the news segment was over.

"Trevor Kaites," he mumbled to himself, knowing it was important. He was sure it would come to him. Hopefully sooner rather than later.

37

WILTON

"Nice of you to join us, Wilton," Mak chided with a smile on her face. "You missed the Zoom call with Tigress and the FBI director—what was his name?" She turned to Sikes.

"Devon Peterson," Sikes supplied. "When you're at home base, office hours start at eight, Rookie."

Stephen's neck reddened. He pulled out a ragged piece of paper that had been torn off a note pad. "I was halfway to the office when I heard the name *Trevor Kaites* on the radio. I turned back around and went to find this list I'd left at home."

"Who is Trevor Kaites?" Sikes asked.

"The latest CEO to lose his life." Stephen looked at Mak. "Remember the case Tigress was working on in New York?"

Recognition dawned in Mak's eyes. "I do. But what does this have to do with—"

"I recognized his name because I took this from Lizzie Taylor's apartment. These are the names of six CEOs of major TV broadcasting networks in New York. The three that were crossed off had already died. Trevor Kaites makes the fourth on this list." Stephen tapped the paper with the names crossed off. "He died this morning."

"You found this in Lizzie's apartment, took it, and you're just now mentioning it to me?" Mak asked incredulously.

"Fill me in," Sikes requested. "Who's Lizzie Taylor and why is she significant?"

"Lizzie Taylor is the CEO of the Entertainment Broadcast Company, EBC. We interviewed her and the people there involved in production because they were the last people to see Selah and Maddox before they went missing. They did an interview for *The Entertainment Today Show*. We wanted to see if anyone knew where they were going next," Stephen supplied.

"That was right before a hired shooter tried to take me out in the parking lot. Rich Landers—"

"Booker's shooter!" Sikes exclaimed.

"As you know, we got Landers, and he admitted it was a last-minute pick-up job. *Kill the female cop,*" Mak quoted.

"Did Rich implicate Lizzie Taylor as the person who hired the hit?" Sikes asked, still trying to puzzle out the connection.

"No, he was always hired through the deep web. As you know, his computer was a dead end. We got the address to where Selah and Maddox were being held from Jason Jones, the limo driver. There were no leads back to Lizzie," Mak said.

"What do you suspect here, Wilton?" Sikes asked. "I fail to see a connection to our case."

"You're right, we couldn't see a connection to our kidnapping case, but I'd like to know why this was in Lizzie's apartment. Does it implicate her in the CEO case?" Stephen asked.

"That's not our case," Mak pointed out.

"It is if Lizzie Taylor becomes number seven on this list of CEOs of major TV broadcasting networks who are dying," Stephen argued.

"How so?" Mak challenged him.

"Well, she could be guilty or she could be a target. I'd like to know why she put together this list and make sure she's not in any danger."

"I bet," Mak snorted.

Sikes raised his eyebrows. "Let me guess, Lizzie Taylor is the most recent *Love 'Em and Leave 'Em* victim?"

"You guessed it," Mak nodded.

Stephen opened his mouth to defend himself when he caught movement just outside the open conference room door. He turned and his eyes connected with the wide, alarmed eyes of Alyah Smith. Her face was pink. She immediately turned and quickly walked out of the office.

For a moment no one said a word, though Stephen knew they'd surmised what was happening.

"You are one busy guy, Wilton," Mak mumbled with raised eyebrows.

"I'll say," Sikes agreed.

"Shit," Stephen said, his eyes sliding closed.

"Let's take a break and reconvene in twenty?" Sikes graciously offered.

Stephen got up to find Alyah.

As it turned out, Alyah was nowhere to be found. Stephen suspected she was hiding out in the women's restroom, but he wasn't brave enough to try going in after her. He called and texted, but Alyah didn't respond.

He'd show up on her doorstep for dinner tonight if that's what it took. She had invited him to dinner so he knew she'd be home. Even with a plan in place, Stephen couldn't quell the panic in his racing heart or his sick stomach.

Yet another relationship ends before it begins?

38

MAK

Mak was sitting in the meeting room ready for the meeting to start back up. If you asked her, Sikes was way too kind to let Stephen go chasing after his new lady of the week while they were in the middle of an important discussion about a case she was trying to get closed. Which is what she found herself pushing toward when Sikes and Wilton finally showed back up.

"Who is going to convince Lizzie that she needs protection?" Mak had argued. "This is a waste of department time and resources."

"But there are loose ends on this case," Wilton argued.

"Not this again," Mak had exclaimed.

"What's the issue with the case, Wilton?" Sikes asked.

"Well, we saved Selah and Maddox, but we don't know why they were taken in the first place," Wilton stated. "Not to mention, someone leaked that Selah was pregnant and very few people knew."

"What does that matter?" Sikes asked.

"It has been bothering me. It feels like a loose string," Stephen admitted.

"You can't talk to the kidnapper because she was killed

before you got there, but did you ask Selah and Maddox if the kidnapper ever expressed a motive?" Sikes asked.

"No, we actually didn't," Mak admitted.

Sikes speared her with his eyes. "Rookie move, Mak. I feel like you should know better."

Mak's cheeks instantly turned pink. She opened her mouth to defend herself but closed it. Instead, she nodded with humility. Had she really been so caught up in the excitement of closing the case that she didn't think to finish off with statements from their *star* witnesses? She had been so black and white about the whole thing. Save the kidnapped couple, check. She didn't think the details through.

"That's another thing. Who killed the kidnapper?" Stephen asked. "Selah and Maddox were huddled in the corner like trauma victims and told us the kidnapper's body had just come falling down the stairs. It's like someone knew we were on the way and took out the kidnapper before she could give us information."

"And the minute *The Fan* showed up dead, it became a murder case. We didn't follow it through to the end," Mak mumbled as she self-discovered and changed her mind. "Can we task the MCPD to solve who killed *The Fan*?"

"Yeah, it leaves our case open, for sure. With the CEO murder case, it sounds like they'll be short-handed, which is why the Attorney General gave the case to us in the first place," Sikes puzzled it aloud. "Any chance the information that you were on your way to rescue Selah and Maddox got leaked somehow?"

"Not by us," Mak insisted strongly.

"Who knew you were en route?" Sikes asked.

"Jonas Petry, Chief Tigress, and the two cops he brought for back up. What were their names?" Mak asked Stephen.

"Bon and Ericks," Stephen supplied.

"Any reason to think anyone in MCPD tipped someone off who sent out a shooter?" Sikes asked.

Stephen shook his head. "I can't see what possible benefit it would be to the MCPD—"

"Well," Mak interrupted. "You did say there's something *off* about Tigress."

"Off, as in arrogant. Not deviant or evil." Stephen shook his head.

"I'm sending you two back. Sounds like we didn't wrap this case up and I'm not putting you on another one until we know this one is done," Sikes announced. "When you come back this time, there better not be any questions or loose ends left. Agreed?"

They nodded but Mak was not happy about this trip. She had really thought they had completed the mission. She had been looking forward to moving on to the next. She'd made a snap judgement of Wilton, comparing him to Booker. *Booker was never this picky about the cases.* Her pride stung that she'd rushed through the final steps, ignored her partner's intuition, refused to listen to him, and got on a plane to come back home.

But if she were really honest with herself, Mak would admit she'd just gotten home and had wanted a little more time with John and Harper. In fact, she only had a small window of time to run home, pack, and let them know she was leaving again.

Mak tried not to feel resentful as she sat stoically beside Stephen later that evening on the plane back to New York. She felt like she was being punished for a job she'd originally thought was well done. She inwardly shook her head. She really only had herself to be mad at, which became an irksome, self-loathing feeling deep inside. It wasn't a feeling Mak was used to.

Still, she could not believe they were going back to New York to offer protection to Lizzie, a woman who likely would not take it. Not to mention, Mak had an uncomfortable suspicion that the shooting in the parking lot shortly after leaving Lizzie's office the first time was a little too connected to Lizzie.

Mak shook her head again, remembering how she'd instantly judged Lizzie Taylor when she'd heard her name before she'd even met her. While Mak was in self-discovery mode, maybe she should figure out why she was so inclined not to like a woman simply because she clearly wanted to be a star.

39

WILTON

Getting back in front of Lizzie Taylor the next morning was proving to be harder than Mak and Stephen had thought it would be. The office manager had called in to announce them, and Lizzie had declared she was *too busy* to talk today. After flashing a badge at the office manager and walking through Lizzie's closed door, Stephen and Mak found themselves sitting in comfortable chairs in front of Lizzie Taylor, waiting.

Today, Lizzie's hair was swept up in a twisted ponytail that cascaded like a waterfall of curls. She wore an elegant black pantsuit with a thin red belt and red stiletto heels.

As Stephen sat waiting for Lizzie to look up from her phone, he marveled that he had no feelings for her other than compassion and concern. While she was beautiful and powerful, Stephen found he preferred the side of Alyah where her walls were down, and she was open to him. He had to force his thoughts away from the mess he'd created back home. The one he'd been unable to fix, not for a lack of trying. He hadn't even connected with Alyah before they'd left. He'd texted, called, and had even shown up for dinner though she hadn't opened the door.

Now, he needed to focus on Lizzie, who had been reading her text for the past few minutes with one finger up to show an air of self-importance. Stephen felt impatient. He pulled the note with the names he'd found in Lizzie's apartment out and slapped it on her giant marble desktop in front of her to get her attention. He caught Mak's glance of approval out of the corner of his eye. Mak hated waiting.

Lizzie looked at the note. Recognition flickered, then a different emotion. Stephen thought maybe that emotion was fear but as she spoke, he realized it was annoyance.

"Where did you get this, Stephen?" Lizzie's voice held a tone. She slammed her phone face down with anger and gave him her full attention.

"You know where I got it, Lizzie," Stephen answered.

"I trusted you, and you went snooping through my apartment?" Lizzie asked. Her eyes were dark. "These are the names of all the major CEOs who happen to be my competition. I'm looking to buy a new network. Those are the men I've been meeting with. If they are crossed off, it's because I already have."

"And the men who are crossed off told you *no*?" Mak asked.

Lizzie shrugged obstinately, then answered with reluctance. "A few didn't commit. They promised to think about it."

"Then they died," Mak pushed.

"Is an item you stole from my apartment without permission admissible in court?" Lizzie demanded, looking at Stephen.

"Lizzie, I don't think you understand the gravity of what's happening here," Stephen replied. "You're a CEO of a major broadcasting TV network. Just like them. You might be a target right now. We can protect you."

Lizzie was shaking her head before Stephen finished the sentence. "No, I don't fit the profile, don't you see?"

"Not really. Please explain," Stephen requested.

"First of all, I'm not a sixty-five-plus year-old guy. Second of all, there's something you might have missed."

"Care to share?" Sarcasm lined Mak's question.

"This is kept under wraps, and I only know about it because my dad started the club."

"What club?" Stephen asked.

Lizzie got up and poured herself a glass of wine. She jiggled a glass at Stephen, but he shook his head. She glanced at Mak in question. Mak shook her head as well.

"My dad went to college with all of these guys. He started a club—"

"A literal club?" Mak interrupted.

"Yes," Lizzie paused, speared Mak with her gaze, then continued. "They called themselves *The Boys of Broadcast*. Literally, I can't make the stuff up. After the third man died, I thought, *Wow, they're all getting so old. They've been in stressful careers their whole lives. And now they're dying.* But now that you're here in my office questioning it, I'm wondering—"

"What?" Mak interrupted.

Stephen shot Mak a look of annoyance.

"Maybe there's more to it. Maybe it's as ominous as you are hinting, and someone is targeting each man in the group."

"We didn't say that exactly," Stephen stated logically.

Mak leaned forward and tapped a fingernail on the note where the name *Trevor Kaites* was written. "This man was still alive when Stephen grabbed this and left your apartment. Had you already met with him?"

Lizzie sighed as she reluctantly swung her gaze to Mak. "I would think you, of all people, would understand ambitious women who work in a male-dominated work environment. Let me explain."

For once, Mak sat quietly, waiting for Lizzie's explanation.

"I invited each man to dinner and made an offer to take over his company." Lizzie sat back down with a wry smile. "Little did

I know they would die within twenty-four hours. I failed to mention it because I thought it would make me look guilty. Either this is one hell of a coincidence or I'm being framed."

"You mean to tell me each of these men died within twenty-four hours after dinner with you and you *failed to mention* that to the police?" Mak repeated.

"That's what I said, yes," Lizzie admitted.

"You're right, Lizzie. That does make you look suspicious," Mak declared with eyes narrowed. "More so because of the obvious admission."

"Mak—" Stephen's voice was soft as if pleading for fairness.

"No, it does. I don't think for one minute you're innocent here, Ms. Taylor. The fact that you're not scared this will happen to you..." Mak shook her head and crossed her arms over her chest. "You should have played it differently. Damsel in distress is more his style." Mak tilted her head toward Stephen.

"Hey!" Stephen protested. "We're on the same team!"

"Are we?" Mak asked through gritted teeth.

"Shall I step outside until you two decide if I'm the bad guy or not?" Lizzie quipped.

"Text Tigress, we're bringing her in for questioning," Mak commanded, looking at Stephen.

Stephen pulled out his phone, the back of his neck red, a sure sign of agitation.

"I couldn't possibly go today," Lizzie answered with wide, innocent eyes. "My schedule is full. Maybe tomorrow?"

"Nice try," Mak seethed.

Stephen glanced at his phone. "Mak, can I talk to you? In the hallway?"

Mak got up angrily and followed Stephen out.

"What?" Mak snapped.

"First of all, I don't appreciate your tone or accusations—"

"I don't appreciate a partner whose vision is clouded and puts me in danger. She's playing you. That was probably her plan. Ever since your one *great night*," Mak made air quotes. "You can't possibly see what's under your nose."

Stephen took a breath to calm himself. "When did I put you in danger?"

"The last time we were here, I was shot at. Coincidence? She didn't have you shot at. It was the *female cop* she targeted. She's having someone else do her bidding."

"But why? We have no proof that she was behind the shooting," Stephen argued, working to push his anger aside and be objective. "The last time we were here, we were on the Selah and Maddox kidnapping."

"Yeah, I'm not sure. But my gut says she's guilty. Not to mention Booker was killed simply because you were interviewing Mrs. Lablanc."

"My brain tells me we need to find the evidence and pissing her off isn't going to get us there," Stephen argued.

"Neither is sleeping with her," Mak snapped.

Stephen shut his mouth.

There was silence as the two stared each other down.

Stephen's phone beeped, interrupting the standoff. Stephen glanced at his phone screen.

"Tigress refuses to grant a room for questioning," Stephen showed it to Mak.

"What?" Mak demanded. She grabbed Stephen's phone and read it.

Tigress: *We've already questioned her. It's a non-starter. Stop wasting tax payer's dollars.*

Mak sucked in a breath. She marched back in and stopped in front of Lizzie's desk. "Don't leave town. I'll arrest you immediately if you do."

Lizzie smiled confidently with a touch of arrogance. "Nice to see you today. Mak, was it?"

"Yeah, or you can just call me *the female cop*. That almost worked for you last time."

Lizzie's smirk faded.

Stephen saw it. Even if for a minute, Lizzie looked scared.

"Hope you brought a bullet proof vest with you, Stephen. Oh wait. Only I need one because she *likes* you."

40

MAK

Mak and Stephen were barely speaking as they pulled into the MCPD building parking garage. Tigress had followed his harsh text with another one requesting they come in and *compare notes*.

Mak turned off the ignition and sat for a second. Her mood was sinking by the minute.

Stephen sat quietly, waiting for Mak to open the door.

"Just tell me one thing, Wilton. What's your motivation behind all that passion for this case? Are you that worried about Lizzie Taylor? Do you really think she's in danger?"

Stephen was silent for a second. "Besides the obvious that we need to solve this case one hundred percent?" Stephen rubbed his neck which was turning a deeper shade of red. "Yes, I'm worried that Lizzie is the most obvious next target in the CEO serial killings. But did it occur to you that if someone else was working with Elle Jones, Selah and Maddox might not be safe yet?"

Mak stared at Stephen, her horror growing. "Right. Of course. That makes sense." Mak threw the door open and got out of the SUV. She must really be off her game lately. She really had thought Stephen was just making this about his relationship with Lizzie.

Though she was annoyed that Tigress had called them in, Mak supposed it sounded reasonable since they were now merging into the MCPD investigation. She expected they would have to calm Tigress down, so he didn't feel they were trying to take over their case. She didn't believe in turf wars. The more the merrier on a case. She just hoped Tigress and the MCPD would feel the same way. They did enlist their help with the kidnapping after all.

What Mak did not expect was FBI Director Devon Peterson sitting at the table of the tiny conference room they were escorted into, which was barely bigger than a closet.

"Devon Peterson, FBI." The man stood, offered his hand to Mak, and his presence seemed to fill the room. He was tall and broad. If Mak had to guess, he was pretty muscular under that button-down shirt he wore. It made sense, he was FBI. Not unlike Tigress, their jobs demanded peak physical condition.

"Mak Cunningham." Mak took his hand and gave it a firm shake. "We spoke on Zoom last week."

"Stephen Wilton." Stephen stuck his hand out as he followed Mak into the room and shut the door. Devon Peterson accepted it. "Nice to meet you in person."

"Have a seat," Tigress commanded tersely.

Mak and Stephen did as they were instructed.

Mak, feeling on edge and ready to get on with the case, spoke first as she sat. "What's this about?" she demanded.

"We were hoping you could tell us, Mrs. Cunningham." Peterson smiled kindly, though his smile was stiff and not quite friendly.

"I go by Mak." Mak crossed her hands over her chest.

"Why are you here, suddenly working on the CEO murder case?" Tigress asked bluntly.

"Ah. Stephen, you want to take this one?" Mak turned to her

partner. "He thinks there might be a connection to the kidnapping case."

Stephen cleared his throat. If he was annoyed by the way Mak tossed him under the bus, he made no indication. He sat forward. "I'm concerned our kidnapping victims might still be in danger. We feel there are some loose ends with the kidnapping case. Unanswered questions. And I can't be sure yet, but I think that case might be connected to the CEO murders."

"Okay." Tigress sat back, a skeptical look on his face. "Let's start with unanswered questions."

"Someone leaked Selah's pregnancy to the press, which was announced at the same time as Selah's disappearance. I can't figure out how that news got out," Stephen puzzled aloud.

"Are you talking about the news story *The Entertainment Today Show* announced mid-case? How did the news that they were missing get out, let alone the pregnancy?" Tigress challenged.

"Stephen told Lizzie Taylor that Selah and Maddox were missing when we went to talk to her. Lizzie Taylor owns an entertainment news conglomerate," Mak volunteered with sarcasm, feeling a little smug.

Now Stephen did shoot her a look.

"Okay, but you didn't tell her Selah was pregnant?" Tigress clarified.

"Right," Stephen nodded.

"Tell me why that matters," Tigress demanded, rubbing his dark crewcut.

"I wonder if the fact that they had information that no one else could have known links someone on her staff at the EBC to the kidnapper. What if it wasn't a one-person job?" Stephen asked.

"You think there was more than one person involved in the kidnapping and that the other person, or persons, could still be out there?" Peterson jumped in. His voice sounded like he was trying to be helpful and put the pieces in place.

"Let's say I believe this theory—and I don't," Tigress snapped. "Who *did* know about the pregnancy?"

"Selah's mom and one of our agents, Jonas Petry, who was watching Mrs. Lablanc when she was in witness protection," Stephen answered.

"Jonas Petry? How well do you know him? Do you trust that he wouldn't sell a story for some quick cash?" Tigress wondered.

"Jonas Petry has been with the US Marshals longer than Wilton has. He's a good guy. I can vouch for him." Mak uncrossed her arms and sat up straighter.

"Not to mention, he took a liking to Mrs. Lablanc. She reminded him of his grandma. He'd have no reason to jeopardize his career like that," Stephen seconded Mak's opinion.

"Okay, so the news got leaked from a doctor or a snoopy reporter. Information about stars gets out all the time. Ms. Taylor has a right to have her network report whatever she wants." Tigress paused to take a breath in.

Interesting, Mak thought. *He's awful quick to jump to Lizzie Taylor's defense.*

"Nothing put out there in that newscast was untrue. Besides, we have Elle Jones' fingerprints on that coaster from the hotel room. She's definitely the kidnapper," Tigress was dismissive. "What else?"

"We never identified the shooter who took down *The Fan*, Elle Jones," Stephen stated. "Where did the shooter come from and why take Elle out before we got there? It feels like someone knew we were coming and didn't want Elle to talk to us."

"Woah, woah, woah," Tigress now sounded angry. "Are you trying to say information was leaked from *this* office?"

"I didn't say that, but you did. You tell me," Stephen said, matching the anger evident on Tigress' face.

"Okay, guys," Peterson stepped in diplomatically. "Point

made, Wilton. Do you have any evidence for us to consider a connection between the two cases?"

"Yeah," Stephen reached into his pocket and drew out the note of CEO names written in Lizzie Taylor's handwriting. He opened it up and laid it on the table.

1. ~~Roger Clamentine~~
2. ~~Jim Tallbott~~
3. ~~Tony Statten~~
4. Tray Walker
5. ~~Trevor Kaites~~
6. Logan Pierce

"What exactly is this?" Peterson breathed in as he looked at it. His voice sounded excited.

"I found this in Lizzie Taylor's apartment," Stephen announced.

"What were you doing in Lizzie Taylor's apartment?" Tigress asked. There was a steel edge to his voice.

Another interesting reaction, Mak quietly observed.

"Lizzie invited me," Stephen announced, matter of fact.

"I see. And she handed this to you while you were there?" Tigress asked. His eyebrows were arched in a silent challenge. His body leaned forward, almost imperceptibly.

Years of training had taught Mak to pick up on non-verbal cues. Tigress was getting angrier and more defensive by the minute. His mannerisms were becoming borderline aggressive.

"Not exactly," Stephen answered.

"Exactly *what* then?" Tigress was impatient.

"I wrote her a note, tore off the top sheet, and this was in the notepad under it. I took it. I didn't even think about it. Something in my subconscious was triggered and I just reacted. Maybe I'd heard the name of one of the CEOs. I just thought this seemed important and I grabbed it," Stephen explained.

"But why were you writing her a note?" Tigress was now rubbing his forehead like he was getting a headache.

"Oh, for the love of God!" Mak exploded suddenly. "Lizzie invited him there for a date. He stayed over. She left him there in the morning. He wrote a note before he left. None of that matters. What does matter is that four out of six names on that list are scratched off. Those men are now dead. When Wilton picked this up, Kaites was still alive."

"A list of scratched names is hardly proof of... anything." Tigress sneered.

"Wilton sees this differently. If you ask me, this implicates Lizzie Taylor in the CEO murders. She might even be linked to the kidnapping because she was the last person to see Selah and Maddox before they went missing. Instead of interrogating us, you need to bring in Lizzie Taylor before she skips town. She knows we're on to her. And with all these questions, you've probably given her time to make her get-away plans," Mak snapped.

"I do see that differently," Stephen argued. "I think she knows she's in danger. She wrote the list because she's keeping track—"

"And psychically crossed off Kaites *before* he was killed?" Mak knew she was no longer presenting a united front, but her temper was getting the best of her.

Tigress' face was a shade of red that could almost be described as purple. He stood up angrily. "Are you in the habit of sleeping with potential murder suspects?" Tigress threw out rhetorically to Stephen.

Wow, Mak thought with surprise, *out of all that information, that's what he's upset about?*

Stephen's mouth dropped. "She wasn't a suspect then—"

"And you," Tigress turned to Mak. "You should know better. You're the senior officer. Yeah, don't look surprised. I looked into both of you. You gonna let a rookie make your calls? Especially one who's objectivity has been compromised?"

Mak stood up to match Tigress and looked him in the eyes. There was a cold calmness to her, and she spoke with quiet calculation. "You wanna talk about objectivity? You sure got emotionally charged when you found out Stephen spent time with Lizzie Taylor. Why would you even care?"

For once, Tigress was speechless. He silently glared at Mak as if daring her to continue.

Feeling she was onto something here, Mak continued. "Your whole demeanor changed when I told you Stephen stayed over. Is your judgement also clouded where Lizzie Taylor is concerned? That would explain why you immediately dismissed us from bringing her in earlier. She's a *non-starter*? Try she might be a *murderer*. You've wasted enough time to give her a head start, too. Who's compromised now, Tigress?" Mak felt justified when Tigress still didn't respond. He just gaped at her like a fish. She decided to push it further to test her theory. She knew people and she had a gut feeling here. "How long were you sleeping with Lizzie before you crossed her off your CEO murder suspect list?"

"That's enough," Peterson stood now too.

"Anyone who *didn't* sleep with our murder suspect or feel an over developed sense of protection for her want to come with me to bring her in for questioning?" Mak challenged. She turned to Peterson. "Guess that leaves you and me. What do you say? Would you like to accompany me?"

Peterson grabbed his jacket and followed Mak out of the room.

"I'm coming with you," Stephen stated. He did a quick jog to keep up with Mak as she and Peterson walked quickly to the elevator that would lead down to the parking garage.

"I have a better idea," Mak tossed over her shoulder at Stephen as she jammed the down button. The elevator opened and the three of them filed on. "You go interview Selah and have another talk with Mrs. Lablanc. You're so worried about who leaked the pregnancy, you can interview them and find out. Also find out if Selah knows why she was kidnapped."

They rode the elevator down in silence. At the bottom, Mak walked off the elevator and into the parking garage.

"Should we really split up right now?" Stephen asked, jogging after her. He looked unsure—hesitant. He glanced at Peterson, who mirrored Mak's impatience. "I can handle this. I can be a professional. The only feelings I have here are urgency to make sure no one else gets hurt."

"That's exactly why I'm suggesting we split up. We might be running out of time. Seriously, Wilton..." Mak walked closer to Stephen and lowered her voice. "When we get back, I'm considering asking for a new partner. If you'd remembered you'd palmed this note when we were here before, we wouldn't have had to come back."

"That's why you're so angry?" Stephen asked.

"I'm fine with traveling for this job. But when I have to leave my family and travel twice to the same place to tie up the loose ends we should have tied in the first place, I get a little irritated. Let's just hope you don't get me shot before this is over."

Stephen shuddered a little. Mak knew he was thinking about Booker—or maybe he was reliving the scene in his head. She also knew she was being unfair. He might be right to question Mak's judgment of cutting him loose right now as the rookie on the case. But she knew he had prior experience. Experience that would not help her bring in Lizzie Taylor. At this point, Wilton would only get in the way of that. So, Mak was giving him a shit assignment—busy work. Stephen knew it too.

Though she was annoyed and acting on it, Mak really was following her gut, feeling that once Lizzie was contained, all would be safe, and everything would fall into place.

That, Mak thought, *might prove to be a bigger challenge than I anticipated.*

41

WILTON

As Stephen traveled to Mrs. Lablanc's home in the Great Green Gardens subdivision, he replayed Mak's words, internalizing them. Had it been his fault that Booker had gotten shot? Was it somehow his fault that Mak had been targeted? Did Mak really think it was Stephen's fault? Stephen felt a cold sweat break out. What if it was?

Stephen knew the danger wasn't over. He couldn't guarantee either of them would come back home without a bullet hole in them, but he sure didn't agree with Mak that Lizzie was a suspect. But maybe it was time to consider that his judgement wasn't what he thought it was when he first entered this profession.

Stephen thought back through his relationship history. He had once arrested Paige—Anna's mother—his *baby mama*, for murdering her own mother. His ex-girlfriend, Carley, had kidnapped Anna and Carley's life had ended in murder. Now, Mak was on her way to Lizzie Taylor's office to bring her in for questioning over the murders of several CEOs.

It was one thing if Stephen's judgement was compromised, quite another if he gravitated to women who were dark and no good to their core. It seemed both were happening at the same time.

Before the Uber stopped outside Mrs. Lablanc's well-maintained brick home, Stephen paid the driver on the Uber app. He jumped out when they rolled to a stop. He walked quickly, spooked by the remembrance of the hit that had happened right here with Booker. As he knocked on the door, he looked down at the very spot where his partner had laid dead. He didn't see Booker's blood anymore. That piece of the wooden deck had been replaced.

The door swung open.

"Stephen!" Mrs. Lablanc exclaimed. "Come on in! Great timing. Selah's here too."

Stephen walked through the door and Selah stood up from the couch where she'd been sitting comfortably. She wore an oversized sweatshirt and leggings. Her feet were bare. Her golden hair was pulled back into a ponytail. Stephen marveled that she looked like a regular person. *She* is *a regular person*, he supposed.

"My hero!" she exclaimed with a happy smile on her face. She gave a little wave. "Have a seat," she plopped back down.

Stephen did as he was told.

Both women stared expectantly at Stephen.

Stephen cleared his throat. He'd never had to tell a victim that he hadn't tied up all loose ends after all. He felt his mood plummet even more.

"Can I get you something to drink?" Selah asked.

"No," Stephen responded quickly. "I'm here because I have a few questions to tie up my loose ends—for the report, you see. Is it okay if I ask you some questions?"

"Anything," Selah grinned and nodded.

"Absolutely," Mrs. Lablanc affirmed.

"Well, Selah," Stephen began. He took out his phone to make notes on it. "When you were being held captive, did Elle

Jones—that's the name of the kidnapper—did she ever tell you why she was holding you captive?"

"Yes," Selah said. "She told us she was working for someone she called *The Boss*. *The Boss* wanted Maddox to fix NFL games. Well, lose some on purpose, throw some games, that sort of thing. She said *The Boss* wanted me to endorse products for them on command, whenever they wanted me to. Elle said she would give us time to decide. We were working through it when her body came hurtling down the stairs."

"Game tampering," Stephen mused. "That's a serious crime."

Selah nodded and flinched. "I wanted him to agree. I was worried about the baby. In retrospect, what they wanted from me was so much easier. I was just supposed to endorse products, act as an influencer. I guess I thought if we said *yes* then, we could find a way out of it after they let us go."

"So, there was a second person involved called *The Boss*?" Stephen asked for clarity. "Any chance *The Fan* and *The Boss* were the same person? Let me explain. I've been in situations before where the suspect had multiple personalities. Did it seem like you were seeing more than one personality from Elle?" Stephen's mind was on Demitri Abbott, the man who was still hiding out there somewhere.

Selah thought more about that. "There were times Elle seemed more frazzled than others. But I wouldn't say her personality had changed. She called herself a fan. Is that what you all called her? *The Fan*?"

Stephen nodded. "She had a history with this sort of thing and had gone MIA for a while. This kidnapping fit her pattern. We thought she was responsible. We just didn't know she was working with someone else. We would also like to find who shot her."

Selah shuddered. "That was terrifying. I can still close my eyes and see her body falling down the stairs, a trail of blood in each place she landed. I can still hear the sound of her body falling and thunking over and over again. I'd never seen a dead body before."

"I told her she needs to find a good counselor," Mrs. Lablanc cut in.

"I will, mom. I just got behind on the tour and Stacia has my schedule booked up. Not to mention, I have a football game to go to." Selah smiled contently.

"Still, you need to put yourself first. You've got the baby to think of now," Mrs. Lablanc chided her daughter.

"Speaking of which, who knew about the baby?" Stephen asked.

"No one," Selah admitted. "Not even Maddox or Stacia."

"I knew," Mrs. Lablanc stated.

"You guessed." Selah smirked.

"How about a doctor?" Stephen asked.

Selah shook her head. "I hadn't gone yet. Maddox didn't even know."

"Selah, can you give me a list of people who work on your team? We met Emily, your publicist, and Stacia."

"Sure. Do you mean bodyguard, backup singers, musicians, and dancers? Or just in administration?" Selah asked, getting out her phone.

"A list of everyone would be nice but I guess I want to know who would have known about your whereabouts? Who kept track of your calendar?"

"Oh, that would be Stacia. She's my PR person, my business manager, my publicist, my tour manager, my everything," Selah said.

"I thought Emily did that," Stephen said, remembering it was Emily who had answered their questions.

"No," Selah shook her head. "Stacia is the one in charge of me."

"You mean in charge of your calendar," Stephen clarified.

"Sure," Selah said with a hint of bitterness and sarcasm.

"What about Maddox? Do you have a list of people who worked with Maddox?" Stephen didn't ask where Maddox was. He knew the big game was coming up and he assumed Maddox would be back in Kansas City getting ready for it.

"Oh," Selah laughed a little. "That's where Emily came in. Emily is Stacia's assistant. Maddox wanted his own person and Stacia thought it would be a good idea to keep his calendar to *maintain control*," Selah said this with air quotes and exchanged a glance with her mother. "So, Stacia promoted Emily and made her Maddox's publicist. He only used her when he was in town, when we were together."

Stephen didn't miss the look Selah and her mother had shared. "You and Stacia don't get along?"

"Oh, it's not that we don't get along exactly," Selah skirted the truth. "Stacia is just classic type A and wants to plan every minute of my day. She doesn't like surprises. Like the kidnapping. She was super annoyed she had to reschedule a few of the tour dates."

"I see," Stephen made a mental note to interview Stacia this time. He'd love to get Stacia's perspective on Selah and what had just happened. "Is she pushing back the tour dates until you recover from what happened? Or will you resume work as soon as the next concert comes around?"

"I haven't decided yet. Can I show you something?" Selah surprised Stephen with her question as she rose in one fluid motion.

"Sure." Stephen didn't know why he bothered to respond because Selah was already walking to her room. Stephen remembered the layout of the house from when he had been there before.

Selah walked into her bedroom. Stephen followed her. He watched her go to a desk in the corner of the room. She opened the drawer, giving it a careful tug. Stephen could see why. The drawer was full of old papers.

Stephen watched as Selah sat down on the floor and grabbed a stack of papers out. She removed the first few sheets, thumbed through them, then handed the papers to Stephen.

Stephen glanced down but his eyes bulged, and his heart rate sped up. He thumbed through the stack. Letter after letter had cut outs of mean things and threats, the type of stuff one teenager might say to another teenager. The words were cut out of magazines. The bottom of each page had a magazine cutout signature that read *The Fan*.

"Selah, why didn't you tell me?" Mrs. Lablanc gasped.

Stephen wanted to kick himself. He and Booker had been here when she was kidnapped, but they hadn't really looked through her things. It's true that they hadn't had a warrant and Mrs. Lablanc had told them *no*, but Stephen could have explained better why they'd wanted to look around. *The Fan* had sent her letters after all.

"How old are these?" Stephen asked.

"I started getting them my senior year in high school. That's when I started getting some attention. I'd won some singing contest and I had a talent scout talking to me. I was booking some small public appearances. Kids were starting to talk and take notice. I didn't tell you, mom, because I was afraid you wouldn't let me play anymore."

Mrs. Lablanc, who had come into the room behind Stephen, nodded as if that sounded right, still looking concerned.

"Is it possible that Elle went to high school with you? Did you recognize her?" Stephen asked. He was still holding and studying the papers.

"She did look familiar." Selah pushed off the floor and stood back up. "I thought it was because she had done my hair for *The Entertainment Today Show*. She said she was a big fan—"

"Wait, she worked for Lizzie Taylor?" Stephen asked.

"Yes, you know Sarah?" Selah responded, sounding surprised. "Well, I guess she goes by Lizzie now."

Stephen felt confused. "Lizzie? Lizzie Taylor, the CEO of EBC?"

Selah laughed a little. "Lizzie's real name is Sarah. Sarah Elizabeth Taylor. I went to school with her. She was my best friend growing up. Sarah and I had a falling out and went our own separate ways before graduation."

"Sarah?" Stephen felt something familiar tugging at his brain. "Hang on," he said to Selah. He left the room and found his way back to the living room where he'd studied the pictures on the mantel the day he and Booker had come by. He found the picture he was looking for and stood in front of it, staring hard.

Selah and Mrs. Lablanc had trailed after him.

"Yep, that's Sarah," Selah confirmed as she stood next to Stephen and followed his eyes to the photo.

Stephen studied the picture and could see the resemblance of the girl in the photo to Lizzie Taylor. He wouldn't have caught it before because he hadn't met Lizzie yet. His heart sank a little more. Another connection to Lizzie Taylor. How long was he going to protect someone who was looking more guilty by the minute? More importantly, why was Stephen constantly finding himself having to protect the bad girl?

"I think you're going to have to tell me the whole story about why you and Sarah had a falling out. Start at the beginning and leave nothing out," Stephen commanded.

"Okay, but then I have to run." Selah smiled, her excitement evident. "I've got a game to catch."

"I don't know if you should leave right now, Selah," Stephen said quietly.

"Don't worry. Stacia hired a new bodyguard for me. She didn't like that the last one listened to me when I gave him the night off. I'll leave when he brings the car around. He'll escort me from the door to the vehicle and everywhere I go."

Stephen had a terrible feeling about this. A flashback of Booker lying face down on the very porch Selah would be walking onto when she left the house took Stephen's breath away. But he was starting to doubt his gut. The one thing that had gotten him this far in life could no longer be trusted.

How could he keep people safe if he couldn't even determine who it was that needed protection?

42

MAK

Lizzie had disappeared. Exactly as Mak had feared would happen. Lizzie was on the run. It was the only conclusion Mak could logically draw. She and Director Peterson had sat outside Lizzie's office for over an hour waiting while Lizzie's assistant made phone calls to every person Lizzie knew in order to track her down. The confusion on the assistant's face was real. Mak completely dismissed the assistant as an accomplice to Lizzie's disappearance.

"She went out for lunch and didn't come back," the assistant had told them. "That was hours ago. She 'no-showed' an appointment. Which is very unlike her."

Mak handed her card to the office manager. "Please contact me if you find Ms. Taylor. It's urgent."

The office manager nodded and took the card.

"Guess we need to put a BOLO out, find Lizzie Taylor, and arrest her," Mak told Peterson.

Peterson agreed and they left the office.

It wasn't until Mak got into the driver's seat that she realized she had somehow missed a text from Stephen.

Stephen: *Got a lot of new information. I'm starting to warm up
to your theory. Lizzie Taylor might just be connected to Selah's
kidnapping after all. Come get me and I'll tell you more.*

Mak hesitated. Time was of the essence here, but she actu-
ally had no leads on how to find Lizzie. She shared the text with
Peterson as she drove out of the parking lot and put Mrs.
Lablanc's address into GPS.

"We definitely need to start the process of alerting all
authorities to find Lizzie Taylor," Mak made the request to
Peterson. "Stephen has information that might implicate her in
the kidnapping too."

"On it," Peterson agreed. He pulled out his cell phone and
started making phone calls as Mak drove.

They arrived at Mrs. Lablanc's house over twenty minutes
later. Mak told Peterson to keep an eye out for suspicious characters as they left the car, warning him to be aware since this
was where Booker had been shot.

Mak bounded quickly up to the front door and knocked.
Peterson was on her heels. Mrs. Lablanc opened the door and
greeted Mak with a smile.

Mak and Peterson quickly stepped inside. Mak was feeling
uneasy already and was unwilling to stand on a porch where
such a horrible event had occurred.

Mrs. Lablanc immediately gave Mak a hug. Mak felt her irritation melting. It was hard to be mad when someone was so
happy to see her.

"This is FBI Director Peterson," Mak introduced him.

Mrs. Lablanc stepped back from Mak and shook Peterson's
hand. Then she turned back to Mak.

"Thank you for bringing my Selah home." Mrs. Lablanc
wiped tears that had formed at the corner of her eyes.

"That's what we do, Mrs. Lablanc. Where is Selah now?"
Mak asked, looking around the room. Her eyes fell on her part-

ner. "Stephen." Mak nodded her head at him, her icy voice making it clear she was still holding a grudge against him.

"Selah left," Stephen said, coming to join the newcomers.

"You let her leave?" Mak tried to keep her voice light for Mrs. Lablanc's sake, but she felt angry all over again. They had a kidnapper and possible murderer out there, God only knew where, and Stephen had let the target walk away by herself?

"She has a new bodyguard who doubles as a driver, and she's on her way out of state. She's going to the big game," Stephen shrugged. "I couldn't keep her here without good reason."

"That's my girl. She doesn't want to sit around and won't let anything hold her back," Mrs. Lablanc chuckled.

"Did you find Lizzie?" Stephen asked.

"Mrs. Lablanc, can you excuse us for a minute? We need to get on the same page and decide where to go from here." Mak smiled quickly. When Mrs. Lablanc nodded and waved them toward the dining room table, the three of them sat at the furthest end and lowered their voices.

"No, we did not find Lizzie. She's disappeared," Mak said through clenched teeth.

Stephen's eyes got big with instant understanding and fear.

"What did you learn?" Mak asked.

Stephen showed Mak the bullying letters signed by *The Fan*. He relayed the conversation he'd had with Selah.

"Your text said you're on board with the theory that Lizzie is our best suspect. I still don't understand. I assume you now think Lizzie *could* be connected to the kidnapping?" Mak asked.

"This is Lizzie Taylor. She and Selah were best friends growing up." Stephen thrust the picture of Lizzie and Selah as kids at Mak. "Her real name is Sarah Elizabeth Taylor. She and Selah had a huge argument in high school because Sarah wanted to take over her dad's company and she wanted Selah to help her. Selah had agreed. They made one of those Goonies blood pacts. Then Selah started to take off and was becoming a singer. An agent picked her up and Selah was already on her way to fame. When Selah backed out, Sarah became irate at Selah for abandoning her. She said Selah was her only hope. Sarah said she'd hate Selah forever and never forgive her because Selah didn't hold up her end of the bargain—"

"Which was what, exactly?" Mak interjected.

"Infiltrate and take over her dad's business, most likely," Stephen answered.

"Most likely?" Mak repeated.

Stephen closed his eyes. "Selah said that she and Sarah Elizabeth had talked about going into business together. The night I was with Lizzie, she told me a sad story about how when she told her dad she was getting her MBA to take over his business someday, he laughed at her. He told her she would never be a CEO because he had already lined up his successors."

"*The Boys of Broadcast* club?" Mak mused aloud, referencing the meeting they'd had with Lizzie after they got off the plane. "Not trying to exonerate Lizzie, but this was high school. Do people really hold grudges for decades? I mean, Lizzie's had a lot of success since then and she did it all without Selah's help up to this point."

"Jealousy and resentment can be a strong motivator," Peterson now broke in. "I've done some profiling with the FBI. Resentments that begin in childhood, such as abandonment of a friend in pursuit of success, if left untreated can snowball into a searing hatred. Add in a dismissive, successful father, who might not have spent a lot of time with her, and Lizzie's entire motivation might be to succeed as a form of revenge against the people who stood in her way or, at the very least, didn't support her."

"Yeah, I mean Sarah told Selah that one day Selah would regret not joining her venture. Fast-forward to the day Selah and Maddox went to the studio for the interview. It was the first time Selah had been in that studio or had seen Sarah in years. Stacia had booked the interview. Stacia told Selah that Sarah had really changed and convinced Selah that Sarah wanted to reconnect—let go of the past."

"Did they?" Mak asked.

"Selah didn't exactly say they became best friends again. But they were in a better place. Selah also told me her kidnapper, Elle, was the same girl who did Selah's makeup for *The Entertainment Today Show*."

"Did she tell you anything else about Elle or their experience with the kidnapping?" Mak asked.

"Yes, Selah said *The Fan* had told them there was someone else involved who she called *The Boss*. *The Boss* planned to let them go if Selah agreed to endorse products and if Maddox agreed to throw games—"

"As in losing them on purpose?" Mak gasped. "That's super illegal!"

"Yeah, sometimes people who do this don't *throw* games exactly, they give insider information like disclosing the ways the players are off—like injuries or sicknesses—you know, to help gamblers have an advantage when placing bets."

"Like insider trading?" Mak's mouth was hanging open. "You knew all this and you still let Selah leave?"

Stephen nodded miserably and shrugged a little. "With a bodyguard."

"We need to go. We can't leave Mrs. Lablanc here," Mak stated. They all nodded in agreement and got up to find Mrs. Lablanc.

"Mrs. Lablanc, I'm sorry, but I don't think you're safe here. You need to come with us to the station. At least until we arrange something more suitable."

"Again?" Mrs. Lablanc's eyes filled with sadness.

"Yes, and please text Stacia and Selah. I think they might still be in danger. We can send an officer over to them. But right now, we need to find Lizzie—Sarah—whatever she calls herself now."

"Before it's too late," Stephen whispered to himself, looking like a lost puppy.

Mak hoped he got it together before he made any more stupid, career-ending mistakes.

43

WILTON

After dropping Mrs. Lablanc off at the station, they picked up Chief Tigress. Tigress, Peterson, Mak, and Stephen were off in search of Sarah Elizabeth Taylor. They were heading to the most obvious place they knew to look—Lizzie's penthouse.

The ride there was quiet. They had already brought Tigress up to speed. There was a terse stillness. The air was charged with unused adrenaline. Stephen's mind was muddled in darkness.

This is all my fault, he thought. *Maybe it's time to turn in the badge.*

The quartet parked and walked quickly into the lobby of Lizzie Taylor's building. Henry, the big brute of an elevator attendant, stopped them before pushing the button. Stephen remembered that he also served as a bodyguard for Lizzie. He wore a black suit and eyed them all suspiciously.

"Hi, Henry," Stephen greeted him.

Henry stared at Stephen for half a minute. "Mr. Wilton, was it?"

"Twenty-fifth, penthouse suite to see Lizzie Taylor," Stephen requested.

The trio behind him waited while Henry eyed them all.

"I'm afraid Ms. Taylor doesn't want to be disturbed." The guard crossed his arms and placed his big, bulky body in front of the elevator.

"I'm afraid you don't get to tell us *no* today, Henry," Stephen stated.

Chief Tigress pulled out the arrest warrant and each officer wordlessly produced a badge. "Do I need to explain what this means?"

"No, sir." Henry pushed the button to open the elevator and the five of them got on.

When the elevator opened into Lizzie's penthouse, nothing looked amiss to them. The penthouse was as immaculate as the last time Stephen had been there.

"Sarah Elizabeth Taylor!" Mak called out in a loud voice.

There was no movement. Henry looked uncertain as he waited for direction from the officers.

"We'll take it from here," Stephen dismissed him.

The elevator doors closed, and the small group began looking around the penthouse. It was fancy but it wasn't big. Stephen turned toward the bedroom door, which was closed.

"Oh no!" Stephen groaned with a deep, guttural tone.

The other officers turned his direction. Someone gasped.

A thin river of blood was seeping out from under the door frame.

Stephen was the first to reach the door. He opened the door a crack but seemed to hit something before it swung all the way opened. He could see her shiny black curls matted with blood before he saw the rest of her body laid out on the floor.

"It's her. Someone call it in!" Stephen shouted, his voice panicked, his heart-rate doubling. He carefully wedged his body through the door and into the room. He knew the truth before he even checked her pulse.

Lizzie Taylor was dead.

She stared at him with unseeing eyes, a wide-eyed, glassy expression of shock frozen on her face. Blood pooled around her head like a dark halo. Her body was lying contorted as if she'd tried to run. But it had been too late. He didn't have to see the back of her head to know she had died from the result of a blunt force object.

Time froze as he stared at her. His heart broke and he felt tears in his eyes. He tried not to look at the bed behind him or to think about their night together. He was feeling all the same emotions now as he had that fateful night not so long ago when Carley died. His sorrow magnified everything. The darkness slammed into his chest.

Suddenly, he remembered that night. The night when he'd gotten to the scene too late. He could see Carley's face as she gasped her last breath. He would see her leaning against the wall, sitting on the floor as black blood poured out of her body. He could see her sightless eyes as the life left her. She'd died in his arms.

"Stephen!"

He heard his name, but it sounded hollow and distant. He couldn't tear his eyes from Lizzie's porcelain face.

"I'm sorry I didn't protect you," he whispered. Though Stephen didn't know who he was saying it to—Lizzie or Carley.

"Stephen?" Mak was suddenly there beside him, shaking him. Stephen wiped his eyes, snapping out of his trance, his training kicking in. He glanced slowly around the room without moving. This was a crime scene. He didn't want to contaminate it.

"There's broken glass on the floor." He pointed to the floor. "Right there by the dresser. She died of blunt force trauma."

Then Stephen left the room. He passed the other officers who were trying to get inside the bedroom.

The elevator door to the penthouse opened and Henry stepped into the room and stood in the corner. He had a clear view of the blood on the floor under the door. His hand covered his mouth, and his face was white.

Stephen approached him. "You really can't be in here. This is now a murder investigation—"

"I know who did this. I'm sorry. I wouldn't have let her up if I'd known."

"Her?" Stephen asked.

"Stacia Lablanc was here. She met Ms. Taylor for lunch here like she has hundreds of times before."

"Lizzie and Stacia are friends?" Stephen asked.

"Yes," he answered.

"Why lunch here?" Stephen asked. "Why not meet at a restaurant?"

"Because not only does Ms. Lablanc run a public relations firm, she's a chef. Cooking is her hobby and the way she relaxes. She got a culinary degree before she went to work for her sister. She'd often whip something up for lunch while she and Ms. Taylor discussed how they would take over the world." Henry smiled sadly as he thought about what must have been an inside joke.

"Take over the world?" Stephen smirked but the bodyguard had gone stoic.

"They wanted to control the media. Set the narrative. Tell the story they wanted the world to believe. I was rooting for them, you know," his eyes were sad. "They had big plans and I thought they'd accomplish a lot. They called themselves the *Manhattan Media Mavens*."

Stephen nearly choked remembering Lizzie's words from earlier.

They called themselves The Boys of Broadcast. Literally. I can't make this up.

"Were they the only two who belonged to this group?" Stephen asked, his pulse quickening. It made sense. Lizzie Taylor was the CEO of a broadcast network, Stacia Lablanc ran a public relations firm. But this sounded like a big goal for two women.

"No, Ms. Elle Jones was the third woman in the group. I haven't seen Elle for a while though."

Stephen gasped, his mind on overdrive. While Elle didn't appear to fit in the group, he surmised her job would have been to wrangle in the talent for marketing and endorsement purposes. "Do me a favor. Let's ride down to the lobby together. We'll need a formal statement from you." Stephen turned, nearly colliding with Mak.

Mak held a broken picture frame in her gloved hand with *Graduation 2009* carved into the bottom right corner. The picture inside the frame was of three very young women, most likely on a graduation trip. Stephen peered closely at the picture.

The three women were Sarah Elizabeth Taylor, Elle Jones, and Stacia Lablanc. Stacia was wearing a tank top with *NYC Culinary Institute* across her chest. Stephen stared at the picture as the mystery began to click into place. Stacia would have been a couple years older than the other two. Was there a reason no one seemed to know Stacia and Lizzie were friends in high school and had remained friends ever since? Had they kept their friendship a secret all this time?

"Mak, you need to hear Henry's story. We were just going down to the lobby. I'd like to get a recorded statement from him," Stephen told her.

The three went to the lobby and found a quiet corner where Henry could still keep track of the elevator and answer their questions. When Henry was done, they dismissed him with the request to stay available in case they needed him to testify later.

Mak shook her head. "We need to find Stacia Lablanc right now!"

"And we need to find Selah," Stephen added, pulling out his phone.

Mak lowered her voice. "When we find Selah, we'll likely find Stacia."

Stephen's heart rate tripled as he considered her words. He feared her prediction might be true, and he knew what Mak wasn't saying.

Would they find Selah alive this time?

Stephen knew if they didn't, he'd only have himself to blame. Just like he was to blame for Lizzie's death.

The lobby doors opened, and Henry pushed the elevator to the penthouse for several officers and a CSI team who'd filed in holding various evidence kits. A group of EMTs brought up the tail.

All those emergency workers would only confirm what Mak and Stephen already knew. Lizzie Taylor was dead due to blunt force trauma at the hand of Stacia Lablanc.

44

MAK

Mak's mind was moving faster than she was driving. Which wasn't surprising given the traffic. She and Stephen had left the other officers to process the crime scene.

"Where are we going?" Stephen finally broke the silence.

"We have to find Stacia Lablanc," Mak snapped.

"Woah!" Stephen said. "Should I assume that this is just another level of intensity for you or is there another reason you're trying to take my head off?"

"What was that back there, Stephen? In the room? It's like you weren't there. You were in the room, standing in front of the door opening. None of us could get in on account of—"

"Lizzie's body lying on the floor blocking the door."

"Right. I must have said your name like ten times. I even knocked on the door a few times before I reached through and shook you. You were just standing there staring at her."

"I don't know," Stephen said quietly. Which Mak decided meant that he really didn't want to talk about it.

Mak was quiet for a minute, feeling her frustration dissolve. "I heard what you said. You couldn't have protected her, you know. You couldn't have saved her. This isn't your fault."

"I'm always too late and it costs them their lives," Stephen said as he looked out the window. They were stuck in another New York traffic stand still.

"What? Is that really what you think?" Mak asked. She was trying to stay mad, but realization was dawning, and she could feel her heart thaw even further.

Stephen nodded.

"I think there might be more to it than that," Mak said with reluctance and maybe resignation, her voice softening.

"Please, do tell," Stephen's voice was sarcastic.

"I'm wondering if you're dealing with PTSD," Mak commented.

Stephen snorted. "I've been doing some variation of this job just as long as you have. I've seen dead bodies before."

"There are dead bodies. Then there are dead bodies of women you care about," Mak prodded.

"Are you adding to the list of reasons why you're planning to request a new partner when you get back? Because I'm perfectly capable of—"

"No, I'm actually sorry about that, Stephen. It's more my fault that we had to come back than it was yours. You tried to tell me something was off, and I didn't listen."

"Oh," Stephen looked surprised.

"Anyway, it's not about that," Mak went on. "Trust me here. I know what I'm talking about. I never told you why they placed me on a mandatory leave."

"Okay." Stephen crossed his arms across his chest, giving her his full attention.

"We were on a child kidnapping case. Booker and me, along with police, and a detective. We had located the child. We were there in the apartment hallway. We had someone with a view into the apartment and we were instructed to stand down. But I couldn't. All I can say is the mom in me took over. It took seven months of therapy for me to admit my perspective was compromised. My emotions took over. I ignored the stand-down orders and rushed in—"

"You rushed in? No way." There was a hint of a smile on Stephen's lips. "I would have done the same thing, you know."

"Well, the child was dead," Mak's voice broke, and tears clouded her vision. She pushed the tears away.

"Mak, that's awful. I'm sorry," Stephen could only think of his own child. He felt his gut tighten.

"We don't know one hundred percent if it was my fault or if the child had been dead for a while. The parents of the child refused to do an autopsy. They put the time of death close to the time I'd rushed in there. I was put on leave as a disciplinary action for disobeying orders. But mostly, they wanted me to work through my issues, so I didn't come back with PTSD. Freezing on a case can be just as bad as rushing in." Mak honked the horn as a car cut her off and almost slammed into them.

"Okay, I hear you. But if that was a PTSD reaction, you have no more worries. I don't know any other women in this state. I'm here with you. Present and accounted for," Stephen promised, trying to snap out of this persistent darkness.

"That's good, Wilton. Because we need to go take this bad guy down."

"Or, bad girl," Stephen corrected.

"Right. But where do we start? If we show up at her office and she's gone, Emily will tip her off."

"Right," Stephen looked at his phone. "FBI and MCPD are requesting we meet them back at the station."

"Okay," Mak said as she made a last-minute lane change which was awarded with some angry honks and hand gestures. Minutes later, they swung into the MCPD parking garage. "Maybe we can take a look through the case files while we're at it. It feels like something is missing."

"Oh we're missing lots of somethings," Stephen said with frustration. "I've never felt more behind on a case before."

45

SELAH

"Stacia?" Selah asked. "What are you doing here?"

Selah was wearing a pair of Prada five-pocket denim jeans with black ankle boot high heels. She wore a tight-fitted white turtleneck with a Kansas City jacket over it. Her blonde hair was pulled up in a ponytail and her signature red lipstick was perfectly in place.

The seats on the jet were off-white leather and some of the most comfortable Selah had ever sat on. It wasn't the biggest jet on the market, but Selah loved the cozy relaxation she experienced in the air. Not to mention, it was reliable. Selah had just been settling in for takeoff and was getting comfortable when Stacia had walked onto the jet. Selah stood, feeling confused, looking into her sister's eyes.

"Hey, Tim," Stacia greeted Selah's bodyguard. "Thanks for all your help, you can go now."

Tim, the bodyguard Stacia had appointed for Selah, nodded and made his way off the plane.

"What the heck?" Selah asked, watching her bodyguard leave. "I need him to escort me to the game."

"You aren't going to the game, Selah," Stacia announced.

"What are you talking about?" Selah laughed. "I am, but you aren't."

"Yeah," Stacia drew out the word, yawned, and stretched in one cat-like motion. "There's been a change of plans."

Selah wasn't laughing anymore. "Cut it out, Stacia, this has been on the books since I got back. You know Maddox and I are trying to make this work. I'm going to the game to support him. And you can't stop me."

"Wanna bet?" Stacia smiled with that cold, calculated movement of her face where her lips curled up but her smile never quite reached her eyes.

"Stacia, what have you done?" Selah whispered with fear in her heart. She felt the energy in the room shift. She suddenly felt afraid of her sister.

"Have a seat, Selah. There's no need for your tantrums and fits this time. Save your energy. You're going to need it." Stacia handed Selah a cup of water as Selah sat back down obediently.

Selah hated it when Stacia got this way. No matter what Selah tried to do, Stacia would always win. Selah had learned to placate her sister and go along with as many of her plans as possible. Selah downed the water, acknowledging to herself that she did feel dehydrated and drinking more water was good for the baby.

"Okay Stacia, the joke's up. We need to leave now or the schedule's going to shift. I'll be late."

"Like I said, you're not going to the game."

"Then where are we going?" Selah switched her tactic.

"We, dear sister, are going to England." Stacia stood with a triumphant smile on her face.

"What?" Selah tried to stand, but Stacia gently put a hand on her shoulder and pushed her back down.

"You might as well get comfortable. This plane is about to leave and there's nothing you can do to stop it."

"Why are you doing this?" Selah asked meekly.

"Simple," Stacia's grin looked evil now. "You are my ticket to freedom. You always have been. I just didn't realize I was going to need you so quickly."

"What are you talking about Stacia? You're not making any sense. You've been a big part of my success since high school. I probably wouldn't be at this point in my career if it weren't for you. But sometimes, you're a lot. You have all the freedom you want. You make great money. You have a fun life. Now, give *me* some freedom and let me go."

"I can't do that, Selah. It's my time to shine." Stacia smiled meanly.

"This game is on the schedule. It's cleared and approved. Stop messing around or I'll miss it!" Selah felt whiney now like she was ten and pleading with her older sister to let her have her cookie.

"We're going to England. Together," Stacia repeated.

"But why?" Selah asked.

"Because after today, I won't be welcomed back into the US as a free woman," Stacia said.

Stacia was talking in code with words that made no sense to Selah.

"Are you kidnapping me? You won't get away with this, Stacia. When I don't show up to the game, someone will find me. They always do." Selah yawned and blinked a little. Her eyes got heavy.

"Oh, I'm counting on them finding us. When they do, I'll finally be able to get rid of them." Stacia walked behind Selah and put her hands on Selah's shoulders.

Selah groaned. Her eyelids shut. "Why do I feel so sleepy?"

"Because I drugged you. That's right, Selah. Take a little nap and before you know it, we will be in England. Home free."

Selah's life was now resting in her sister's hands.

46

WILTON

"Someone's made themselves cozy," Tigress stated with attitude while walking into the conference room. Peterson followed behind Tigress.

Both Mak and Stephen had the files open and spread out in front of them and were busy getting up to speed on the CEO serial killer case. Stephen was leaned back in his chair, his feet on the table, reading an autopsy report from the most recent murder victim, Trevor Kaites. Stephen ignored Tigress.

"This indicates Kaites died of complications due to diabetes," Stephen took his feet down and put the autopsy report on the table in front of him and tapped on the line that said *Cause of Death*.

"That's weird," Mak said. "The autopsy for Roger Clamentine says the cause of death was a heart attack."

"And Jim Tallbott died of a stroke." Stephen looked up at Tigress and Peterson. "How in the world did you figure out these guys weren't dying of natural causes and they were actually being murdered?"

The room went silent. Peterson looked uncomfortable. Tigress swung his gaze to Peterson.

Peterson sighed and leaned over to close the conference room door. Then he turned his attention to Mak and Stephen. "That's a good question and a long story. The short of it is we had been tracking Jim Tallbott for a while. He had some shady dealings happening. Then we stumbled upon the name *The Boys of Broadcast*—"

"Lizzie Taylor's dad started that group when they were all in college. She was under the impression it was just a white, male privilege group designed to exclude her and any other women." Stephen sat up, giving Peterson his full attention.

"It was far more than that," Peterson continued. "And thanks to the handwritten note you found at Lizzie's place, we now know all the members and can broaden our search for illegal activity. So, thank you for that," Peterson said. "The illegal activity is part of a bigger, ongoing investigation. Each time I identified a new member in this group of criminal activity, they would turn up dead. It seemed too coincidental. As you know, we partnered with the MCPD to try to head off the next victim."

That's working well for you, Stephen thought sarcastically while thinking of Trevor Kaites, but he kept his mouth shut. He had to remind himself that turning over the note earlier also might have saved Trevor's life.

"So, you established a pattern of CEOs who had been in this good ole boy society, a male privilege club, who were doing illegal things and then dying. These are old guys with health issues. How do you know they aren't just dying of natural causes?" Mak asked.

"The timing," Peterson answered. "They all died within a short period of time from each other."

"And now Lizzie is dead," Stephen asserted.

"We're talking about a serial killer. Lizzie doesn't fit the pattern. Lizzie was killed by blunt force trauma. Her death was unplanned. It was a crime of passion in the moment by a desperate person who simply reacted. She's a young female. She was not connected to these illegal activities and didn't die of natural causes," Peterson stated.

"So you are going off a hunch? A working theory that these men are connected and therefore were murdered instead of dying of natural causes?" Mak looked surprised. "Are you trying to fit a theory into the circumstances?"

"These are bad men, Mak," Peterson defended himself. "Insider trading, racketeering, blackmail—"

"Then they should have been in jail, not out in the open where they could be targets of potential enemies," Stephen stated.

"Again, we had a name—*The Boys of Broadcast*—but we didn't have names and addresses. Each time we uncovered one of the men, he turned up dead."

"You know, *The Boys of Broadcast* sounds awfully familiar to another group we uncovered, Stephen," Mak said smugly.

"Sure does," Stephen said as if he was about to reveal the secrets of the universe. "It sounds like a group called the *Manhattan Media Mavens*—"

"I can tell you two think you're about to solve the crime of the century. So, go ahead," Tigress mocked. "Impress us."

Mak and Stephen exchanged a look.

"Stacia Lablanc is behind the whole thing—the kidnapping, the CEO murders, and Lizzie Taylor's murder. Maybe even Elle's murder," Mak stated. "She didn't do it all alone, but now she's the only one left. And the more time we spend in here, the more chance we have of losing her."

"Where's your evidence?" Tigress argued. "We can't get an arrest warrant to go get her based on *your* hunches. I hope you're wrong because if you're right and it's Stacia, she's probably with her sister, Selah, as we speak."

Mak's eyes bulged at the possibility.

"Wait, wait, wait," Stephen said. "We do have some

evidence. Mak found a broken picture frame with Stacia Lablanc, Lizzie Taylor, and Elle Jones in high school partying together in Mexico. Two out of three of them are dead. Who does that leave?"

"It's not enough," Peterson warned.

"Okay, how about this? We have a recorded testimony of Henry, the bodyguard in Lizzie's apartment—"

"Some bodyguard," Tigress quipped.

Peterson shot him a warning glance.

"Anyway, Henry sees who visits Lizzie's apartment. Henry told us Stacia Lablanc was the last person up to that apartment before we found Lizzie dead. He said he let her up because they meet there for lunch frequently. It turns out Stacia has a culinary degree and would whip something up for lunch often."

"Yeah, that's incriminating," Peterson admitted with a nod. "It puts her in the apartment at the time of death."

"Also, we grabbed Lizzie's calendar when we went back to her office earlier. She keeps a paper calendar, if you can believe it. If we can confirm that Lizzie met with each man in her apartment and Stacia made them dinner, we can connect Stacia to the murder of each man."

"How does making a man dinner connect her to murder?" Tigress asked with cynicism.

"Because each of these autopsy reports have one thing in common," Mak said as she gathered them all from the files placed on the table. "High levels of sodium found in their blood."

"Which means...?" Tigress still looked skeptical but seemed more interested now.

"Sodium nitrite poisoning. The reason I know about this is there's a rise of sodium nitrite suicides in our area. We had a case last year where I learned a lot about it. There's a lethal amount of sodium nitrate—2.6 grams—that when consumed, causes death. It's rare to consume that much on accident. It's an odorless powder," Mak educated.

"How would one consume that much unless it was on purpose?" Peterson asked.

"It could easily be dissolved into a salty alcoholic drink," Mak said.

"Go on," Tigress nodded to the report in front of Mak.

"Each man had high traces of sodium nitrite in his blood stream. Too high. They didn't die of heart attack, stroke, or diabetes. They died of sodium nitrite poisoning within twelve hours of when they would have had dinner. Lizzie admitted to Stephen and me that she'd kept the fact that they'd had dinner with her from the police when they'd interviewed her initially because she knew it looked bad that each man died shortly after having dinner with her," Mak finished with a smug smile.

"If you really listen to people, sometimes they will accidentally admit guilt. Maybe Lizzie was thinking about confessing their crimes," Stephen said.

"Only the person who was involved in the murders—Stacia Lablanc—didn't want her to go to the police so she took Lizzie out of the picture," Mak finished. "Is that enough for a warrant?"

"Yes, but there's still no time!" Tigress said. His voice now sounded urgent. "We'll bring her in for questioning. That's the only way we can get her legally. For now. I can get the warrant started, but we need to find her immediately."

"How do you propose we do that?" Mak asked. "Stephen and I almost went to her office, but if she's not there, Emily, her assistant, will likely tip her off that we're looking for her."

"Divide and conquer," Tigress answered. "We'll all split up. I'll go to Stacia's office. Peterson, you head to Stacia's home. Mak and Stephen, you go to Selah's jet just in case Stacia's trying to make a get-away."

Tigress held up one finger and left the room for a few

minutes. He came back with a copy of Stacia Lablanc's information, including her vehicle on file, a picture of her driver's license, and her home address.

Tigress told Peterson the name and address of the building where Peterson could find Stacia's office.

Peterson nodded and left the room.

"I'll go get that warrant started." Tigress left the room.

Mak and Stephen stared at each other.

"I don't know where Selah keeps her jet, do you?" Mak asked. Then she smirked. "Never thought I'd hear those words come out of my mouth."

"I remember seeing it in the file we were working from the kidnapping case." Stephen picked up his phone and dialed Deputy Director Sikes. He quickly caught Sikes up to speed and asked for the information. Stephen wrote the address down and hung up the phone.

"Got it, let's go." Mak picked up the post-it note.

They raced out the door together. Every minute from here until they found the murderer would be crucial. Stephen just hoped it wouldn't be too late.

47

WILTON

The traffic in New York was practically at a standstill when they headed out. Stephen could see Mak getting more and more agitated as time ticked by. He could recognize the signs because he felt the same way. He rubbed the back of his neck feeling sure it was beet red right now.

Newark Liberty International Airport, the place where Selah stowed her jet, was already a forty-minute drive. One could get away with a lot of things in forty minutes. Things like murder. This was a time when they could really use some police sirens.

Finally, after a forty-minute drive became fifty minutes, driven in tense, near-silence, they arrived. Stephen had called ahead and had airport security explain exactly where Selah kept her plane. Due to staffing issues, there wasn't an officer available to go to the plane, but they were able to get air control to agree not to approve a takeoff before they arrived.

Using the directions security had given them, Mak and Stephen pulled right up to the private runway where the jet sat. The jet had pink words stenciled on the side, *Pretty in Pink*, named after Selah's upcoming tour. Stephen was surprised to see the ladder to the jet was still touching the ground.

"Requesting backup," Mak announced over comms. "Stacia's vehicle is at the airport."

"Don't let them take off," Tigress commanded. "I'm on my way."

She rolled her eyes. "Ya think?" Mak smarted back on comms. "You'll be able to hear everything that goes down."

Stephen pulled out his phone. He hit *Record*. It was an old trick that had never failed him.

The day had turned cold and gray. They got out of their car. Stephen pulled his gun. Mak did the same. They made their way to the stair ladder.

Why was this so easy? Stephen wondered. *Why was the ladder still down?*

Stephen and Mak walked up the stairs cautiously. The stairs were a little steeper than they looked so Stephen had to look down to keep his footing. It had started to spit rain. He watched patters of rain hit the steps as he climbed. They had called ahead to stall the plane from take-off, but Stephen wondered if it was the pilot who'd left the ladder down for them. The door to the jet was even open.

The warmth of the plane rushed over Stephen as he boarded. His feet sunk into the soft, lush carpeting on the floor. He could see overstuffed, off-white leather chairs around the plane that looked equally comfortable and a matching couch with fluffy pillows all over it. There were two solid wood tables bolted to the floor. There was a smell that reminded him of fresh-baked cookies with a hint of cinnamon.

Relief filled him as he immediately spotted the tall blonde. She was standing with her back to the door, looking out the window. Straight blonde hair hit her shoulders. She was wearing a black sweater and dark blue jeans with a pair of black Doc Martins on her feet.

"Oh, Selah, what a relief! You're okay!" Stephen breathed as he entered the plane.

"Wow, this is nice!" Mak exclaimed coming in right after Stephen, talking over his comment. Her eyes roamed the open lobby area. "This is big enough for a party of fifteen to come hang out."

"Selah?" The woman at the window turned to answer Stephen with anger flashing in her eyes. "Don't ever call me that again." The woman who turned to face Stephen was not Selah. Stacia Lablanc was a dead ringer for her sister. In fact, Stephen had to wonder if they'd ever traded places on occasion due to double-booked events or to trick paparazzi.

"US Marshals Wilton and Cunningham. Stacia Lablanc, you are under arrest for the murder of Sarah Elizabeth Taylor and possibly Elle Jones. Put your hands up," Stephen said in an authoritative voice with his gun pointed at Stacia.

Possibly? Mak mouthed to Stephen with a raised eyebrow.

To their surprise, Stacia started laughing. "You're too late," she said triumphantly. She swung around a high-backed swivel chair to reveal an unconscious Selah.

"Oh gawd! Is she dead?" Mak moaned. "Stacia, did you kill your own sister?"

That's when Stephen saw it. The glint of metal. The sharp point of destruction.

"No, but I will kill her if you come any closer. Lower your weapons." Stacia swiftly put the knife she was holding to Selah's throat.

Stephen weighed his options. He thought about the 'guns at a knife fight' saying and sighed. If Stacia really wanted to hurt Selah, she could. With the simple flick of her wrist. *If I could just edge closer to her without her noticing.* He just hoped Mak could keep her talking.

"Whatever you've done, we can help you. Just come clean." Mak's voice was soft and pleading in a tone Stephen had never heard before. He might even call it a nurturing mom voice.

Stacia laughed again. This time it was a short bark. "You

sound just like Lizzie." Stacia's voice went up an octave as she mocked her former, now dead friend in a high-pitched voice. *"It's over Stacia. I can't do this anymore. They're on to us and we need to come clean."*

"Is that what Lizzie said to you? Is that why you killed her?" Mak asked.

Stacia shrugged. Then she looked sad for a minute. "I actually didn't mean for that to happen. I just got so angry, you know? We'd been working on this plan for so long—we had steps, like a business plan. We were so close," Stacia's voice came out in a wail. "It was finally all happening. At the exact moment when it was coming together, Lizzie wanted to bail on me and leave me holding the bag. Well, this was *her* plan. It had always been *her* plan. At first, I thought it was a crazy one, too. But then it started to make sense, you know? We had some bumps along the way. Selah here wouldn't go along with us. We needed her. She was the marketing piece. Do you know how powerful influencers are? Her endorsements would have been everything. It would have been the missing piece!"

"Is that why you kidnapped Selah?" Mak asked. "Was it for revenge or was it to get her to do what you wanted her to do?"

"Both," Stacia sneered.

"So, Selah knew your plan and refused?" Stephen asked.

Stacia barked a bitter laugh. "We knew better than to trust my stupid little sister with our *whole* plan. Besides, we were just in high school back then. We didn't have the details in place. We had a vision. Strong, powerful women who would never be passed over again."

"That's what you were? Passed over?" Mak asked.

"Hell, yes. I'd always been passed over. For her," Stacia pressed the knife to Selah's throat.

Stephen held his breath.

"We never told Selah so much that it was necessary to take her out of the picture. If she refused to help us voluntarily, we'd make her. We figured out a different way that she could help us out. But it all really came together when she started seeing an NFL football player. That was like icing on the cake. Can you imagine? Fixing games, along with sales endorsements, would have put us and our newly-bought networks in the gold. We were this close," Stacia's fingers pulled apart an inch. "We would have gotten away with it, too."

Stephen was a little shocked by the arrogance in Stacia's words. There was no way this plan would ever have worked. Did the three of them—smart, powerful, talented women— really think the only way to succeed was to kill, control, and manipulate by way of the entertainment industry?

"How would the plan work exactly?" Mak asked.

Stephen wondered if Mak was stalling until backup arrived.

"Lizzie, Elle, and I would each own a network. Well, Lizzie would own them, and we would be partners running them for her. We would grow them in our way. A new, modern way to capture American entertainment. Bring everyone into this century."

"What does that mean?" Mak asked.

"The men who own the majority shares of those other networks were over sixty. They were the epitome of the patri-archy. Times have changed. It's time to let women shine. Cut out the dinosaurs—the old, white men. Hire a staff of millen-nials and Gen Z. We had so many plans!" Stacia wailed as the reminiscent smile fell from her face.

"Stacia, those aren't terrible goals," Mak said. "But your execution of them was."

"Tell us about the plan to take over the networks. Was it always intended to be a hostile takeover?" Stephen asked.

"Well, no. Lizzie offered a helluva good deal to buy them out. They refused. They laughed at her. At first, we only needed two more networks. But they were so rude! They said things like *she'd never live up to the legacy her dad had left*. They called her *an idealistic little girl*, that kind of thing."

"I'm confused," Stephen said. *Just keep her talking...* "Don't networks have boards? You can't just take it over, right? They would have to vote you in. Didn't you think this was all rather ambitious?"

Stacia was already shaking her head. "Remember these guys were ancient. They owned the majority share of the companies to the tune of fifty percent. It was in *The Boys of Broadcast* contract. If any of them sold, it would have to be to a relative of someone in the group."

"You thought you'd invite them to dinner and get them to sell their share to you?" Mak asked. "But they didn't?"

"They made the biggest mistakes of their lives." Stacia smiled meanly.

"What mistake was that?" Stephen asked.

"They underestimated Lizzie." Stacia shook her head and snapped. "No! They underestimated me!"

"And it cost them their lives?" Stephen asked.

Stacia waved her hand like she was dismissing that.

"Wait, Stacia. Don't downplay that. That was the most brilliant part of your plan. Did you come up with it?" Mak's voice held awe. "You went to culinary school, right? You knew how to salt the food just right to spike the sodium of men who already had heart and blood pressure issues. You made it look like an accident."

"Well, that's not the reason I went to culinary school. Cooking is my passion and I'm good at it. It's like a weird little hobby no one knows I have." Then Stacia bowed a little and smirked. "But yeah, that was me. Only, regular seasoning wouldn't have been enough. No one noticed when their Bloody Mary's got a little saltier." Stacia smiled smugly. "Mom thought I wouldn't amount to much. She thought Selah would have all the success. Well, I was on my way!"

"Until Lizzie tried to stop you?" Stephen asked. A faint warning bell went off in his head. *Why is she admitting all of this so freely?* he thought as his eyes flitted to the open airplane door and back. Then he knew. *She's not planning to let us live. Any of us.*

"And Elle. Elle was stupid. Her job was to find 'star power' to lend influence to our venture. Only, she wasn't any good at it. She had resorted to kidnapping. She had already gotten caught before. She was about to get caught again. I had to serve her up Selah and Maddox—"

"What do you mean *serve her up?*" Mak asked. "You told Elle where they would be and had her in position for the right time to kidnap them?"

"Yep!" Stacia smiled now. "But Elle got nervous and irresponsible. Not to mention, she'd broken the code by bringing her stupid, loud-mouthed cousin in to help. Said she couldn't physically move an NFL player by herself."

"So, you killed Elle—"

"I didn't kill her." Stacia wagged her finger.

"But you had someone do it for you," Mak stated.

"Had someone do it," Stacia confirmed.

"Killed Lizzie—"

"Lizzie's death was a mistake," Stacia corrected sadly.

"Killed Roger Clamentine, Jim Tallbott, Tony Statten, and Trevor Kaites, all CEOs of major broadcasting networks."

"That was natural causes, sodium overload, old age, loneliness—whatever you wanna believe there," Stacia made her eyes wide with feigned innocence.

"But the intention was to kill them so you could take over their networks," Mak said conversationally.

Stephen had taken advantage of each time Mak posed a question by inching his way closer to Stacia.

Stacia shrugged impishly.

"Yes, but you said you only needed two more networks to run," Mak was definitely stalling.

Any minute, Stephen feared, *those doors will shut. After that, they'd have a hard time taking control of the situation.*

Stacia shrugged. "We got excited. Lizzie thought she could run them all. And she could have. With our help. We would have been unstoppable."

Stephen was close enough now. He hit Stacia's arm with a karate chop on the inside of the elbow that was holding the knife, which caused her elbow to bend and the knife to go flying.

Selah's eyes fluttered open.

Stephen put his gun against Stacia's arm.

"Stacia Lablanc, you are under arrest for the murder of Elle Jones, Sarah Elizabeth Taylor, Roger Clamentine, Tony Statten, Jim Tallbott, and Trevor Kaites."

Selah let out a surprised squeak. "Stace, what's he talking about?"

"Shut up and drop the sweet and innocent act," Stacia hissed. "Grow up!"

"Don't worry, Selah. You're safe now," Mak said. "Your sister is going away for a long time. She can't torture you anymore."

Tigress walked through the door of the jet with his gun drawn.

"It's okay, we got things under control," Mak greeted.

"Drop your weapons," Tigress snapped.

"She already did," Stephen grinned with relief.

"Glad you could make it," Mak quipped sarcastically.

"We're all on, please shut the door," Tigress called loudly to someone unknown.

Mak whipped around in surprise.

There was an airline pilot in the cockpit. Had he been there the whole time? Had Stacia paid him to go along with her scheme?

The door shut to close them all on the jet.

Mak felt panic set in.

Tigress walked right up to Stacia, who was still standing beside Selah. He pointed his gun at Selah's head. The cool metal of his Glock touched Selah's temple.

Selah gasped and let out another squeak.

"I said drop your weapons," Tigress repeated, clearly addressing Mak and Stephen.

Shock registered in Stephen's brain for a second before he dropped his gun.

Mak dropped her gun beside Stephen.

"Kick them away," Tigress commanded.

Mak and Stephen obeyed.

"You okay, baby?" Tigress asked as he gave Stacia a quick kiss, his eyes still trained on Mak and Wilton.

"I am now. I had to tell them my whole life story just to stall long enough..." Stacia seemed to sag with relief. "What took you so long?"

"You weren't with Lizzie. You were with Stacia?" Mak stated the obvious conclusion as it played out. How had her intuition been so wrong?

"Okay, don't say another word, baby. We're gonna get you off this continent."

"Over my dead body," Stephen said, launching himself at Tigress.

Mak's mouth dropped open as she watched Stephen. It was his turn to be the incredibly impulsive partner for once.

Startled, Tigress swung the gun, and a loud shot rang through the small space, rendering them all temporarily deaf.

Stephen crumpled mid-air and hit the floor with a groan.

48

MAK

Stephen's moment of sheer stupidity was all the distraction Mak needed. She jumped between Tigress and Selah.

"Selah, get out of here!" Mak yelled.

Selah got up and ran for cover. They heard the bathroom door open and lock behind her.

Mak threw a roundhouse kick at Tigress. Her foot connected with his hand. His gun went flying. It had landed toward the back of the plane. Tigress was caught off balance and his solid, muscular body knocked into Stacia, sending her flying. Stacia landed on her bottom and smacked the back of her head on the corner of a table. She passed out. The back of her head dripped blood on the floor, ruining the posh carpet.

"Don't move!" Mak shouted when she was back on both feet.

"Hey, what the hell is happening right now?" Peterson's voice came over comms. He sounded bewildered and out of breath.

"Peterson, you're alive," Mak said, feeling relieved. "Did you get that confession?"

"Yes, are you all still alive?" Peterson asked.

Mak's eyes flew to Wilton who hadn't gotten up yet. She didn't answer Peterson. Her stomach twisted. She turned back to Tigress. Hands in fists, Tigress was squaring off. Mak jumped into a boxer's stance, pulling her fist up to protect her face as she bounced on her toes into a split stance.

"You didn't kill Peterson?" Mak asked, relief flooding through her body. She swung a jab at Tigress who weaved under it.

Tigress grinned pure evil as he jabbed back. "Didn't have time. Sent him to JFK airport."

Mak jumped back but then quickly sprang two steps closer to Tigress, connecting a hook to his jaw. Taking advantage of catching him off guard, she followed it up with an uppercut to his chin.

Tigress doubled over and Mak took the moment to go for the guns she and Wilton had kicked away. She put one gun in her holster and swung around in time to catch Tigress getting up, trying to catch his breath.

Gun trained on Tigress, Mak walked to Wilton, bent over, and felt for his pulse. She let out a sigh of relief. His pulse felt strong. But she didn't think they were safe yet.

Mak straightened and kept the gun trained on Tigress. She rattled off the actual address of the airfield for Peterson. "Our boy Tigress is in bed with Stacia Lablanc. He tried to take over the plane, but I'm holding him at bay. Wilton is down. Could use your help here, sir."

"On my way," Peterson said.

Mak took out her handcuffs and threw them to Tigress. "Put them on. No funny business."

Tigress surprised her by doing exactly what she asked.

Mak bent and found the handcuffs Stephen was carrying in his back pocket. She yanked them out and walked over to Stacia, whose eyelids had started to flutter. Mak tugged Stacia up. She sat Stacia in a seat as far from Tigress as possible, gently pulled

Stacia's arms behind her back, and cuffed her to the chair. Then Mak went in search of something to stop Stacia's head from bleeding. She found a dishtowel in a cabinet and applied pressure to the back of Stacia's head.

Mak cited the Miranda rights to both Tigress and Stacia.

Selah peeked out from her bathroom hiding place. "Is it safe?"

Mak put her hand up to motion that she stay back.

Selah didn't listen. Once in view of her sister, her lip quivered. Tears sprung to her eyes. She came to stand in front of the now alert Stacia Lablanc.

"How could you do this?" Selah asked Stacia, her bottom lip trembling.

Stacia rolled her eyes and turned away. "I'm not saying another thing without a lawyer."

"Oh, that won't help you now, Stacia," Mak said cordially. "We have your confession. You and Tigress are through. You might as well answer her question."

Stacia turned angry eyes to Tigress. "This is your fault!" she screamed. "You said you'd take care of them. I didn't think what I said would matter."

There was a tense staring match between Stacia and Tigress. Finally, Stacia swung her gaze to Selah.

"Do you really hate me that much, Stacia?" Selah asked. Tears dropped down her face.

"Look at you right now," Stacia snapped. "You're weak. You're pathetic. Always the good girl. The *mommy-look-at-me* girl. Well, some of us aren't as lucky as you. Some of us have real skills and just need to be given the opportunity to use them."

"But you hated Sarah growing up," Selah crossed her arms and leaned against the hallway wall.

Stephen groaned.

Mak dropped the towel on the floor and flew to his side.

"Are you okay?" Mak asked. She could hear Stacia snarking

meanly at her sister. She cared less now that Stacia was in hand-cuffs. She focused on her partner.

"I did until one thing bonded us," Mak could hear the bitter-ness lining Stacia's toxic words. "Senior year, after your big fall out. After you broke your word and abandoned her. We hated *you* more than we hated each other."

Stephen patted his stomach. "Took the wind out of me but that's all." He opened his shirt to reveal a bulletproof vest. The bullet was lodged right where his sternum was.

"Thank God!" Mak exclaimed. She could hear sirens in the distance.

"Two minutes out," Peterson's voice assured her on comms.

"Boy, was I glad to see you when I opened my eyes. You were the first person I wanted to see alive on this plane," Stephen admitted with a smile.

"Careful, Wilton. You might actually develop a healthy, platonic friendship with a female. That would really change your world."

"Admit it, you're happy to see me, too," he grinned.

"I'm happy you're alive," Mak told him with sincerity.

"Let's get off this plane," Stephen said as he pushed into a seated position.

"I couldn't agree more, partner."

49

WILTON

Anna's karate tournament had been a huge success. Anna had performed her katas perfectly. Stephen had to admit he was impressed by Anna's blocks, kicks, and elbows. Everything seemed precise and her skill-level at her age was inspiring.

As Stephen watched her, he felt a sense of pride. Then another emotion stirred and overpowered him. He was confused. Why did Anna complain about this so much when she was clearly a natural?

Stephen also noticed out of the corner of his eye how Paige and her husband, James, juggled twin newborns. As usual, when he was around them, he pictured himself juggling twin babies with his daughter's mom. He'd lived with Anna and Carley for a year while raising Anna. One toddler had been a handful for him. Or maybe that was just a strong-willed toddler like Anna.

During that time, Paige had been placed in protective custody. Without Carley, he didn't know what he would have done. Despite all Carley's best defenses, he fell for her. That year was the closest Stephen had come to feeling like he had found his happily ever after.

I just picked the wrong girl. Stephen sat up straighter as he continued watching Anna's performance. But his mind was wandering. That was it. Maybe there was nothing wrong with him. It was okay to want a wife and children. He just needed to pick the right girl.

"Stephen, you okay over there?" Paige whispered. She had a baby on her lap and was swiping snack crumbs from the stadium bench. James was on her other side performing the same actions with a baby on his lap.

"Yeah, actually," Stephen said, snapping out of his inner thoughts. He stretched a bit. "Do you care if I take Anna out to ice cream after this? Just the two of us? Karate was my idea and I just want her to know how proud of her I am."

"Of course," Paige said, her eyes on the end of the ceremony where they were handing out belts.

Stephen positioned his phone camera and snapped a picture. Then he recorded a video of them awarding Anna her yellow belt.

As the ceremony came to an end, Stephen's phone buzzed. He glanced at the screen.

Mak: *Hey, are you going tonight?*

Stephen sighed. In truth, he was exhausted. The office was having some party tonight. Stephen hadn't stuck around long enough to find out what it was about.

He had to immediately get in his car and drive after the plane landed in order to make it to Anna's tournament in time. He'd barely made it. That kind of stress wore him out. He hadn't considered that the hard, taxing case they'd just closed might be lending to the wear down.

But during his long drive, his mind kept returning to Alyah. She'd remained silent all this time. He wondered how she would respond when they saw each other again.

Stephen scooped up his daughter and put her on his shoulders when he saw her.

"I got my yellow belt, daddy!" she squealed.

"I know! I saw every minute of it!" Stephen beamed. "I'm so proud of you!"

Paige and James echoed the sentiments.

Stephen was really comforted knowing that if Demitri Abbott found Anna one day, maybe she'd be able to defend herself. He hoped Anna would be fully trained if that happened.

They went out the door and Stephen took Anna to his car.

"Where are we going?" Anna asked.

"I'm taking you for ice cream!" Stephen announced.

"Yay!" Anna yelled.

Paige came over with Anna's booster seat. "Don't keep her too long, Stephen. She has school tomorrow."

"Don't worry," Stephen said as he watched Anna jump in his car and buckle up. "I have to be back at the office for some big thing they're having."

Paige clicked her tongue. "Always working."

"That's where I'm at my best," Stephen responded.

"I know," Paige kissed him lightly on the cheek.

There was a time when that would have tripled his heart rate. Now, Stephen just felt a sad resignation. The better man had won. He looked up and gave a wave to James who was just getting behind the wheel of their SUV.

Stephen got in the car. "Ready for ice cream?"

"Yeah!" Anna yelled with her hands raised.

"What are you gonna get?" Stephen asked as he navigated out of the parking lot.

"Orange, chocolate, and mint!" Anna said.

"Ew, gross!" Stephen smiled at his funny little child. That was one thing he could praise her mother on. She sure did allow Anna to just be who she was.

"It's not gross, daddy," Anna said. "Orange, good. Chocolate, good. Mint, good."

"But mash 'em altogether? No good!" Stephen groaned.

"You'll see. You'll like it if you try it," Anna said in a sing-song voice.

And he did. And he was right. The combination was no good. But, to Anna's credit, she ate every last drop of it.

It was harder than usual to say good-bye to his precocious daughter. He knew he was going to have to try to see her more often.

But as he fielded yet another text from Mak pleading for him be at the party tonight, he wondered how he would be able to balance home and work life.

50

WILTON

Stephen thought an office party on a Thursday night was overkill. But he knew the evenings weren't sacred in this business. He hadn't been required to come back for the party. But the truth is, Stephen was so comfortable with the people he worked with, he had to admit they were his only real friends. He'd been so busy trying to get to Anna's event, he hadn't stopped to ask what the party was for.

It turns out, it was a celebration for him and Mak. They were the new office heroes having cracked a case that had become an even bigger case, and they had solved the whole thing. There was a banner. There was cake. There was beer.

There was Alyah.

She stood in the corner of the room talking to Mak, looking beautiful in her casual, tight blue jeans, low-cut red cami that clung to her curves, and long-sleeved sweater jacket that hung open. Even the matching suede red high heels on her ankle boots did nothing to boost her short frame.

Stephen's heart beat fast as he remembered the last time he'd seen her. It was after Mak had teased him about Lizzie. He'd turned to see Alyah standing there with wide eyes, alarm evident. She'd clearly overheard what they'd said and had left the office abruptly. He'd followed her but hadn't found her. He'd shown up for dinner at her house, but she hadn't opened the door.

Then he'd gone out on assignment. Alyah hadn't answered or returned any of his phone calls or texts while he'd been gone. He'd finally given up trying.

As if she felt him staring, Alyah looked up and locked eyes with him. Stephen moved forward slowly as if she was a deer and he was afraid to spook her.

Someone clinked glasses and Alyah's eyes broke contact with his and dragged to Deputy Director Rob Sikes, who was calling for a toast. No, he had an announcement.

Reluctantly, Stephen turned and gave Sikes his attention.

"First of all, great job to our two newest partners, Mak and Wilton!"

The office erupted into clapping and cheers.

"To be honest," Rob admitted as the room settled. "I didn't know if they would kill each other or work well together—"

"We didn't know either!" Mak shouted in high spirits.

The room erupted in laughter.

"But with the good comes the bad. That's how the universe stays balanced after all. I have a sad announcement to make. Our District Attorney, Alyah Smith, will be leaving us. She has accepted a position in Washington, DC, and will be leaving effective immediately."

This was met with *boos*.

Stephen's eyes flew to Alyah. Her eyes were on his. Though there was a smile plastered on her face, there was a sadness in her eyes. A swarm of people mobbed her, and Stephen slipped out the door.

He sat in his car in the parking lot next to her car. She had to come out sometime. He fidgeted with his phone a bit. Then he looked around, watching people file out of the US Marshal building.

Finally, Alyah walked out of the building and toward her car. She looked more beautiful than Stephen had ever seen her and more unattainable.

Stephen got out of his car and met her at hers.

"I can't, Stephen. I just can't," Alyah said. She tucked a wayward piece of waving hair behind her ear. Her dangling earring glittered in the moonlight.

"I'm sorry. I called and left you messages. I texted. I don't know how many times and how many different ways to tell you that—"

"Then, stop," Alyah interrupted. "So, you were with someone before you were with me. We're all adults, Stephen. It's not even that big of a deal."

"Then, what? Why won't you talk to me?" he asked, his face revealing the bewilderment he felt.

"Because even though it's not that big of a deal and it's nothing you did to me, it still bothered me. Greatly," Alyah admitted, her green eyes troubled.

"Again, I'm—"

"Don't say it!" Alyah gently covered Stephen's mouth. "This promotion is bigger than all of that."

"Then why don't you look happy?" Stephen wanted to touch her. He wanted to pull her into his arms and erase the fear he saw in her eyes.

"Accepting a promotion to be a DA in Washington is a really big deal. This will make my career." Her words were like a death proclamation, and they landed abruptly on the pavement and lingered in agonizing silence at his feet.

Stephen's brain flipped through possible responses knowing the best one would be to congratulate her, support her choice, and let her go. But Alyah wasn't looking at him. He lifted her chin and looked into her eyes. He could see tears in the rim threatening to fall.

That's when he understood her true intention. "You're running away."

Her eyes snapped up to his. He could see her anger there.

"Not everything is about you, Stephen!" she snapped.

"Yeah? When did you get this job offer?" he challenged.

"It was an open offer. Four months ago, and I turned them down. They told me the job is mine if I change my mind. And I did. I took this job because I was looking for closure with Carley. And I got it."

"Why not just stay? What are you afraid of?" Stephen asked, bypassing her explanation.

"I'm afraid of—" Alyah started, paused, and started again. "I'm afraid that one day I'll look back and regret not taking a job in Washington because I would always wonder what might have happened with my career."

Stephen felt like he had been slapped. This really wasn't about him. Another woman who he'd fallen for was leaving him. And this time, he couldn't even fault her for it.

Instead, Stephen leaned down and hugged her. "I'm happy for you, then," he whispered in her ear.

Alyah shivered. She turned her head toward him.

Stephen tilted his.

Their lips connected in a powerful explosion of feelings and emotions. Stephen would follow her to the ends of the Earth if only he could.

Alyah broke the kiss and took a step back.

Stephen felt instantly cold and alone. "When do you leave?" he asked.

"The end of the week," she whispered.

He nodded. "I'm not gonna lie. I'll miss you."

Alyah nodded. "Goodbye, Stephen." She lifted her chin and turned to her car. She got in, started the ignition, and rolled down the window. "Did you ever open that envelope you got at the funeral?" she asked.

"No, I didn't," Stephen said. Truth be told, he had forgotten all about the envelope that Trevan Collins had handed him at Booker's funeral. In the excitement of the case restarting, he'd left it right where she'd last thrown it in his car. He glanced in the back seat. It was still there, unopened.

"What are you waiting for?" She tilted her head to the side.

"I don't know," Stephen said. But he did know.

"You can't be afraid of the unknown. You need to face it head on. Whatever is in that envelope, I'm positive you can handle it."

"Thanks, Alyah." He watched her drive away. He watched until her car was out of sight. He'd been busy since he'd been back and hadn't seen her until tonight. At least she'd said *goodbye* to him in person.

Stephen got in the car and grabbed the envelope he'd thrown in the back seat. He thought of Trevan Collins, the man who had handed him the envelope after the funeral. He also saw the license plate number scrawled in his handwriting on the envelope. He forgot he'd written it down after driving by Trevan's car. He needed a way to look up Trevan in case he had questions for him.

Stephen took a swig of water from his water bottle and opened the envelope. He pulled out a large, letter-size picture and started coughing on his water, which went down the wrong pipe when he saw the photo.

Though instant tears streamed down his face as he tried to catch his breath, Stephen could not look away from the photo. It was a picture of his brother frozen in time moments before his death. From the angle of the photo, Stephen could see a close-up of his brother's profile and a man who was holding a gun to his face. This was the man who pulled the trigger minutes later. He didn't need to see the date and time stamp to know this was seconds before his brother was murdered. Which made this man the murderer.

He studied the man holding the gun. The boy who had been convicted of killing his brother had gone to juvie and was already out. This man was not that boy. That boy had grown up, having served the full sentence.

But he was not the man in the photo. Stephen knew because Stephen had sat in the courthouse as they convicted his former classmate, Davey Stinnert, for the murder of his brother. Stephen had never seen the man in this photo before. Had they sent the wrong person to jail for the murder of his brother? Why was this just now coming to light?

Stephen studied the picture harder. He suddenly had a million questions about his brother's death when before, he and his family had thought it was an open and shut case. It looked like he would be paying a visit to Trevan Collins after all.

Anger, confusion, and grief warred inside of him. Maybe he wouldn't get the girl in the end. But he would always get the killer. That was what Stephen excelled at. If they'd put the wrong guy behind bars for the murder that had inspired Stephen's career, he'd find out. If it was the last thing he ever did.

The End

WHEN SHE VANISHED

If you liked *When They Disappeared*, order book 2 in A Mak and Wilton Thriller series—*WHEN SHE VANISHED*.

PROLOGUE
LACY

Lacy Donovan jogged up the steps to her tiny one-bedroom, one-bath bungalow, careful to avoid the rotting side that led up to her door. She juggled her keys, a bag of groceries, and her phone, which was tucked between her ear and the crook of her neck. As the darkness set in, she walked inside, suppressing a shudder from the February chill.

"I'm fine, mom, really," Lacy said for the fifth time during the call. *I know I'm only nineteen,* Lacy answered her mom in her head, feeling exasperated. *And yes, I am on my own for the first time.*

Lacy could acknowledge her mom's point. Lacy *was* cute, little, and had the body of a slim yoga instructor. Lacy was aware she turned heads when she *flipped her long, blond ponytail over her shoulder.* But what *really sealed the deal,* according to her mom, was Lacy's *big, innocent blue eyes.*

Not so innocent anymore, mom, Lacy thought as she finally popped her front door open. Lacy had been on too many dates by now to say that. She was living her own life in a different state. She even refused to tell her mom where she lived.

When Lacy first tried to move out, she'd quickly discovered

rent was out of control. Then Lacy found this place, and it had been a steal. Until she saw it in person, of course. The pictures on the rental site showed a cute little home at the back of a fifty-acre property where one other home—the home of the landlord—sat a good half a mile away.

The reality of the tiny home was peeling paint outside that looked like it had once been seafoam green. The place was smaller than she'd thought it would be. The front stairs were rotting and a little slanted. There were obvious shingles missing from the roof. The windows had been painted shut, which limited the air flow through the place.

But the wooden door was solid, so that was a plus. Not to mention, it had all the amenities inside that she needed. It had a living room, a kitchen, a bedroom, and a bathroom. The structure was sound, and the doors locked. But the house was not fit for entertaining. Nor did she think that she'd be able to convince anyone to come visit her any time soon on account of where the home was located.

The fact that her tiny home was secluded in the country at the back of someone's property should have made her feel safer —less findable. But it didn't. Truth be told, where she lived creeped her out most nights. But there was no way she was going back home now. She'd made her choice and she would live with it.

Lacy listened to her mom prattle on about how much they missed her. Lacy caught the hints of manipulation that her mom dropped into conversation. She wanted Lacy to come back home. Her mom thought she was so subtle. But she wasn't.

Lacy was so intent on her mom's words that her brain missed important details upon entering her home. She didn't register that something was wrong the minute she walked through the door. She dropped the groceries on the kitchen table and started taking off her shoes. The first odd thing she noticed was a picture that hung crooked on the wall. Then she saw the couch cushions were pulled sideways and some were thrown to the floor. Drawers were dumped out and tables were overturned. Messy piles of Lacy's belongings lay on the floor underneath the drawers.

"Mom, I'm gonna have to call you back," Lacy said as she hung up on her mother mid-sentence. "Why would someone come all the way back here just to rob me?" Lacy speculated aloud to herself.

Lacy backed out of the still-open front door, her hand positioned on her cell to call 911, until she bumped directly into something solid and dropped her phone. She froze in place when she realized she'd bumped into a large human resembling a wall. A big, hulking giant of a man stood behind her, breathing loudly through his nose. She could smell his hot breath on the back of her neck as he loomed over her.

Before she had time to process the situation and run, the man grabbed her from behind, his arms in a tight bearhug, circling around her upper body and rendering her motionless. Lacy twisted slightly and saw that the man had tanned, leathery skin with a thick, light pink, weathered scar that ran from the corner of his mouth down his chin.

This is so much more terrifying than it is on TV, she thought. But this wasn't happening on TV. This was happening in real time, right here and now. She'd do well to use her brain to focus on escape. That couldn't happen because Lacy couldn't move. Her body had frozen up.

All thoughts slammed to a halt, freezing her with immobilizing fear. Then Lacy felt her feet lift off the ground. His arms were so tight, she couldn't breathe. She felt herself being carried backwards and down the steps, away from her tiny home. Then she realized that her feet were dangling. She began to kick and flail her legs about, connecting with his shins several times.

"Shit!" her captor growled. He lost his grip and dropped Lacy.

Lacy gasped as she felt herself fall. Her tailbone instantly ached with a burst of pain as her bottom connected with the ground. She could see the black Brooks tennis shoes the man wore.

Before Lacy could get a shoe on the earth to spring up and run, the man threw a fist at the back of her head. She felt a throbbing zing radiate down her skull to her neck. She saw stars, then darkness, but only for a minute. Or was it longer?

When she gained consciousness, Lacy realized she was upside down. Her body was moving but not by her own volition. She opened her eyes and lifted her chin. She could see the red, clay dirt moving quickly underneath her. Her arms dangled a few feet from the ground, and she tried to move them or flail them to fight. Then she saw the rope tied around her wrists. Perhaps in denial, Lacy attempted to move her fists, but they were bound tightly. She must have been out longer than she thought.

Kick! her brain shouted at her. *Get free!* Lacy tried to move her feet but could not.

She heard a laugh so low it almost sounded like a growl and reminded Lacy of pure evil. That's when she figured it out. Her captor had thrown her over his shoulder. He tightened his grip on her. In that moment, Lacy lost all hope of getting free.

She shifted her focus from escape to surveying her surroundings. Trying to ignore the way the blood ran to her brain and made her feel dizzy and the way her head throbbed, Lacy made an attempt to figure out where she was going. There was nothing around but woods bordering the property. Was that the smell of impending rain? What had she been thinking to move so far out of civilization and isolate herself like this?

Where was he taking her? Lacy couldn't see her bungalow anymore, but she knew it must be somewhere behind her. The only other home on the property was the hulking mansion that sat out front about half a mile to the north of her. Was he taking her to the mansion?

Her question was answered when her body abruptly stopped moving. He shifted her weight until he held her like a baby in his arms. Then he let her fall on her bottom roughly enough that she was sure she would have a bruise tomorrow. She saw the man open a hidden hatch in the ground that was indistinguishable from the rest of the property—all red clay with minimal grass around until it opened up like a storm cellar.

Lacy blinked a few times to clear her eyes. She had a hard time comprehending what she was seeing. The man had opened a trick door that had looked like solid ground minutes before. When he pulled on a latch, it had become a door to some underground hole. She couldn't even see how he'd opened it. There was nothing around to indicate where this place was.

"Don't get any ideas. I'm going to untie your feet." The man carefully unbound the rope from her ankles. Her muscles tensed when he bent down and shoved her toward the ledge, his large hands digging into her back and hips until she was sitting on the edge of a giant hole in the ground. Her feet dangled over the pit.

"Down," he ordered. He sounded out of breath, the only indication that carrying her body had been hard for him.

He grabbed her still-bound wrists, picking her body up with one powerful movement, and swung her to the hole. Her arms were in a point over her head, her legs dangling freely, suspended over darkness. Lacy gasped as she looked down. She could not see the bottom.

He released his grasp and let Lacy fall. Less than a second later, she hit the ground and landed in a heap. She'd fallen a good five feet from where she'd been hanging. Unable to catch herself because her hands were tied, a sharp, instant pain registered where she landed on her left hip. She cried out in surprise and agony upon impact. She heard, rather than saw, the door above her fall shut with a muffled thud.

Everything had seemed to be moving in slow motion, but now she realized it had all happened fast. Like lightning speed. One minute she was on the phone with her mom walking into her house, the next minute, Lacy was trapped underground.

She began to cry.

A hand touched her shoulder. Lacy screamed, whirled her head around, and dug her feet in the ground, awkwardly scooting herself backward.

A young woman sat down on the floor next to her and stared at her. Lacy noticed the woman was her age with a sunken appearance, gaunt cheekbones, eyes that looked too big for her head, and thinning hair.

"It'll be okay," the skeleton woman said. It seemed like the effort to get out that hoarse croak took all her energy. The woman put her hands on Lacy's and began to untie the knots at Lacy's wrists.

"Where am I?" Lacy asked. She looked around and gasped. It was dark, but there was some sliver of light coming in from somewhere above her. It must have been a full moon because it cast a circular light on the ground in front of Lacy's feet. Three more sets of eyes peered at her. There were other women, all in various stages of starvation and dehydration. Lacy's breath caught in her throat. She felt afraid. She wasn't sure if she was more scared of the women or the possibility that she might be looking into a future mirror.

Lacy could see that these women were dying. She wondered if they knew how bad a state they were in. They must have been here for a very long time and were perhaps delusional. One of those women had just assured Lacy it was going to be okay.

But it wasn't going to be okay unless she could find her way out. She could only guess what her mother would say to her now.

I told you, Lacy. It's not safe for pretty girls like you to live alone.

Lacy had ignored her mother. She had decided she knew better than the woman who had raised her. She'd moved to a place in the middle of nowhere with no forwarding address just to spite her mother.

Now Lacy would pay the steep consequences.

1

WILTON

Stephen held the Glock 19 in front of him with both hands. He adjusted his grip, his left hand under his right hand, holding his gun firmly. His finger rested against the barrel of the gun, not on the trigger. Not yet. Stephen was trained to keep his finger off the trigger until he was ready to shoot.

Know your target and what's beyond it.

In this instance, Stephen's target was the outline of a person on a piece of paper hanging fifty yards away in the outdoor shooting range. Beyond it was a big, open field with green, rolling hills for miles. He took a deep breath in and smiled. He loved the smell of gunpowder that lingered in the air.

Stephen shifted his focus back to his paper victim. His stance was perfect, if he did say so himself. He stood wide and staggered with his weight shifted slightly forward, his footing solid. There was a slight bend in his elbows.

He lined up the site on his gun, then squeezed the trigger and shot off five rounds. The pop of his gun sounded hollow and far away in his noise-cancelling headphones. He hit the bullseye every single time, demolishing the place right in the center where the heart would have been.

Stephen looked over to see his partner finishing her rounds.

Mak looked up in frustration and peeked from around her booth and over at Stephen's target.

Stephen grinned, feeling like a little boy proud of his accomplishment.

"Show off," Mak said, gritting her teeth.

Stephen moved over to invade her shooting space. He eyed her target critically with a lifted eyebrow.

"What? I was close," Mak defended herself, her voice pitching upward.

"Close enough to have my back in a gunfight?" Stephen challenged.

"It's not fair," Mak whined. "This left-eye dominance thing sucks!"

Stephen nodded. "I have an ex-girlfriend who has the same problem, which gave her a hard time hitting the target, too. You either need to train your right eye to be stronger—"

"How?" Mak interrupted impatiently.

Stephen closed his left eye and mimed picking up a book to read.

"Ugh! One, I don't have time to read. Two, I can't sit still long enough," Mak sputtered.

"You wanted my help," Stephen shrugged.

"Right, but I wanted a quick fix. I don't have time to train my eyes—"

"Eye," Stephen corrected her. "And my running skills aren't exactly improving overnight, either."

They had several foot chases during their first case, proving Mak could easily outrun Stephen. While it was true Mak was slim and athletic, Stephen had been surprised by the powerhouse of speed she possessed. Mak always had to wait on him to catch up. In the meantime, Mak had already apprehended the perp before Stephen even got there. At some point, Stephen realized he needed to improve his stamina and speed.

That's why they created a running regimen after their last case. The plan meant meeting up with Mak before the sun came out to run several miles a day four days a week. They'd created this habit months ago. Just when Stephen started to feel comfortable, Mak leveled up the intensity by increasing her pace or adding another mile.

Before he'd met Mak, Stephen had prided himself on his cardio. Now, with his calf and quad muscles screaming at him from their latest sprint at the end of their hour-long run that morning, he'd never felt more out of shape.

"Improving yourself is not supposed to be easy. If it were—"

"Everyone would do it," Mak interrupted.

"I was going to say I'd be a superhero," Stephen grinned. He wasn't going to say that at all. He just secretly wished she would learn her lesson about interrupting all the time. Though, he did think her habit might be getting a tiny bit better. That, or maybe Stephen was just getting used to it.

Mak racked her gun and dropped the magazine.

"You done for the day?" Stephen asked in surprise.

"We've been here for two hours. Let's give it a break," Mak decided.

"It's been one hour and twenty-five minutes. But I'm going to let you call it because we only ran for an hour this morning," Stephen quipped and made a face as he walked over to put his gun away.

"Oh, did you want me to go easy on you?" Mak called to be heard over the wind that seemed to blow in small microbursts. Her ear coverings were a basic, low-quality grade she had rented from the shop.

Stephen smirked at her. His expensive headphones dulled the loud gun shots but made Mak's words clear enough that she didn't have to yell. "You, go easy on me? That's laughable!"

Mak rolled her eyes as she zipped up her US Marshal jacket.

The sun was shining today, but there was a slight chill in the not-quite-spring air.

"How's Alyah?" Mak asked when they were on their way out to the parking lot.

Stephen took a deep breath in and blew it back out. "There's really nothing to tell. She's in DC, and I'm here. I call her, leave long voicemails, and she responds by text days later. Another one..."

"Bites the dust," Mak finished.

Stephen's mind wandered as he thought about Alyah, the beautiful petite brunette with a sharp temper when on the wrong side of her and a warm heart when on the right. Which he had managed do, and he'd thought about little else ever since.

District Attorney, Alyah Smith, had taken a piece of Stephen's heart with her when she transferred to Washington, DC, to further her career. Stephen had a theory that Alyah was running away from the feelings she had for him. He knew this had to be true, because he had the same feelings. But they hadn't given him the nickname *Love 'Em and Leave 'Em Wilton* at the office for no reason. He had a reputation for moving through relationships too quickly. Burning out of them was more like it.

Mak got into the driver's seat of the Range Rover with the impressive *US Marshal* stencil across the door. Stephen grudgingly got into the passenger side.

"You could let me drive sometimes you know. Partnership means working together," Stephen grumbled.

"Do you know how to drive?" Mak asked with wide, innocent brown eyes. She ripped her rubber band out of her shoulder-length auburn hair, smoothed back the pieces that the wind had blown, and pulled it back into a neater ponytail. Mak was pretty in an unassuming way, but she didn't know it. Nor did she seem to care.

Stephen laughed but found Mak regarding him seriously in her position of authority behind the wheel. "Of course, I know how to drive. I drive to the station every day."

"But do you *really* know how to drive?" she asked. "Like with speed and precision?"

"Yes," Stephen answered in his best dumb jock voice. "Stephen can drive."

Mak snorted and let out an exasperated sigh. "But have you ever raced?"

Stephen's eyes bulged. "Like illegal street racing?"

"Yes."

"No. Have you?"

"Yes."

"I don't believe you." Stephen's skepticism was evident by the way he raised his eyebrows.

"I could take you to a street race tonight." Mak glanced at Stephen, then back at the road, her eyes serious.

"You're kidding me," Stephen gawked at her.

"I'm not. My dad is a pro street racer."

"Huh. Let me guess, you raced to get daddy's attention growing up?" Stephen smirked.

"No, Stephen, I'm a daddy's girl. I didn't *try for* his attention, I always had it," Mak's voice sounded icy and defensive now. "I raced because I wanted to, and I loved it. The adrenaline rush—it's like nothing you've ever known before."

"I'll take your word for it," Stephen said wryly.

"Oh, Stephen. Just once I'd like to see what would happen if you lost control."

"Sorry to disappoint. It'll never happen," Stephen promised.

"Never say never," Mak said.

"That's something you think would be fun to see? Me losing control?" Stephen felt confused.

"Not necessarily. It happens to the best of us. It's just not the end of the world when it does," Mak shrugged.

"Sounds terrible. I think I'll sit that one out," Stephen shot back.

"Might not have a choice. You need an outlet, a way to stay healthy, or it's inevitable. You just..." She mimicked the sound of an explosion and mimed it with the hand not on the steering wheel.

Stephen's phone buzzed before he could answer. He pulled it out of his pocket as Mak drove into the parking lot of the building with the words *US Marshals* in bold lettering across the top.

Stephen wondered if the awe of being a US Marshal would ever wear off. He hoped not. He felt like he had the job of his dreams. But he knew his dream job was going to get tough again real soon because Deputy Director Rob Sikes had just texted him and Mak.

They had a new case.

ALSO BY ADDISON MICHAEL

A Mynart Mystery Thriller series is ghostly suspense with psychological elements. If you like complex heroines, paranormal twists and turns, and gripping suspense, then you'll love this dark glimpse into the psyche.

Book 1 - *What Comes Before Dawn*

Book 2 - *Dawn That Brings Death*

Book 3 - *Truth That Dawns*

Book 4 - *Dawn That Breaks*

Book 5 - *What Comes After Dawn*

The Other AJ Hartford - A phantom on a train. A mysterious kidnapping long ago. Can she connect the dots before all her futures disappear forever? If you like good-hearted heroines, ghostly phenomena, and nail-biting high stakes, then you'll love this mind-blowing adventure.

A Mak and Wilton Thriller series is a pulse-pounding crime thriller series with a strong female lead, stimulating twists, and relentless suspense.

Book 1 - *When They Disappeared*

Book 2 - *When She Vanished*

Book 3 - *Why He Lied*

Book 4 - *Why She Fled* - Releases July 31st!

REVIEW REQUEST

If you enjoyed this book, I would be extremely grateful if you would leave a brief review on the store site where you purchased your book or on Goodreads. Your review helps fellow readers know what to expect when they read this book.
Thank you in advance!

~ Addison Michael

ABOUT THE AUTHOR

 Addison Michael is the oldest of six siblings. She grew up with a golden reputation and a well-hidden dark side. Writing became her outlet. Addison's dark side emerges in the crime and mystery thrillers she writes today. She lives in the Midwest and believes in writing what she knows, so her stories are often set in the Midwest region. From cabins surrounded by acres of desolate woods to rural police departments and eclectic personalities, Addison Michael captures the essence of small-town living.

You'll find the following tropes in Addison Michael thriller books:

- Cabin in the woods
- You can't go home again…
- Unreliable narrator
- Kidnapping/missing person
- Addiction/recovery
- Femme fatale
- Serial killer